THE LONG GOOD BOY

Also by Carol Lea Benjamin

✦

THIS DOG FOR HIRE

THE DOG WHO KNEW TOO MUCH

A HELL OF A DOG

LADY VANISHES

THE WRONG DOG

THE LONG GOOD BOY

A RACHEL ALEXANDER AND DASH MYSTERY

Carol Lea Benjamin

Walker & Company ✸ New York

First published in the United States of America in 2001 by
Walker Publishing Company, Inc.

Published simultaneously in Canada by Fitzhenry and Whiteside,
Markham, Ontario L3R 4T8

ISBN 0-8027-3364-6

Series design by M. J. DiMassi

Printed in the United States of America

For Victoria and Stephen Joubert, *mishpocheh*

Acknowledgments

For the sharing of information, opinions, and great stories, my thanks to the late Lee Brewster of Lee's Mardi Gras, Janine Adams, Peter Fenty, Emma Jean Stephenson, Mark D'Alessio, David Schneider, Nick Brous, and the hookers of the Gansevoort Meat Market.

For advice, encouragement, and taking care of business, thanks to my agent, Gail Hochman.

My gratitude also to all the good people at Walker & Company for their skill, humor, and warmth; to Job Michael Evans and Wayde Vickrey for incomparable conversations, then and now; to Daneil Hu for the *tui na*; to Stephen Lennard, my favorite husband; and to Dexter and Flash for bringing Zen into the office. Good on ya, one and all.

Trying to define yourself
is like trying to bite your own teeth.

—ALAN WATTS

THE LONG GOOD BOY

1

I Know What You Mean

SHOULDN'T have been awake, but it was one of those nights. I was in the garden, with Dashiell, watching the blue-black sky, waiting for dawn and the false feeling of safety that comes with the light. When my cell phone rang, I sent Dash for it, wiped it off on the leg of my jeans, and flipped it open.

"I got to get to sleep," someone said.

The wind blew. I shivered. The dry yellow leaves that had clustered against the back wall of the garden lifted and eddied.

"I know what you mean," I told her without bothering to ask who she was or who had died this time.

"What I was wondering," she said, a heavy smoker, a rich, raspy Lauren Bacall voice, "is if you're going to the run with Dashiell tomorrow."

He was over at the back wall, poking his big head into the pile of leaves, trying to figure out what had made them move.

"Who wants to know?" I asked.

"Never mind that for now. This is about work. For you."

I waited for more. She waited for me to comment.

"This here's Rachel, right?"

"Yes."

"Well." Pleased with herself.

I had a nearly overwhelming urge to talk, to tell her that maybe I was awake because the wind had made the windows rattle, that the noise had gotten me up. Or maybe not— maybe something else, the holiday blues arriving earlier than usual this year, before Thanksgiving this time, ask if she ever got them, and if she did, what she did about it. I could have gone with it, told her the story of my life. Four in the morning, you'll talk, period. You'll order a pizza to talk to the deliveryman. You'll say anything to anyone who'll listen.

Instead I said, "Two-thirty."

"No good."

"Then when?"

"Before work. Eight o'clock."

"That's less than four hours from now," I said, more to myself than to her, thinking I wouldn't get any sleep at all, a hell of a way to start a case.

"Not *that* eight. The other one."

"Eight P.M.? But you said—"

"Right. I'm a health care professional. Night shift."

"Okay. Eight P.M. it is, but then not at the dog run. Too many aggressive dogs late in the day. Name another spot."

"You the fussy one. You name one."

"Farther west okay?"

"Whatever."

"Abingdon Square Park, Twelfth and Hudson." I figured it wasn't all that far from St. Vincent's Hospital. If that's where she worked. If not, then the hell with it. Let her take the subway.

"You got it."

"How will I know you? I mean, just in case someone else decides to take a load off at eight o'clock, enjoy the scenery."

"Are you kidding? You don't got a dog to exercise, some other pressing reason to be out, you staying inside, watching

HBO, you're not sitting out in no unheated park. It's November, woman. Where you been, hibernating?"

"Still."

"Girl, you too much with your questions. Take something, okay? Help yourself relax. It's not gonna be your problem. I'll know you. Okay?"

"And how will you do that?"

She sighed. There was some whispering then, but her hand must have been over the mouthpiece, because I couldn't make out the words.

"Honey, you was described, in detail. No stone was left with moss on it. You wanna skip the park, walk around the Village with your dog, keep moving to keep warm, it don't make no difference to me, I'll find you, jus' make up your mind. What I can't do is keep standing here yammering about it. My feet's killing me."

"Okay. Abingdon Square it is. And what did you say the job was?" Wondering what kind of a person calls at this hour of the night, wondering what she had in mind for me to do.

"You see what I mean about you? I din't say. But it's undercover investigation. What'd you think I was goin' to say, nucular physics? We'll tell you all about it tomorrow."

"We?"

But there was nothing more. The line was dead.

2

I'm LaDonna

I SLEPT for three and a half hours, from just after light to nearly eleven A.M. Then I shopped for organic meat and vegetables for Dashiell and me, did the laundry at the main house while checking to make sure no one had broken in and that all systems were operational, the job that gives me a rent I can afford. I raked the last of the fallen leaves, trimmed back the herbs for winter, and vacuumed the cottage from top to bottom. At a quarter to eight, Dash and I headed over to Abingdon Square, the small triangular park where Hudson Street and Eighth Avenue play kissy-face for just a moment.

I sat to the right of the Twelfth Street gate so that I could see both entrances, turned up my collar, opened the *Times*, holding it high, the way you do when you read in the subway, except there the paper gets folded like a road map in large accordion pleats so that you don't take up the room of three people. Here, alone on a park bench, I spread the paper out and slumped down behind it. Very B movie. Not to mention pointless. I was not only the only person there with a pit bull, I was the only person there. Besides that, it was way too dark to read.

I didn't have long to wait. She was on time. Rather, they were on time. I knew they were my clients the moment they showed. It wasn't the white uniforms either, because, truth be told, they didn't look much like nurses.

The one holding the dog, a wirehaired mini dachshund the color of bread crust sticking halfway out of her short, red leather jacket, had big hair, loose, frizzy, and a shade of blond that was closer to white than yellow. Her skin was pale, too, coffee with much too much milk in it. She wore a short, tight, shiny black skirt, lacy stockings, and pointy-toed stiletto heels. Her compatriots, one on each side, weren't wearing white either. The biggest one, head and shoulders above the other two, was wearing a halter top and matching miniskirt in a floral pattern, a faux fur jacket over it, her bronze hair piled high on her head, loose curls falling forward against her shiny ebony skin. In the light from a streetlamp, I could see she had glitter along her prominent cheekbones. A nice touch. I thought I might try that sometime. The smallest of the three, her skin the color of walnuts, eyes as small and dark as currants, wore spandex, a kind of cat suit, except the pants ended mid-thigh, as if she were about to do a cross-country bicycle race. But had that been her plan, the shoes were all wrong. They were little strappy things with the highest heels I'd ever seen, heels as sharp as needles that made a metallic peck-a-dee-peck sound as she approached, like a hungry chicken with a stainless-steel beak. Me, I couldn't sit in those shoes, let alone work as a health care professional in them.

They spotted me and tottered over. I dropped the paper onto the bench, stood, and smiled. Or maybe I gaped. Who knows?

The big one stuck out her enormous hand. I felt sure she was going to say her name was Alice, because Lord knows, I was in Wonderland. But I was wrong.

"I'm LaDonna." She was tall, dark, and gorgeous, six-one, maybe even six-two in stocking feet. Only she wasn't—she wore thigh-high pink boots and matching lipstick. We shook hands, her grip, like her broad shoulders and narrow hips, at odds with the message her outfit was trying so desperately to convey.

"Chi Chi," the frizzy-haired one said. "And this here's Clint." She jiggled the dog. "Same deep-set, dark eyes." She nodded slowly. "I could go for him," she said.

"Aren't his blue?" the one in the cat suit said, wagging one long finger to and fro.

"Whose?"

"Clint's."

Chi Chi looked down at her dog, then shook her head. "No way. They brown."

"I meant—"

"What?"

The one in the cat suit shook her head. Never mind, her hand said.

Chi Chi shrugged, turning back to me. "Did you see the one where he risked everything for the hookers?"

"I did," I told her. "I loved it."

One hand to her chest, long, iridescent purple nails. "Me, too. The Un something, am I right?" It was the voice from the phone. "This here's Jasmine. She won't tell you herself. She won't speak up 'less you make a mistake. Then she jump in, point it out to you, make sure everyone knows how smart she is. One year of college." Chi Chi nodded, then knocked my third client with her hip.

Jasmine had one arm bent, her pointer on her heavily rouged cheek, the elbow resting in her other hand. She looked me up and down.

"She needs work," she said. "But she has potential, I'll give her that. Turn around."

I did, Dash standing up, then sitting down again, confused. He wasn't the only one.

She pushed back her long, blue-black hair with one finger—well, one long press-on nail that matched her lipstick and eye shadow—a little over the top for me, but as she'd already pointed out, what did I know? "She's lucky," she said to the other two. "She's got small feet." She turned to me. "Unless you need a tiara or a butt lifter, you don't need Lee's, size thirteen and up. You can go to Eighth Street. You can go to Barney's or Jeffrey, you got money to burn. What are you, an eight narrow?"

I looked down at my red Converse high-tops, then back up at Jasmine without answering. I thought I'd wait for the Mad Hatter to show before saying anything further.

"Shoes tell a lot about a person," LaDonna said. "Your shoes can give you away in a heartbeat."

"Yeah," Jasmine said. "You know what they say. There are only two kinds of women wear red shoes." Now they were all looking at my sneakers. "And you ain't no Spanish dancer."

The three of them fell apart laughing, like it was the funniest line ever delivered.

"At least the color's a good choice," LaDonna said, arms folded, one long finger tapping her Adam's apple.

"Can we get serious here—"

"We are serious, girlfriend. Dead serious. We're trying to save your life, so you can save ours. We're saying, you've got to look the part, for your own safety. And you've got to check them out, too. Look at *their* shoes. When you get the chance. You see cop shoes, you don't talk money, you beat it the hell out of the car, fast as you can. Of course, some of them, no way you're going away without they get a free sample first." Jasmine shrugged. "Cost of doing business."

"Look, you're way ahead of me here."

"She's right," Chi Chi said. "We need to start on page one. You're already in the sequel."

I sat. She sat to my left and took one of my hands in one of hers. For some inexplicable reason, the gesture touched me. LaDonna sat on my right, her eyes way too bright, as if she were about to cry, or just had. And even though I was cold, wearing much more than she was, she was sweating. They all were. Jasmine squatted in front of me. How she did that without tipping over in those shoes I'll never understand.

Chi Chi did the talking. "One of our friends got killed a couple of weeks ago. Nothing's going to be done about it. You understand how that works, don't you? We was told you would."

"Who—"

She scowled and flicked her hand at me. "I already tol' you, you ask too many questions. Jus' listen, okay?"

I nodded.

"Remember a few years ago, this transvestite Marsha got herself killed on the Christopher Street pier?" She patted my hand. "Remember what happened then?"

"Nothing."

"Our point exactly."

They all nodded. Jasmine pushed her hair back again.

"Our friend, someone got her with a box cutter, right across her throat." She drew one finger across her own neck to illustrate, in case I hadn't gotten the picture.

"I'm sorry."

"People think because we engage in commercial sex work, means we're trash," LaDonna said. "They think we're not worth shit, we don't have lives. Or feelings. This is what we do, it's not what we are."

I nodded. Enthusiastically.

"Anyways, we waited to hear something and din't. So then her brother called the precinct to inquire about the case, and they tol' him it was most likely a john and how are they going to find him, it's not like he left his business card or anything."

"But you don't think it was a john?"

"Did I say that? What I'm telling you is that they're not going to do anything. I mean, din't they say that themselves, to her brother?"

"Does she have other family, or just the one brother?"

"There's no brother," Chi Chi said. She was looking down

at our hands. She was mumbling. "She was alone. That's why it's up to us to find out who did her."

"But you said—" I stopped when I knew what was coming.

"It was me," she said, letting her voice drop. "I had to try to find out. She was a good person, you know, God-fearing. And she was our friend."

I nodded again. "What was her name?"

"Rosalinda."

"Pretty name."

Jasmine smiled. "For a while, she was Gypsy Rosalie. She was taking dance class, at the Y. She wanted to be a stripper."

"Hence the name."

"Yeah," she said. "Like you said. Hence the name. And can I give you a little tip here? Cut the 'hence' shit when you're on the stroll, okay?"

"When I'm on the—"

"This was just her day job," LaDonna said.

"So to speak."

"Yeah," Jasmine said, "and eighty-six that one, too."

Before I could even phrase a question—being careful to omit "hence" and "so to speak" from my vocabulary really slowed me down—Chi Chi leaned closer. "What we want," she said, "is for you to find out *who*. Okay?"

"What we want," LaDonna said, "is to know how much for finding out *who*. Always good to get the money squared away up front."

"And if you take Visa, Discover, or American Express," Jasmine said.

"I—" Things were moving too fast to stop and think. Perhaps I was still trying to process the phrase "when you're on the stroll."

"Only kidding," Jasmine said. "It'll be a cash transaction. That's the only way we do business." She unzipped the front of her cat suit, reached into her bra, and took out a wad. LaDonna stuck her big hand up her short skirt and brought out another. I turned to Chi Chi, who was pulling Clint out from underneath her jacket. He had a jacket of his own on, also red leather. With a zippered pocket. She opened that and took out a third wad of cash.

"We have to know," she said. "And we're willing to pay to find out."

"And then what? What happens if I find out who?"

They were all paying attention, all giving good eye contact, but for a change, no one had anything to say.

I held up one hand. Dashiell lay down, though it hadn't been meant for him. "Look, I'm not going to find this person and have you execute him."

"What about to protect the rest of us? What if he's going to do it again? What if it wasn't about Rosalinda specifically, but there's someone out there gets off on killing hookers? What about that? At least if we know what the guy looks like, then we're safe." She began to put Clint back inside her jacket, but her hands were shaking. When she looked up, there were tears in her eyes. "If *you* got the information to the cops, well, that's one thing. If we said, Hey, we know who killed Rosalinda, do you think they'd lift a finger? You think they give a shit about us?"

I sat there thinking for a minute, the three tranny hookers watching me, no one making jokes now.

"So what's your take on this? Do you think it was a customer?"

LaDonna shrugged her massive shoulders.

"Could it have been another hooker? Are you guys territorial?"

No one answered.

"A pimp? Setting an example for the rest of his girls?"

I waited.

"No? Not a pimp? They're nurturing, gentle, like the good mothers none of us had? That's what I've always heard, so no way, if that's what you tell me, I'm going to feel you're being less than honest."

Pregnant pause.

"I take it you're not going to set the record straight for me."

Nothing.

"Okay, so you don't think it was her pimp?" I looked from one to the next. Mount Rushmore was more expressive, a bit less terrified, too. "If you don't tell me the truth, how am I going to help you?" Wondering if they were capable of doing that, even as I asked.

Clint sneezed.

"Whatever you tell me, it stops with me. Client privilege. You know what that is? So, Rosalinda, did she do something to piss off her pimp? Hold out money? Sass him? Someone, anyone? The pimp, he decided to put the fear of God—"

"We don't know. That's why we hiring you," Chi Chi said in a voice so low I had to lean closer to hear her.

"It could be it was a wife," LaDonna said, "didn't take to her husband's little habit."

I looked up at her.

"They's all married."

"Not all," Chi Chi said. "Maybe most."

Jasmine shook her head. "A lot of them aren't. Sometimes they say they are, even when they're not. They complain about a wife they may or may not have. This guy, he says, my wife, *she* wouldn't do that you put a fucking gun to her head. Who knows, he's really got a wife or not? This ain't exactly St. Patrick's Cathedral, people coming around to confess the truth, ask for forgiveness."

LaDonna nodded. "You work undercover, right? At least, that's what we was told."

I looked up at her, down at Jasmine, sideways at Chi Chi.

"You're kidding, right?"

They shook their heads.

"We'll take care of you. Don't you worry," Jasmine said.

"You'll be with me," LaDonna said. "I'll never let you out of my sight for one minute."

I looked back up, thinking for the moment of something

my sister had once said, about how I seemed to be looking for better and better ways to get myself killed.

"So you think it was family?" I asked.

"Or another hooker," Chi Chi said. "They's some out there, they're crazy. Desperate. Kill you soon as look at you."

"Could be something else entirely," LaDonna added, "something we ain't thought of."

"Hence we hired you." That Jasmine was one smart-ass broad.

"Right. What about the meat market? Is there any chance—"

"The meat market's not even open when we work," she said. "Case closed."

"Right," I said, "and anyway, there's all that rich tradition behind you, of hookers working in the same area as the wholesale markets, here, Hunts Point—"

"What about the pig man?" LaDonna whispered out of one side of her mouth, ignoring me, bending so that she was talking right into Jasmine's ear.

"The pig man?" I asked.

"He's just a customer, some butcher Rosalinda did once or twice. That don't have nothing to do with anythin'," Jasmine said.

"So what's his name, this pig man?"

"I already said, it don' have nothin'—"

"We don't kiss and tell," Chi Chi said.

"Truth is," Jasmine said, leaning forward, "we don't kiss, period. It's unsanitary. You never know where someone's mouth's been."

"So she never mentioned the name? Not even just his first name? The place of business? Nothing? She just referred to him as—"

"The pig man." All of them together, Tranny Hookers Local 101, my new employers.

They were a sad-looking group. Despite the quick repartee, the fancy outfits with matching shoes, tattoo covers, press-on nails, glitter, the pancake makeup, rouged cheeks, painted mouths, misery was shining in their eyes, to a man. And something else, too, perhaps more than just a hint of the craziness they accused others of. I know I should have been scared, sitting with them the way I was, no one else around. But somehow I wasn't. At least, not enough. For some reason I can't explain, something in Chi Chi's voice had touched me, and I knew before I met her that whatever it was she needed, I'd be with her all the way, in a straight line, right up until the end.

"So he sells pork," I said. "This we know."

Chi Chi nodded. "We're pretty sure that's so." She looked around, shifted her feet, twitched one shoulder, checked to see if Clint was okay. "He sells pork," she repeated, forcing a laugh, as if to say, Sense of humor like mine, I was ready for *Late Night*.

Jasmine pointed to her head. Well, truth be told, to her hair. "Smart," she said.

"Like we was told," Chi Chi added. Too loud.

"By whom?"

I could hear soot falling. I waited a bit longer, but no one had anything to say.

"Chi Chi, last night you mentioned that someone recommended me. I need to know—"

"You don't *need* to know. You *dying* to know," Jasmine said, more to them than to me. "Don't you know the old saying, Curiosity killed the cat?"

"I had some trouble with Clint. He was going in the house, and I called this dog trainer. We got, you know, pretty friendly, and when I told him what happened, he was real sympathetic, you know, about the possible danger to the rest of us, and he said, You have to find out who did this, and I know just the perfect person for the job."

I felt as if I'd swallowed a cake of ice. Dashiell began to whine.

"What was his—"

"Like we already tol' you," LaDonna said, lifting her big hand like a stop sign, "that part of the discussion's over. We don't kiss and tell. Our lips," she said, pursing hers for just a moment, "are sealed." To emphasize the point, she turned a tiny, imaginary key, then tossed it into the dark night.

3

Hey, Baby

WHEN LaDonna, Chi Chi, and Jasmine left for work, I headed home with so much cash, all in fives, tens, and twenties, I had to divide it in half to fit it into my jacket pockets, wondering all the time how they got their hands on so much money, and if they'd all soon turn up dead because of it. They'd insisted they hadn't held out on their pimp to pay me. Yeah, yeah. Maybe the money was from rent collected on some of their properties, book royalties, or winning the lottery. Again and again, they'd said that this was what they wanted, shoving the money at me, telling me they had to know who did the killing. When I told them I didn't need this much up front, that half of it would have been too much, they insisted I take it anyway. "We don't do layaway," Jasmine had said. "We pay in advance." I had the feeling that if I didn't take the money, someone else would. One way or another, they wouldn't be able to hold on to it.

When they started out of the park, Chi Chi hung back, fussing with her dog, letting him down for a pee, adjusting the strap on his coat. She gave me her cell phone number, reminding me she already had mine, my house number as well. Who the fuck was going to believe this? I thought, and then I got one more surprise, Chi Chi leaning forward and giving me a kiss on the cheek before running off to catch up to the others, already on the corner, waiting for the light to turn green.

It wasn't quite ten, and the restaurants along Hudson Street were still crowded with middle-class people eating ricotta ravioli or swordfish steak with capers and white wine. The video store was just closing, the last two customers leaving with rented movies to slip into their VCRs after they slipped into bed with snack food and soda at the ready. The Golden Rabbit had taken in the cut flowers and put them in the window, parchment-colored roses and tiny purple violets, red carnations with sprigs of white baby's breath, too cold to leave them out at night this time of year. And a few blocks north and west, where my clients had headed, the corners were dotted with working girls, girls who shaved their faces even more carefully than their legs, at least those who hadn't gone through the pain and expense of electrolysis. Rosalinda had just finished hers, Chi Chi had said, thirty-two sessions. It cost a fortune, but it was an investment in your future, she'd told me. I'd wondered how much of a future any of them had. While I was safe at home starting my research, they'd be leaning into the cars that stopped to shop the merchandise, making deals, risking their lives.

You never know when you get in a car, you going to come out again, Chi Chi had said right before they left. Oh, you come out, LaDonna said. The question is, you step out or you dumped out.

They'd given me six thousand dollars. The way I lived, that was enough to pay the bills for several months. I tried not to think about what they'd had to do to earn it, nor what they were figuring I was going to have to do to keep it. They didn't know the secrets of my trade any more than I knew theirs, and that was exactly how I thought things would stay. I had no way of knowing then how wrong I was.

On the way to Abingdon Square, I'd put out all the old newspapers and magazines for recycling. When I got to where I lived, I picked up the package by the string to bring it back in. This time, I held the stack as far away from my body as I could. Without checking carefully, I was pretty sure most of the neighborhood dogs had added to all the news the *Times* saw fit to print. In fact, I'd just stopped Dashiell from filing his own story.

In the yard, I opened the cord and pulled out the first two sections of the papers for the end of October and the beginning of November, leaving the rest piled up near the stairs. Once inside, I took them up to my desk and began to look for any mention of the murder of Rosalinda a week and a half earlier. There'd been nothing the last few days of last month, but when I got to the first of this month, I found something else of interest.

It was an article on the first page of the Metro section reporting the gangland-style execution of the manager of one of the meat plants, a Kevin Mulrooney, thirty-eight, who'd been found, bound and gagged with silver duct tape, hanging from one of the meat hooks. He'd been shot once in the heart, and again in the back of the head. Better safe than sorry. Mulrooney, it said, had been the manager of Keller's since the retirement of the previous manager two months earlier, and fellow workers said he was making "innovative changes" in the way Keller's operated.

I skimmed the rest quickly—Mulrooney was survived by his wife and kid, yadda, yadda—left it to the side, and began paging through the next days' papers until I found a follow-up piece, just a paragraph near the end of the Metro section saying that two men, Andrew Capelli and Joseph Maraccio, had been arrested and charged with the murder of Kevin Mulrooney three nights earlier. Both Capelli and Maraccio—who were employed by the CityWide Carting Company, which had, until a week prior to the murder, carted the trash from Keller's—denied any knowledge of the crime.

There was a short quote from the mayor calling the crime a throwback to the days when the mob ran the carting industry, saying he had reiterated his vow to make the Gansevoort and Hunts Point markets as squeaky-clean as he had made the Fulton Fish Market. Yeah, yeah.

I cut out the articles and put them aside, going back to the last week in October and starting again to look for mention of the death of a transvestite hooker. Fat fucking chance.

And found yet another piece of interest. The day after the report of Mulrooney's murder, there was a short piece near the back of the B section in an article called "Metro News Briefs."

COSTUMED MAN FOUND DEAD AT WATERFRONT

Sanitation workers, beginning the massive cleanup following the Greenwich Village Halloween Parade, found the body of Angel Rodriguez, 26, dressed in a long white gown and holding a small wand, sitting up against the chain-link fence where their vehicles are parked, at Gansevoort Street and the river, a spokesperson said. Mr. Rodriguez, who had lived in the Bronx, died of a wound to his throat. Police said no weapon had been recovered and that no suspect was in custody.

I thumbed through the B to B phone book, found the address for Keller's, grabbed my sheepskin coat and Dashiell's leash, and headed for the meat market. Dashiell was thrilled with the extra walk, pulling out in front as if he knew exactly where we were going and had to get there yesterday.

Keller's was off the main drag, on Little West Twelfth Street. You might think, since I lived on Tenth Street, that it would be only a few blocks away. But that's not how the Village works. Going north from Tenth Street, you run into Charles Street, where the Sixth Precinct used to be, then Perry, where there used to be a garage that fixed Rolls-Royces and Bentleys. After that there's Eleventh Street, but before you get to West Twelfth Street, you hit Bank and Bethune.

Farther east, to make things even more difficult, West Twelfth Street runs into West Fourth Street, and a street called Waverly runs into itself. In addition to that, West Twelfth Street stretches all the way across town, nearly from river to river, but Little West Twelfth Street is another story. It runs for only two blocks, bisected by Washington Street, where the transvestite hookers stroll. I passed a few of them on the way to Keller's—two on the corner near the deli on Gansevoort and Washington, a lone one across the street near the now-closed dry-cleaning shop—but didn't see *my* hookers, which at this point was fine with me.

There was a dump of a little diner on the southwest corner of Little West Twelfth and Washington, Hector's Place, Inc., where the butchers could snag a greasy burger or some take-out coffee. They probably had sweet rolls, a breakfast special, "homemade" soup, but I wasn't about to check the menu. I turned left and started checking the numbers, though it was difficult to see them in the dark. Walking under a sidewalk bridge at one point, the street strewn with trash, I saw something dark moving quickly from across the street and disappearing into one of the buildings on the side I was on. Sure enough, when I got to where it had vanished, the sign said Keller's. And under that, Fine Pork Products.

I stood there for a moment just looking at the place where Kevin Mulrooney had been found, executed, and refrigerated, wondering if I'd found the pig man that easily, and if I had, if his death had anything at all to do with Rosalinda's death.

I dialed Chi Chi's cell phone.

"Chi Chi?"

"Who's this?"

"Rachel."

"I can't talk now. I'll call you back."

"Hey, baby," I heard her say, the phone no longer close to her mouth. Then: "Come on, honey, give me jus' a minute, an' I'm going send you right to heaven. This here's real important." I heard a car door open. "You home?" she asked.

"No. Call my cell phone."

I crossed the street, moving around to keep warm, understanding why the hookers did those little dances, that it
wasn't only to attract attention but also to keep from freezing.
I wanted to put a little distance between me and Keller's so
that I could see the whole building and also distance myself
from whatever ran across my path moments earlier, as if
whatever it had been was the only one of its kind.

It was a smallish building, two stories high, made of
wood, an anachronism if ever there was one. The windowless
ground floor was probably all refrigerated, and upstairs,
where there were three small windows, that would be where
the offices were, where the manager did his paperwork and
made innovative changes.

Was that also where the pig man met with Rosalinda once
or twice?

I shivered, pulling up my collar and jumping around in
place, glad I was off the main drag and hoping no one would
drive around the corner and ask me, "How much?"

I looked around for a grate in the sidewalk, which is
where a lot of the homeless slept, trying to keep warm on
whatever heat escapes the basement where gigantic trans-
formers step the electricity down from 1,000 to 110 volts to
make it usable in big buildings' lines, a process that gives off
tremendous heat. But I was kidding myself. There were no
skyscrapers here. I was in the wrong neighborhood for sidewalk grates, and anyway, if there were any here, there would
probably be hordes of rodents streaming in and out of them.

Twenty minutes later, my cell phone rang. I fumbled it
open without taking off my warm gloves.

"What?" she said.

Time is money.

"Angel Rodriguez," I said.

Silence.

"Chi Chi?"

"Where'd you get that name?"

"The *New York Times*. November 2. Small piece in the Metro section. Just a paragraph about a twenty-six-year-old male in a white gown, carrying a wand—"

"She was twenty-eight."

"I'm just telling you what I read in the paper."

"And it said her name?"

"No, Chi Chi. It said *his* name."

"And you—"

"Put two and two together."

"Which is like what you do, right?"

"Right. It's like why you and LaDonna and Jasmine hired me."

"No need to be sarcastic. Just because I'm a hooker don't mean you shouldn't treat me with respect. What do you want me to do, get a job in retail? You think I could be on the floor at Jeffrey, or at Bloomingdale? You think someone wants me out front anywhere?"

"Sorry—I'm just cold standing out here in the street."

"Honey, you don't know from cold. You just a beginner." I heard her light a cigarette. "Gave these up last week." She stopped to exhale. I could hear her blowing the smoke out, hear her sighing. "And the week before that. I ain't go no willpower."

"There was a butcher killed the same night, Halloween night. Worked at Keller's. You know Keller's?"

"I mighta passed it once or twice. It's around here, right? What, on Thirteenth Street, or somethin'?"

"Little West Twelfth. So, was he the pig man you all tried so hard not to mention tonight?"

"Was who?"

"The dead butcher. Kevin Mulrooney. Was he the pig man?"

"No. No way."

"How can you be sure? You said you didn't know his name."

"She might have mentioned a first name one time."

"She might have?"

"Yeah. But I got a lot on my mind, you know? Shit."

"What happened?"

"My smoke went out."

"Yeah, well, Chi Chi, my friend, what was the first name Rosalinda might have mentioned? Can you help me out here? I'm working for *you*. I'm not the enemy."

"I can't recall, but I know it wasn't Kevin. You said Kevin, din't you?"

"Right. Think, Chi Chi." Whatever she was smoking was not helping the conversation one little bit.

"It was like a Polish name, far as I can remember. Kevin's Irish, right?"

"Try a little harder, Chi Chi. Try to remember."

"I'll get back to you."

"Chi Chi, if you want me to do this for you—"

"Hey, baby, you goin' out?"

"How much for the both of us?"

"Both of youse? What are you, crazy? What'd you think, just because I'm a prostitute, you could do anything you dream up, like I have no say in the matter, like I'm too stupid to know what's a good idea, what isn't? Get lost, two at a time." Way too loud, one word eating the next.

I heard the car peel out.

"Wanda'll do 'em. Wanda, she don't care. She used to work with this girl Susan, but she's dead already. They called her black-eyed Susan, she got beat up so much. Mostly—"

"Chi Chi, I'm still here. Talk to me."

"I *am* talking to you. I'm saying Grace," she said. "He asked Grace to do them, she'd take off her size-thirteen-and-a-half shoe and give him two at a time on his stupid, bald head. Grace, she don't take shit from no one. Ebony, she a whole 'nother story. Ebony got a screw loose. Everybody says so. Had her face done, you know, like Rosalinda did, but Ebony, she didn't do her upper lip. Said it hurt too much. It was too sensitive. Can you imagine! She spend all that money, she still look like shit. What's a little pain matter? In this business, appearance is everything."

I heard another car. Business was brisk.

"Look, can we do this later? I gotta earn a living."

I thought she hung up, because for a while I didn't hear anything. Something black and low to the ground moved across the street. I yanked Dashiell's leash, and we headed for the corner.

Then she was back. "Don't be like that, baby. Yeah? Up yours, too."

"Chi Chi?"

I heard a horn honk. "I'll call you in the morning," she whispered. "Hey, baby. I'm goin' make you feel *real* good, ya hear?" And then the line went quiet. Two cars passed Little West Twelfth Street. I could see Chi Chi's near-white hair as the second one went by.

The rat aside, I had a lousy feeling about Keller's, about Chi Chi's convenient memory loss, about life in general from where I stood. I checked my watch. It was nearly midnight. Keller's wouldn't be open until just before dawn, and when it was, no way was someone going to talk to me about the death of their manager. I needed to get in there when they were closed, check their paperwork, see what I could find out. I shivered at the thought. There were more rats than people in New York City, a denser population here in the meat market than, say, the Upper East Side. But that was just an educated guess.

I wondered if there were rats in the cellar at Keller's, the answer a no-brainer. I wondered if any of them came upstairs, especially when the place was quiet, the way it was now, the way it would be when I was in there, reading what was in their files, quiet as a little mouse.

I wondered if they moved around much in broad daylight. But what if they didn't? I couldn't either. Like the rest of the denizens of this street, I'd have to do my work under cover of darkness.

I walked back to Keller's again, staying on the opposite side of the street, passing by and going all the way to the end of the block, to West Street, where the wind picked up my scarf and almost carried it away. About a third of the markets on Little West Twelfth Street looked as if they'd closed not just for the night but for good. More and more of the markets were moving to Hunts Point in the Bronx, another neighborhood of wholesale food suppliers and drugged-out hookers. I'd have to come back in daylight to make sure, but some of the buildings looked deserted; a few were even starting to go to seed.

The building to the right of Keller's, my right, that is, had a sign that said they sold rabbit, grouse, pheasant, and other game. The one on the other side, the one closer to West Street, to the river and that punishing wind, to where Angel Rodriguez's body had been found, looked deserted; no vehicles outside, a heavy padlock on the door, one of the windows upstairs broken and not even repaired with cardboard and tape. All three structures as similar as they could be, aside from their signs.

I walked back to the corner again, now looking to see how I could implement my next good plan, hoping I could do it without freezing to death. At least the hookers got to get into warm cars. They didn't just stay out in the street the way Dash and I were doing.

Alert for movement, even paper swept up and sent tumbling by a gust of wind, I checked out both sides of the street for a place that would let me see without being seen, then thought of a place where I could get warm until the time was right to settle into my hiding place.

4

She's a Virgin

I SPENT a few hours at Florent, the all-night bistro a block away on Gansevoort Street, eating steak frites, then nursing a glass of wine and writing down the questions I needed to answer, watching the clock as I worked. I wanted to be back at Keller's at least an hour before they opened, but since I hadn't tested access to my brilliant hideout, I gave myself forty-five minutes extra, hoping the steak and red wine would keep me warm while I secreted myself and waited, probably for nothing.

Back at Little West Twelfth Street, I looked for the best way to climb up to the top of the sidewalk bridge that protected the first half of the block—from what, I couldn't be sure. Sidewalk bridges are used to protect pedestrians from falling debris when, in compliance with Local Law 10, owners have contracted to have the brickwork repointed and cornices made secure. But none of the squat old buildings that housed meat markets, or used to house meat markets, on Little West Twelfth Street were being repaired. And anyway, I didn't think Local Law 10 applied to such low buildings. I thought it was for high rises since it was passed after someone was killed by a falling piece of cornice from a tall building. Nevertheless, in keeping with the general chaos of the market, the bridge was there and appeared to have been in place for years. Had there ever been razor wire along the top, luckily for me, it was long gone, but the supports looked sturdy. Whether or not the top of the bridge was, I was about to find out. The bridge went from the building line at the corner to the building just past Keller's. For my purposes, assuming I could get up there without killing myself, and that the bridge would hold me, it was perfect.

I found a wooden box down the block and brought it back to the side farthest from the corner, hoping that this way I wouldn't be seen. Little West Twelfth Street was off the stroll, and at this hour there was no one around, at least not that I could see. I placed the box next to the far, inner leg of the bridge, standing it on its side to give it more height, then gingerly testing it out. I was still short of where I could reach the top and hoist myself up. Then I got a better idea.

Like all the bull and terrier dogs, Dashiell can scale a nearly perpendicular wall and leap astonishing heights, even without a running start; the muscles he sports are not just for show. I remember once hiking with him on a steep mountain trail, astonished at how fast and graceful he was, moving up the mountain not on the zigzagging path the way I did, slow and unsure of my footing, but by going straight up like a mountain goat, his mouth open in a grin, happy to be using those powerful muscles on something that actually required them.

I pulled the box way back, found some boards and concrete blocks, and made a sort of platform a few feet back from the bridge. Then, leaving Dashiell's leash attached to his collar but dropping the handle, I backed him partway down the block and told him to wait. Next I got between the platform I'd created and the bridge, bending slightly forward to round my back, hoping like hell Dashiell would understand what I had in mind for him. I told him *hup*, and he took off, barely touching the platform as he ran. I heard the board creak, then he was on me, his back feet digging into my waist, his front paws lightly on my shoulders. I never even had the chance to wince at the thought of what those nails would do to me when he took off, it was all so quick. But the sheepskin coat was thick enough to protect me. He seemed to fly over my head, and then the bridge sighed, arcing slightly under his weight, dust and bits of mortar and God knows what else falling to the garbage-covered sidewalk beneath. When I looked up, he barked once. He was peering over the edge, his flews hanging down, his forehead creased, impatient for me to join him. I was comforted by his approval of my plan, even knowing that no one but a dog would think I was doing a wise thing.

Moving the box close again, I stood on it and reached for Dash's leash. With one hand finding purchase in the structure and the other on the leash, I told him to back up; between us, me climbing, Dashiell pulling, I was lifted up to the top of the bridge. It moaned, and held.

After checking the surface out to make sure that none of the boards was broken, and brushing off as much of the debris as I could, using one of my gloves as a whisk broom, we lay side by side, facing Keller's, and began what I now hoped would be a fruitful vigil.

He showed up at ten to four, parking and reparking his car to get it exactly where he wanted it, a case of obsessive-compulsive disorder if ever I'd seen one, then whistling as he unlocked and removed the padlock from the door, locking it back onto one of the handles, then disappearing inside. At first nothing happened. We waited. A light went on upstairs. We waited some more.

I heard Clint before I saw her. As she passed under the bridge, picking her way through the trash, the dachshund began to growl, then bark. Dashiell stood, sending a shower of dust and small stones down between the slats. I signaled him to stay and held my breath, hoping this wasn't all for nothing, hoping she wouldn't look up and see us through the openings between the boards that made up the floor of the bridge, wonder what I was doing there, and abort her current project.

I heard Chi Chi shush her dog. Moments later she stepped out from under the bridge, tiptoeing through the parking area out front as if there might be someone around who shouldn't hear her, Clint still grumbling deep in his throat, Dashiell's tail stirring the air behind us as he stood next to where I was lying, still as ice.

I watched her stop at the door to fix her hair, running the fingers of one hand through that big, near-white mop of pubic-like curls, wiping the corners of her mouth where lipstick tends to smudge, pulling up her panty hose, and doing something distinctly unladylike in the vicinity of her crotch.

She pulled Clint out of her jacket and let him down, bending and whispering to him. I saw him lift his leg and immediately get scooped up again and tucked not back into her jacket but under her arm.

She reached for the door and pushed it open, disappearing into the dark. Then a hand came back out and pulled the door closed. In the quiet, I could hear it click shut.

I let out my breath. I was no longer feeling cold. I looked straight across to that lit-up window now, thinking that if either of them looked out, they would be able to see Dashiell standing on the bridge. So I tapped the board in front of him, and when he lay down, I put an arm across his wide, warm back and waited again.

After ten or so minutes I changed my mind, deciding to abandon my hiding place before Chi Chi appeared. When she stepped gingerly out into the parking area in front of Keller's, stopping to put some bills inside the pocket of Clint's coat, I was across the street. But she didn't see me. She picked her way under the bridge and headed back toward Washington Street. Until her phone rang.

"Who's this? LaDonna, this you?"

"No. It's Rachel."

"What you doing up so late?"

"Waiting for you."

"What you mean?"

She'd stopped walking, but she wasn't looking around. She stood in the dark under the sidewalk bridge, her back to me, Clint's little rump sticking out beyond her elbow, his tail hanging straight down like a plumb line.

"I'm across the street."

Now she turned, frantic, until she found me with her eyes. I stood there watching as she crossed the street, putting Clint down when she got there.

"What you doing, spying on me?"

"Exactly."

"I can explain."

"I thought you might be able to, but it would have been a hell of a lot simpler for you to tell me what's going on in the first damn place."

"It's not what you think."

"And what is that? What do I think, Chi Chi?"

"That it's all about the money. Well, it *is* steady money. I admit that. He pays real good. Better than most." She unzipped the little pocket in Clint's coat and pulled out two twenties and a ten. "Sometimes, some of 'em, you know, when it's slow out and I really need the money, they pays me five. Two even, one time. I had to. I didn't have enough for the subway. The night before, I'd been run in, beat up. I was really hurting, and I needed somethin' for the pain, you know. But here, I get what I'm worth." She held up the money a second time. "And I can use the bathroom after, freshen up, make myself look good for the next customer."

"That's not what I was thinking."

"No?"

"I was thinking that there's a chance, just a chance, that he's the one who killed Rosalinda and Mulrooney, and that you're taking your life in your hands when you see him like this."

"It couldn't be him."

"Why not?"

"It jus' couldn't."

"Because—"

"He never hit me, not even once. He doesn't have much of a temper. She lucky, his fiancée."

"You never heard the expression, Revenge is a dish best served cold?"

"Wha's that supposed to mean? That he did it? That he killed Rosalinda?"

"No. It means you don't need a hot temper to murder someone."

"That's not how it is with us." She was shaking her head so vigorously, Clint began to bark. "You shut up," she told him. "You could wake the dead, that mouth of yours."

"So how is it with you?"

She looked exhausted. Even with all that makeup, freshly applied at Keller's, she looked used-up and ready to fold, struggling to keep her eyes open.

"It's in the heat of the moment. Like someone finds out." She just looked at me, to see if we were on the same page.

"And?"

"They might stiff you. 'Cause you cheated them, they say. You tricked them, pretending to be one thing and really being something else. This one guy, he catches me off guard, you know what I'm saying? And he goes, 'Oh, my God, it's a man. Do I finish?'"

"What did he decide?"

Chi Chi rolled her eyes. "Paid me, too. But some of them, they feel like a fool, and they gets pissed something fierce."

I nodded.

"That's the least of it, not paying. They get so mad sometimes." She shook her head. "Sometimes you got to go to Emergency. You can't work for a couple of days. Means you can't eat, or nothing. Means you could lose your home, have to live in some abandoned car, take a crap next to a tree, like you was a dog. Could be, your luck runs out, it's worse than that. Like what happened to Rosalinda."

"You're saying it was a john who did her?"

"I'm saying—" She sighed. "I'm saying, some people, you put one over on them, they feel . . ." She seemed to blank out for a second. Then she began to shake her head. "Look, I'm telling you the truth. You listening?"

"I am."

"You injure their pride, some of them, it makes them mad enough to kill. You understand what I'm saying? It's a guy thing," she said, reminding me she knew whereof she spoke. "Look, we gotta go. I promised Vinnie."

"Vinnie? That's your idea of a Polish name?"

"Whatever."

I watched the ten float down to the sidewalk. Chi Chi didn't seem to notice.

"The only thing he cares about is I jus' gotta make sure none of them sees me when they come on."

"The other butchers?"

I pointed to the bill, and Dashiell picked it up. I took it from him, held it up to show her, and put it in the pocket of Clint's jacket.

"Right. They would, you know, never let up on him, he did it with someone like me. He couldn't stay working there. The truckers, well, that's a whole other story. They get what they want, and that's the end of it. No one knows but the two consenting adults involved. You get my meaning?"

I nodded. "The payer and the payee."

"Yeah."

"You're saying it's a cash transaction with no repercussions."

She nodded.

"Hey, the guy's been driving since fucking Iowa or some other godforsaken dump with dead pigs in the back. He's got needs. He's human, right? So for twenty, thirty bucks, he feels like a million. Not a bad return on his money. End of story. No one from the pee hole where he lives is gonna give him a hard time, because no one from there knows nothing. They never left there in their miserable lives, and if they did, this is the last place on earth they'd show up. Sometimes that's what I think it is, Rachel."

She stumbled, and I caught her elbow.

"The last place on earth?" I asked.

Chi Chi sighed. "I want this trick, I gotta be prompt arriving and get out prompt, he says. That's all. And one other thing."

"What's that?"

"We maintain the illusion. He don't wanna find a dick in his hand unless it's his own."

"Got it. So this is the pig man you didn't want to talk about?"

She nodded. "Look, we gotta talk somewhere else. I can't stay here. It's getting to be time."

"For them to open?"

"Yeah. For the rest of them to come. And the truckers. I might do some of them down the block, but they see me here, it's a whore of another color. They could run me over soon as look at me. Get it?"

"I do," I told her. And I did.

"Far as they're concerned, we're all—" She moved the air with her hand.

"Interchangeable?"

"Trash."

Walking back toward Washington Street, I remembered seeing an article in the Horatio Street newsletter the winter before saying some of the tranny hookers were living at the Gansevoort pier, burrowing into the piles of salt used to melt the ice after a storm or getting into the trucks, sleeping there, nowhere else to do it, just trying like hell to survive however they could.

The first of the delivery trucks was parked around the corner, backed up perpendicular to the sidewalk. There was a patrol car just turning off Fourteenth Street, heading our way,
doing a slow crawl. Chi Chi saw it, too. She grabbed my arm
and pulled me across the street, pushing me back under the
sidewalk bridge. Then she turned to face west, pulling up her
collar, like that was going to fool New York's finest.

"Okay, boys. Sun's almost up," came blasting over the
loudspeaker. "Back under your rocks. NOW."

Chi Chi's arm in mine, we walked west, into the wind off
the river, my face feeling numb in no time.

"He engaged, Vinnie," she whispered as we passed
Keller's. "And she's like very religious, his fiancée."

I nodded.

"She's a virgin."

"What?"

"Means she never done it."

I whistled. "No shit?"

She shrugged, her shoulder rubbing against mine. Aside
from the hair, we were the same height, at least with those
heels she was wearing.

"Anyways, that's what he says she says. Him and me, it's
jus' until they get married and he gets to do her."

Under cover of darkness I rolled my eyes. "Touching."

"No, really." She laughed. "I give him a month. No, two
weeks. Then he's on my cell, bobbing and weaving, telling me
a tall one, why he's gotta see me."

"First Rosalinda, now you? A long engagement."

"She wants a June wedding, a long white gown, six brides-
maids, he said, the whole package."

"So how did this happen, Rosalinda was killed and you
started doing Vinnie?"

She opened her mouth, but I stopped her.

"The truth this time, since obviously you do kiss and tell.
At least, you tell. Otherwise, how would you have known how
and where to contact Vinnie the pig man after Rosalinda—"

"She was my roommate, Rosalinda. She did, you know, tell me some stuff. Mos' of it you don't want to talk about. You don't want to think about it. It's jus' a living, what you have to do to pay the rent and eat, pay for what else you need."

"But this was different?"

"Right. Because you could clean up, go to the bathroom, like a person. 'Cause you knew, no matter how slow the night was, younger hookers on the stroll, taking your work away from you like candy from a baby, whatever, at least you'd get your fifty."

"So how did the transition occur?"

"What do you mean?"

We turned onto West Street, holding each other tighter against the wind.

"Come on," I said, heading for the corner. "Let's get something to eat. Let's get out of the wind."

"What did you mean?"

"The transition? How did you start"—I stopped, fishing for a euphemism, changing my mind—"after Rosalinda was killed?"

"I'd done him before, once when she was sick. She had a bad reaction to some hormones. The doctors, they never ask what else you taking. They didn't say, don't take this, you on that. She was feeling bad, up all day throwin' up. She tol' me to go. She didn't want to lose it to crazy Ebony or Alice. Alice, she'd steal your eyeballs out of your head, you don't pay attention. She's got car phones, gloves, cigarettes, even the change from the ashtray, anything she sees in a car's not nailed down, she takes it."

"Alice?"

"Mmm. Yeah. So Rosalinda, she says, You go do him. Tell him I sent you."

"And you did?"

"Right."

"When was that?"

Chi Chi shrugged, pulled out a cigarette, lit it, cupping the match in one big hand.

"And what about the night she was killed? Had you done him that night?"

She shook her head. "No way. Only when she tol' me to. And after."

"After she'd died?"

"Yeah. After that."

For normal people, people who were asleep, it was still Friday night. But technically it was Saturday, so Florent would be open. They closed at five A.M. during the week, but on weekends they didn't close at all. You wanted rillettes at four in the morning, salad Niçoise at five, you knew where to go. We took a table in the front corner, sent the dogs under it, and ordered soup, holding our hands around the bowls when they came.

When the waiter began to back away, Chi Chi grabbed his sleeve.

"Now I need a burger, honey."

His skin was a light reddish brown, his long dreadlocks pulled back in a ponytail.

"Rare. With fries."

He nodded, his face saying, What the fuck do I care what she orders. Burger, fries. He heard it a hundred times on every shift. How enthusiastic could he be, a New York waiter? Especially since none of them were actually waiters. They were all supporting their art, waiting on tables while they waited for a big break, star opposite Julia, get a long run on *The Sopranos*, go from nowhere straight to the top.

"And don't be stingy," Chi Chi said, "you hear? I'm starved."

He turned to leave.

Chi Chi grabbed his sleeve again.

"And a rum and Coke," she said. "Soon as you get a chance." She watched him walk away.

"Cute butt," she told me, one hand over her mouth.

Despite her flirtatiousness with the waiter, in the harsh light of the little bistro, Chi Chi looked defeated. Or sour. Maybe both. I could see how rough her skin was under the thick pancake makeup, but I couldn't see the shadow of a beard. Apparently one of the things she'd used all that money on was hair removal, a pretty normal business expense for transvestite hookers.

"So what's the rest of his name, this Vinnie person?"

Chi Chi shrugged. Then she excused herself to go to the bathroom. I ate some soup and looked around. When she came around the corner from the john, way in the back of the long, narrow room, I could tell immediately that something was different. She bounced toward me, stopping at three other tables to chat, bending over and whispering at one, tossing her head way back and laughing at another, sitting on an empty chair and picking up a handful of some woman's fries at the third, feeding it to her boyfriend. I was pretty sure when she landed in her own seat across from me, Chi Chi wouldn't be looking sour any longer.

"We don't use last names, and neither do they," she said, as if I'd asked her Vinnie's last name seconds rather than minutes ago. She picked up her spoon, looked at the soup, then pushed the bowl across the small table. The rum and Coke came, and Chi Chi began to drink, holding it even when she put it back on the table, tapping her nails nervously against the sweating glass.

"I'm going to need to get in there, to see if I can find anything connecting the two murders," I said.

"What? Into Keller's?"

I nodded.

"No problem. You can take my place tomorrow."

I raised a hand in protest, but Chi Chi took my hand in hers with a surprising tenderness, bringing it down to the table. She leaned forward and lowered her voice. "He's not *attached*," she said, "leastways not to me. He wouldn't care if you did him. In fact, he might like a change, s'long as you promise to—"

"Get in and out on time."

She nodded and smiled, pleased I was such a quick study. I shook my head. "I don't think so."

Chi Chi shrugged. "We can split the money, if that's it." Scowling.

"That's not it."

"Then what? Oh, I get it. Okay, keep it all. I'll live."

Something about her eyes scared me. I looked away for a moment, thinking how nice it would be to be home, asleep in my own bed.

"It wouldn't help, Chi Chi. I need to be in there alone, not when Vinnie's there. I need to look through files and papers. Look, you have your way of working, and I have mine. There has to be another way for me to get in there when they're closed. I need a little time to figure that out."

"This Mulrooney, he never met Rosalinda. He never even laid eyes on her. What you think you're going to find in there?"

"I don't know, but coincidence gives me a funny taste in my mouth," I told her, immediately regretting my choice of words. "They were both killed the same night. And she had a connection to Mulrooney's place of business. Maybe that's just what happened. Maybe those murders were two separate—"

"Word is, he was killed because he changed trash companies. He comes in, brand-new, first thing he rocks the boat." She shook her head. "Dumb." She pulled out a cigarette and lit it, cupping it in her hand and holding her hand down at her side, like at five in the morning someone was going to give a shit, was going to tell her not to smoke. "Rosalinda, she didn't have nothing to do with the carting industry, and like I told you, she never met Mulrooney. Vinnie had her out of there long before Mulrooney showed up for work."

I nodded. "Still. I'm not going to tell you how to do your work, and you're not going to tell me how to do mine, deal?"

She shrugged one wide shoulder. "I was jus' saying, is all."

"If it's nothing, no connection between them, fine. I'd be

less than responsible to you and LaDonna and Jasmine if I didn't check it out."

When the waiter brought the burger and fries and put it down in front of her, Chi Chi looked confused. Then she pushed the plate toward me, as if I'd been the one who'd ordered it. It sat there getting cold until the check came. There was a moment of awkwardness, but Chi Chi insisted on paying, picking up Clint and pulling the money out of the little pocket in his jacket, leaving a generous tip.

"They's in a cash business, too," she said. A little too loud. Half the people in the restaurant had turned to look at her.

I got up, then sat down again.

"Chi Chi, you're going to see Vinnie again tomorrow morning?"

"Yeah. Why, you change your mind?"

"How many times a week do you see him?"

She shrugged. "Whenever he aks me to."

"Well, on average, what is it, two times a week, three?"

"Yeah, around that. Sometimes four."

"Where the hell does he get the money to pay you fifty bucks a pop, three, four times a week?"

"Sometimes from his pocket, sometimes from the cash box."

"The cash box?"

She nodded, as if to say, Where else would he get the money from but from Keller's not so petty cash, what was so unusual about that? "That's what he say, You wait here, Chi Chi, I'm short today. I go get your money from the cash box."

"But you never saw it, the cash box? It's not in the office?"

"Uh-uh."

"He goes somewhere else to get the money?"

"Um-hmm."

"But you don't know where?"

"Uh-uh. 'Cept one time. Usually he puts the money on the edge of the desk." She sniffed and wiped her nose with her hand. "But this one time, he touched me. I was picking it up, and he grabbed my arm and pulled me toward the door. It was getting late, he said. I had to go. And his hand, it was ice cold."

One more thing to check at Keller's.

Outside, I headed east. Chi Chi just stood there watching me go. When I got to the corner, I turned back. She was still there, the wind pulling that blond hair across her face, hugging herself to keep Clint against her chest, her knees slightly bent, toes pointing in, looking small and lost.

5

I Cocked My Head

I CLOSED my coat and headed home, the streets dark and deserted, only an occasional light on in the buildings I passed, some insomniac waiting for dawn, the way I sometimes did, or an unusually early riser, someone who went to the gym before work, had a crying baby, suffered from bouts of acid reflux. A small blue sedan pulled up near the corner of Greenwich and Charles Streets, and a squat, dark woman in a hooded sweatshirt and long parka got out, pulled a stack of the *New York Times* off the backseat, and headed for the lobby of the closest building. Other than that, I was alone, no one rushing off to work, walking the dog, reparking the car. Today and tomorrow, you could forget about the car. Monday you'd be out again, trying to snag a legal space, your life controlled by alternate-side-of-the-street parking regulations.

When I got back to Tenth Street, I unlocked the wrought-iron gate, closed it behind me, and unhooked Dashiell's leash, thinking about what I'd seen earlier, until I realized what was right in front of my eyes, Betty running to meet Dashiell, the door to the cottage ajar, and Chip standing on the top step. I'd forgotten he was coming over.

"How long have you been here?"

"Since midnight. I had a ten-o'clock in Chelsea. I tried your cell phone. Didn't you get my message?"

I shook my head. I hadn't looked.

We walked inside, and I told him about the call from Chi Chi, and some, but not all, of what the girls had told me in the park, leaving out, among other things, the part about the dog trainer who had given her my name. Not a problem. It couldn't have been Chip. We told each other everything.

Didn't we?

Then Chip was saying something, and I wasn't listening. I was thinking about all the things I'd never told him, starting with the cleaned-up story I'd just related, and segueing to other things, to the parts of myself I hadn't shared with anyone. Why had I thought, even for a minute, that Chip didn't also have parts of his life he kept to himself, secrets he wouldn't share, even with me? If I'd learned anything doing this work, it was that you never knew anybody, not even the people you thought you knew best.

The door was still open, the sky now the most incredible blue I'd ever seen.

"I can't stop trying to figure out how I'm going to get into Keller's," I said, "without actually taking Chi Chi's place."

"Good thinking."

"What is?" I cocked my head, a result of living with dogs for so long.

"Not taking Chi Chi's place."

"Oh, that. No kidding." I looked at my watch. "I've got to get cleaned up and get back to work."

"You just got home."

"Well, you know what they say, a man works from sun to sun, but a woman's work is never done. It's six-thirty. The market's open, and I have to try to buy a couple of pork chops for dinner."

"I thought they only sold wholesale. Anyway, I'm working tonight—"

"Me, too," I said, grinning. "And this morning."

Now he was grinning, too. "Nick and Nora Charles?"

"Sure. If you have the time. I'll be ready in ten minutes."

"Give me fifteen. I need a cup of coffee."

"I'll make it seven," I told him. "We'll get take-out and drink it on the way."

6

Vinnie Looked Annoyed

THERE was a heavyset man in white, a transparent shower cap covering his hair, a hard hat over that, standing next to what looked like a semi full of dead pigs, its back doors open and facing the entrance to Keller's. A thinner man, his hair as black as tar, long, pointy nose, stood next to him taking notes on a clipboard.

We'd left the dogs home. I'd changed to a clean jacket and taken a purse, for God's sake. We approached the younger guy, the one with the clipboard, and smiled. He didn't. Perhaps it wasn't us. Perhaps it was the sudden, violent death of the manager that had him on edge.

"We were wondering if we could get some pork chops," Chip said, trying to sound as nerdy as possible. "We've just moved in," he said, pointing back behind him, as if we lived in one of the refrigerated plants across the street, "and we heard—"

"This is strictly wholesale." The tag on his white coat said V. Esposito. "You want two pork chops, try D'Agostino's."

"But we heard—"

"Ottomanelli's. Bleecker Street. Not here."

"Vinnie," the chunky guy called out. "You checking the order in or what?"

Vinnie shook his head, no way were we doing business with him, and walked away. Standing where we were, we could see partway into the first-floor, stainless-steel walls, giant vats for grinding meat or making sausages, several guys in white walking around in rubber boots and a hose snaking along one wall, for the afternoon cleanup. Two men from the truck were carrying in boxes. On a rack inside the truck, whole carcasses hung on hooks, like coats in the back of a classroom. At the bigger plants, on Washington Street, the apparatuses on which the carcasses were hung in the truck attached to the ones outside the market, and the meat rode inside the way clothes circle around at the dry cleaner, swinging ever so slightly from side to side as the machine sent them in for processing. Those places had permanent metal canopies that housed the moving hooks, not only to get the meat inside quickly and efficiently but so the butchers could work outside, rain or shine, in relative comfort. At Keller's, if it was raining, snowing, hotter than hell, you were out in the weather until the order got checked in, no two ways about it. Two more men came out from inside to help with the morning's delivery, a short, stocky young guy, kinky blond hair sticking out from under the net under his hard hat, and a dark guy with a sweet, round face he hadn't shaved in three days. I couldn't read their name tags.

We were still standing there when a tired-looking guy with a little mustache, a beret on his unnaturally dark hair, showed up, pulling a handcart. Vinnie nodded to him and bellowed to someone inside.

"Carl, bring out Charlie's order."

Charlie looked at Chip and shrugged. "I tell him Charles." He pronounced it *Sharl*. "He calls me Charlie."

Chip opened his mouth. Vinnie looked annoyed. "He's buying for a restaurant. Hotels and restaurants, that's what we do. We don't sell to individuals."

"This is so interesting," I said. "Okay if we take a peek inside?"

Vinnie turned back to the truck to check off the next eight boxes. I took that as a yes and stepped closer to the door, careful to keep out of the way of the truckers. That's when I saw it, a small flap of heavy black rubber to the left of the door, hidden by the truck from where we stood. There was a trash can in front of it, to conceal it when the truck wasn't there, not something they wanted to advertise.

The cold air from inside rolled out like the waves at high tide. I shivered, then turned when I heard a noise behind me. The big guy with the thick neck was headed my way, a scowl on his face.

"Are you the manager?" I asked him in my sweetest voice. Then, before giving him a chance to answer, I made my plea again. "Do you ever make exceptions?" I whispered. "We could even come back later."

"Lady, you're going to have to step back. Insurance regulations. Hard-hat area." T. McCoy tapped his with his knuckles. "You could get hurt, hanging around here."

I nodded and backed away, taking one last look at the building before picking my way back to where Chip was standing. I took his arm and pulled him toward the street.

"There's a pet door. I'd bet big money it's for a cat. I can just about guarantee they need one. Could also be a way for me to get in there."

"Excuse me. You're going to fit through a cat port?"

"Uh-uh."

"You're thinking of hiring on a midget?"

"Uh-uh."

He was heading toward Washington Street, and I pulled him the other way.

"Where are we going?"

"I want to check out the building next door. When I was here last night, it looked vacant."

We walked a few steps past Keller's to the identical building next door, the one with the broken window on the second floor.

"What do you think?" I asked him.

"Looks deserted."

"That's what I thought last night, but I couldn't be sure, even with the broken window. Hell, for all I could tell in the dark, it could have been broken ten minutes before I got here. But if it were operating, it would be open now."

"There's not even a sign."

"Of life?"

"No, a sign saying their name and what they sell."

We walked across the parking area to take a closer look, the door padlocked, trash and papers blown up against it.

"Perfect," I said.

"For what?"

"You said you didn't want me to take Chi Chi's place for a night, right? Anyway, even if I did, I couldn't check out Keller's paperwork with Vinnie there watching me."

"That was Vinnie, the guy we spoke to?"

"Unless there's more than one Vinnie working there."

"So, go on. What's the deal with this place?"

"I thought I might ask Chi Chi to see if there's any way Clint could get me into Keller's, like a sliding back door held closed with a stick, I should be so lucky, or a window on the second floor he could unlatch. Look at the little one up there to the right. Doesn't that look like a push-out window, maybe in a bathroom?"

Chip looked up at the small window I had indicated.

"Could be."

"Well."

"Well, what?"

"I'm sure I can get in this building. Probably not much in it to protect at this point. Even if I have to climb up and break a window—"

"Are you crazy? You could go to jail for that."

"You worry too much. Listen, if I can figure out how to get in here, and if Chi Chi will let me work with Clint—"

"Back-chaining."

"Right. I'll teach him what to do in this building, then when he's got it, I'll send him into Keller's when it's closed, through the cat port. He can unlatch the window for me, and I can get in, check the paperwork, satisfy my curiosity, and both of us will be out of there long before Vinnie shows in the early morning."

"How did you say you were going to get up to that window he'll open for you?"

"I'm starving," I told him. "How about some breakfast?"

I began to walk, heading back to Washington Street for my third visit to Florent in the same day, though in truth it seemed like ages since I'd been there, sitting with Chi Chi, listening to her spin the truth until neither one of us knew what was real and what wasn't.

But didn't I do that, too, I thought, stopping and waiting for Chip to catch up, even when I wasn't on the job?

7

You Don't Think It's Possible to Be Fooled?

I DON'T know why I was hungry. I'd had a steak, green beans, and thin, crisp French fries in the middle of the night, part of a bowl of soup a few hours after that, then a small, sweet clementine in the morning, which I'd peeled and eaten on the way to Keller's while Chip sipped his coffee and ate a croissant, the flakes of pastry floating from his mouth to the front of his jacket like snow. But when my bacon and eggs came, I felt I'd become Dashiell, the smells filling my senses separately and together, so that even the odor of the butter on my toast seemed to saturate my mouth and I longed to dip my head, as he would have, and eat until everything was gone, licking the plate until it was clean, then, my forehead pleated with wrinkles of concern, beg for more. Had Chi Chi slipped something into my soup when I wasn't looking? No, it couldn't be that. Her little trip to the bathroom had had the opposite effect on her. She'd lost her appetite.

"What does this Clint dog know?" Chip asked, lifting a hand to get the waiter's attention, then pointing to his coffee cup.

"He's housebroken."

"How long do you think it will take you to teach him what he needs to know?"

"Don't know. All I've seen him do so far is ride around in Chi Chi's jacket. And possibly take a leak on command."

"That's a good sign. At least she taught him something."

"The thing is, I won't know how complicated the job will be until I get inside the building next to Keller's. Assuming the layout inside is the same, that'll tell me how far he'll have to go, what's involved in opening the latch, if that's what turns out to be best. At this point, I'm not even sure there's a way he can let me in."

"Wouldn't it be infinitely simpler to have Chi Chi leave the latch open for you, right before she leaves?"

"She could. But I doubt it would stay open. I'm sure they do a walk-through before closing up. Anyway, if it's always locked, and they find it open, Vinnie will know who did it, and it could cause a lot of grief for her. That's the last thing I want."

"What about a night watchman? Wouldn't that put a kink in the plan?"

"Can't be one. Vinnie wouldn't be able to have a tranny hooker visit him if there was a watchman on duty. And if, say, there was one, but he left when Vinnie came, I would have seen him. And I would have seen lights on somewhere. But there weren't any. Not a one."

"When will you try the empty building?"

"Tonight. If it looks good, maybe I can start Clint tonight, too, assuming Chi Chi lets me."

"She will."

I looked at him, doubt I'd tried so hard to quash creeping back. What was wrong with me? Any one of a dozen of my old trainer friends could have given Chi Chi my number.

"What makes you so sure?" I asked.

"Well, I'm not sure. But from what you told me, she needs to know who did this. They all do, don't they? Before another one of them gets killed. Why would she hire you, lay all that money on you, and then not cooperate?"

I shrugged. "Who knows? I can't presume to understand her, or any of them."

"They're just people, Rach."

"Get real. Yeah, they're people. But they're also drug addicts. I mean, think of how you are in the morning before you get that first cup of coffee. Think of how badly you want it. Now multiply that by ten thousand, and figure every day you have to earn enough money so that you can have what your body is screaming for, and every day you might not, you might get arrested, you might get beaten up, you might get your money stolen, you might get your throat cut. You ever talk to a tranny hooker?"

He nodded.

"You did?"

"Yeah. At Hunts Point. I was protection-training a Shepherd for one of the plants out there. I used to take him by their walk sometimes, see how he'd react to people on drugs, get him to be steady with it when it had nothing to do with him. Great dog. He was a Vinnie, too, by the way, a German import."

"With an Italian name?"

He nodded.

"I thought those were straight hookers at Hunts Point."

"Mostly. But there were a couple didn't look like women to me."

"Too tall?"

He nodded. The waiter filled his cup. Chip thanked him.

"No hips?"

He nodded again.

"Feet too big?"

"Way too big."

"Still, you can't be sure."

"I didn't have to be sure. I wasn't buying."

"Who do you think does?"

He took a sip of coffee, put the cup down, and took my hand. "How would I know that, Rachel?"

"Oh, I figured when you were there, working Vinnie, maybe you saw some of the johns, got some idea."

He shrugged. "Sure. It's a busy place. I saw lots of them."

"And?"

"How can I make a judgment, looking at some guy behind the wheel of a car in the dark? What could I know about him, just from that?"

This time I shrugged. "Old, young, fat, thin, good-looking, ugly, messy, neat?"

"Yes."

"All those things?"

"Except neat. And good-looking." He took a sip of coffee. "Most of them were pretty seedy looking, unkempt, you know what I mean?"

"Chi Chi tells me a lot of the johns are fooled. She says they don't know—"

"That the women they're hiring are men?"

I nodded.

Chip shook his head.

"You don't think it's possible to be fooled?"

"I didn't say that."

"Well?"

"I think the people who are fooled want to be fooled."

I turned and watched our waiter heading toward the pass-through to the kitchen, the stiffness of his legs, the way his narrow hips moved, the way Chi Chi walked, only not quite so over-the-top. A moment later he was back with our check. He put it in the middle of the table. It's no longer PC to give it to the man, even if you're absolutely certain who's a he and who's a she.

When I got home, I tried to sleep but couldn't. I kept thinking about how I say one thing when I'm thinking something entirely different, something unrelated to the conversation, something a thousand times more urgent, more real than the words coming out of my mouth.

Was my sister right, saying this work was changing me,

and not for the better? Isn't that what happens to cops after a while, that they look at the whole world as a crime scene, that they become so paranoid they shoot an innocent person reaching for his wallet or the keys to his house, all the faster if that person happens to be black?

And then I thought about the hookers, trying to find out who had killed Rosalinda. Was it to protect themselves? Or was it to get a little justice, one of the many things absent from their pathetic, lonely lives? There'd be no family to help, and the cops didn't care. They only had each other. And for now, they had me. I stayed awake a long time, thinking about the people who say they care, and the ones who actually do. Then, at last, pressed tight against Dashiell's back, I was able to sleep.

8

You'd Be Real Popular

WALKING Dashiell along the river in the late afternoon, watching the way the last light of the day turned the color of the water nearest to us silver and a deep aqua on the Jersey side, I tried to figure out the best way to get into the building next door to Keller's and, in particular, what I would need to take with me. Of course, this was New York City. I could carry an aluminum ladder through the streets without getting a second glance. A ladder would be nice. I could climb up to the second story, break the bathroom window with a rock, open it, crawl in, and plot out the path Clint would have to take to open the latch at Keller's.

For a moment, stopping while Dashiell found something particularly interesting to investigate, I wondered how much I'd have to teach the little dog before I started his work in the empty building. If he was only housebroken and hadn't even been taught to sit on command, he wouldn't know how to listen to human language, let alone how to work.

Not only that, Chi Chi might not want to give him up for a few days. But no way, if she didn't, was Dashiell going to fit through that cat door. If Chi Chi turned me down, I'd have to come up with a whole new plan.

We headed north again, and as we got closer to the meat district, I thought about my night's work again. The door to the closed plant had been padlocked. Even if I could cut the padlock, that wouldn't be a good idea. It would be too visible. A broken window, that happened in a deserted building, especially in cold weather, but a cut padlock could bring police to check out the building. I'd been cavalier with Chip, but I surely didn't want to get arrested. Nor did I care to explain that I was there preparing a dog to help me break into the market next door so that I could look through their files.

The small window seemed my best bet. I hadn't checked the back of the building, but since the lower floor of all the markets were refrigerated, there surely wasn't going to be a window there. The next question was, short of carrying a ladder to Little West Twelfth Street, how was I going to get up to the second floor?

We crossed the highway at Gansevoort Street, running to avoid getting mowed down by traffic. Even starting out as soon as the light turns green, you need to move pretty fast to get all the way across before the light changes and the traffic peels out. Once safely on the other side, we headed north again, then east when we got to Little West Twelfth Street.

In the fading light of afternoon, I noticed something I hadn't seen before. The name of the business had been painted across the top part of the building, over the second-floor windows. It was faded almost to nothing by now, and in fact, I had to stand slightly to the side to see the words—Jeffrey's Fine Poultry, established 19-something-something, the last two numbers of the date gone completely, as was Jeffrey himself. Of course, this wasn't Jeffrey Kalinsky, who owned the fabulously expensive shop on Fourteenth Street. This place wasn't for the sensibility of folks who went to his shop for two-hundred-dollar T-shirts and twenty-two-hundred-dollar Gucci leather jackets. Even in its heyday, this Jeffrey's wasn't a place for the overly sensitive. While the animals weren't slaughtered here, the scent of fear and the rank odor of blood permeated the buildings, despite the high-pressure hoses and steam-cleaning machines that were used daily. Fourteenth Street was fast becoming a place for people who didn't contemplate the source of the sauce-covered delicacy on their plates, at least not what happened prior to the time when their own butcher took a delicate, pink piece of veal, pounded it flat, and wrapped it carefully in brown paper. They didn't imagine the food they were eating when it was part of a living, breathing creature. Who does? But on Little West Twelfth Street, you couldn't escape the knowledge that what you were eating for dinner had once eaten dinner itself.

The small window I'd assumed was a bathroom was off to the right. On the left side of the building there was a tree, one of those hardy plants that survives against all odds, cracking the sidewalk to make room for its trunk as it grows, its roots snaking their way around rocks and shale as they burrow deep into the ground in search of water. We walked over to it, and Dashiell gave it one more obstacle to overcome for survival. I hadn't spent a lot of time climbing trees since I was a kid, but I had the feeling I could do this one. In fact, standing there charting my path from branch to branch and then to the roof of the old chicken market, if I wanted to get inside, this looked like my only real shot. I pulled out my cell phone and dialed.

"Who wants Chi Chi?"

"I do. It's me, Rachel."

"Yeah? You found out something already?"

"No, not yet. But I need your help."

"I give you anything you need. What's up?"

"I need you to describe the inside of Keller's. I need you to tell me every last detail, first the layout in general, how many rooms there are and where they are, where the stairs are, where the bathroom is, okay? And then I need you to de-scribe the windows, how they lock. Can you do that?" I asked,

remembering how one of the detectives at the Sixth told me
that sometimes, if they cleaned up well, hookers could be
great on the witness stand because they were very good at
noticing small details; like cabdrivers, they had to assess people very quickly to know if doing business seemed safe. Of
course, to help me with the information I needed, Chi Chi
wouldn't have to look middle-class, which was a damn good
thing. But she would have to use that ability to remember details about a place rather than a person. I waited for her answer, listening to her blow her nose, cough, spit, light a
cigarette. Then she walked me through, from the front door,
through the refrigerated first floor, the bodies of the dead pigs
hanging cold and silent in rows, as if they were waiting on
line for something. "But they're not," she said. "Shape they're
in, their waiting days are over." She took me up the narrow,
wooden staircase to the office on the right, describing the
messy desk, the row of files, the computer and printer, even
the phone, "black, three lines." And finally, Chi Chi described
what she called "the ladies," only there weren't any working
there. In fact, in all my walks through the meat district, I'd
never seen a female butcher, nor any other woman, other
than a transvestite hooker picking her away around the
clumps of fat, the occasional kidney, the barrels of bones.

"What about the windows?" I asked.

"None downstairs. Regular whatdoyoucall'ems in the two
offices."

"They look like double-hung windows from the outside.
The ones that slide up and down."

"Yeah, whatever."

"What about locks?"

"Those turn thingees on top of the lower window."

"So it's possible, if I'm desperate, to break the glass, turn
the lock, and get in that way."

"Not possible."

"How come?"

"The glass of those windows, it's got wire in it, like

chicken wire. I don't think you can break that kind of glass so easy. 'Less you bring your hammer."

"What about the bathroom window?"

"No wire. Just that kind of glass you can't see through."

"Frosted glass?"

"Right."

"What about the window? How does it work—like the others?"

"No. It opens out. You get what I mean? It doesn't slide up. It opens like a little door for a midget and it's got this hinge, locks up tight if you push it all the way open, you know the kind? So you want the window to stay open and not blow closed on you, like if the weather's warm, you push it all the way. Because it will." Pause, inhale, exhale. "Blow closed."

"Got it."

But she wasn't finished. "Or if it stinks too bad. I got to tell you, in case you got to go, it's filthy, the sink, the toilet, the floor. Mens. They never think to spray a little Fantastik, wipe things up once in a while. But it beats the street. That's for sure."

"And what about the lock, Chi Chi?"

"A latch. You know, like on a screen door. What's up?"

"I have to get in there, remember?"

"Oh, right. You wanna check out the paperwork."

"Right. One more thing, the toilet?"

"Seat's always up."

I laughed. "No, not that. But that's good you told me that. That helps a lot. What I want to know, is it next to the wall with the window?"

"Right there. Those butchers, they can sit on the pot and smoke, knock they's ashes out the window without getting up. Me, I'm an inch or two too short. You, too. But you don't smoke anyway, so no problem, and the way they keep the place, you could use the floor."

"Chi Chi, you're fantastic. You ever want to quit hooking, I'll hire you on."

"Same here, Rachel. You get dolled up right, honey, you'd be real popular on the stroll, especially if you go blond, like me. They's some of them, they come here, it's more convenient for them than the Bronx, but they got a yen for white meat. Hard to find on this stroll. Some pale PRs, you know, but that's about it. Your skin, your blue eyes, you go blond, you'd clean up."

I laughed, and she did, too. "I'll keep that in mind."

By now it was dark, and I could get to work. I told Dashiell to stay and reached for the first low branch on the tree, which was just a bit too high for me to get, the same inch or two that would prevent me from sitting on the toilet at Keller's and using the window as an ashtray. So I went back out to the sidewalk and found the box I'd used the night before to get up to the sidewalk bridge. With that, and one of the boards for an extra inch, I was able to reach the branch with both hands. Holding on, I walked myself far enough up the trunk that I could climb onto the first branch. From there, it was easy. I had the building on one side, the tree on the other, and braced one way or the other, found places to step until I was up on the old, flat roof of Jeffrey's Poultry Market.

Testing the roof first with my hands, then gingerly with one foot, I carefully walked across to the other side, knelt down, and looked over the front. Even though it was only a two-story building, everything swirled in a most unpleasant way, starting with my stomach. From the roof, the bathroom window seemed much farther away than it had from below, and with my problem with heights, I didn't think there was any way I could lower myself to where it was, break the glass, undo the lock, and get inside by this route.

I backed up and stood. That's when I saw it, way in the back of the roof, the moonlight reflecting off something. Crouching again so that I'd be less obvious, even on the dark deserted street, I duckwalked to the back of the roof and found a small skylight. I could see from there that the building abutted the one behind it. A skylight would be the only way to get natural light or ventilation for a room in the back of the building, a way to make an inhabitable space more user-friendly. The glass part of the skylight had screening in it, like the windows next door. But the frame looked old and rusty. I slipped my hand into my jacket pocket and took out my pocketknife, wedging it under the frame and jiggling it around.

9

He's My Right-Hand Man

Look at you!" Chi Chi chided. "You was absent the day they taught personal hygiene? You don' even know to take the dust bunnies out of your hair before you meet up with a friend?" She reached forward, bent my head down, and began plucking things out of my hair, as if we were chimps reinforcing our social status.

"Chi Chi," I said, my chin on my chest as she picked and brushed at my hair.

"Ssh. I'm not finished. Whatever you got to say, it could wait till you look proper." Her hand slipped under my chin and lifted it, the way a mother does to a child who may not be telling the truth. "Better," she said, but she looked scared, and when I opened my mouth, she put one finger to her lips and then began on my jacket, thoroughly absorbed in the task at hand, or so it seemed. "I got friends coming soon, and I don't want you to embarrass me, have them ask me all kinds of questions." She shook her head. "Where you get so dirty? Where you been?" Afraid of what my answer would be, but asking anyway.

"That's why I called you. That's what I have to tell you about. Next door."

"Um-hmm." She brushed something off my cheek.

"Next door to Keller's."

"The rabbit place? What you doing there?"

"Other side."

"But—"

"Exactly. It's closed down. Kaput. Gone and all but forgotten. But it's exactly the layout you described, for Keller's." When she looked confused, I added, "They're twins, Chi Chi. They're all but identical."

"So? They don't got identical files, do they?" Despite the fact that we were alone, no one else anywhere near the corner of Hudson and Fourteenth Streets, she looked around for applause. Everyone's a wit.

"No—but here's the thing. I thought I was going to have to ask you to lend me Clint so that I could use the deserted building to teach him how to get me into Keller's, but now I don't have to do that."

"Say what?"

"There's a skylight. In fact, I can get to Keller's roof from the roof next door, jimmy the skylight, get into the office at Keller's, and—"

She was shaking her head.

"Slow down, sugar. There's no skylight at Keller's."

"Yes, there is. In the back. To give the back room light and air. I saw it. I was on their roof, just a little while ago."

She was shaking her head again, the wind pulling that near-white hair across her face. She brushed some out of her mouth, checking to see if it had lipstick on it before letting it go.

"Now, listen carefully. Whatever's behind the offices, you know, where you said, in the back of the building, it's locked up tight. I tried that door once, the first time I was there, thinking it was the bathroom." I opened my mouth, but she kept right on going. "No, honest. It's not like there's a sign on the head. They just got one. Unisex, Vinnie said. I see where you at, but you wrong. I didn't steal nothing. You think I'm a hooker, makes me a thief." She shrugged, sighed, and looked away. "Fine. I'm a thief, a liar, too. But I'm telling you this, you fall into the room in the back, that's where you be stayin', bitch. That door's locked. You don't take my word for it, try it and see. And I sure hope you can get back *up* to that skylight, because that's the only way you're getting *out* of whatever's there."

"Shit."

"You can say that again, my own client acting like I'm—"

"Can it," I said. "That's your paranoia. I never said you were a thief. And I never thought that."

"Well."

"Then it seems I will need Clint."

Chi Chi put her arms around herself, squeezing so tight that Clint began to growl.

"It's just for a few days. I'll give him back."

"He my signature," she said, looking away from me, trying to make me disappear.

I touched her arm. "He won't get hurt, Chi Chi. I promise."

"He's my right-hand man. I can't."

"No, Chi Chi. For the time being, I'm your right-hand man. I'm the one you're counting on, to find out what I can, to keep you and your friends alive."

"What you need him for? You got your own dog."

"There's a cat port at Keller's," I began, telling her how Chip and I showed up to buy two pork chops. She stepped closer and leaned toward me. "My dog's way too big to fit through it. But yours, he's perfect. I bet he's smaller than the cat that uses it. What I'm going to do is start at the bathroom window next door to Keller's, and as fast as I can, I'm going to teach Clint to open the lock so I can get in the window—"

"But you already got in, by the skylight."

"Just listen. After he knows the lock, I back him up, say to the door of the bathroom, and teach him to go from there, close the toilet seat, hop up on top of it, nudge the lock open, see? Then we back up some more, to the stairs, then, eventually, to the place where the cat port is in Keller's. The place next door doesn't have one, so I'm going to have to teach him to go through one at home."

Chi Chi looked confused. "You have a cat?"

"No, but I can approximate a port for him and teach him to go back and forth."

She nodded, looking down at Clint, then back up at me. "You know how to do all that stuff?"

I nodded.

"I thought you was a detective, a private eye is what we was tol'."

"I am. But I used to be a dog trainer, before I got married."

"You liked it, dog training?"

I nodded. "Very much."

"Then why you stop doing it? Your husband rather you do this, run around with hookers in the middle of the night with dust bunnies in your hair?"

"No. No more husband. And I don't know why I didn't go back to dog training. I just didn't. But now I can use what I know to teach Clint how to unlock the window for me."

"Then one evening when they're closed, he goes in and follows the route you taught him, lets you in, right?"

"Exactly."

"Then how you going to get into that window, once he opens it for you?"

"I haven't decided yet. There are a number of possibilities."

"You afraid of heights, am I correct?"

I nodded.

"I thought so. Not exactly a plus in your line of work."

"No one's perfect," I said.

"Speak for yourself, bitch."

I was worried about that very hole in my plan myself, but

even if Clint were a genius, it would still take time to teach him everything he had to do. So I had a few days to figure out how to get myself into Keller's via that small bathroom window.

"I could give you something," she said, as if she'd been reading my mind.

"What do you mean?"

"I could give you something, you could climb down from the roof into the window, you wouldn't feel no fear."

"I don't think so."

She looked confused again. "Something out there to help you, you don't want it?"

"Yeah," I said. "The only something I want is him."

"When?" she said.

"The sooner the better."

Chi Chi unzipped her jacket and lifted Clint out, handing him to me.

"He likes chicken," she said, "but only the white meat. And no cheese. It gives him gas."

"I'll take good care of him," I told her.

"He eats grapes," she said, "but you gots to take the skin off first."

We could hear them before we saw them, two hookers, arm in arm, coming around the corner.

"Hold on to your wallet," Chi Chi said. "The one on the left, the redhead, that's Alice. She goes to the gym every day." Chi Chi rolled her eyes. "She says, you work the streets, you better be able to protect yourself. Only, *she* the one you need protection from. She a klepto. She steal easy as you breathe."

"What about the other one?"

But the way their big feet ate up the distance between us, it was Alice, staring at me, who spoke next, not Chi Chi.

"Who she?" Her wrist bent, one long, mahogany finger pointed in my direction. There was maroon polish on her nails, a white daisy painted near the tip.

"Dog groomer," Chi Chi said. "She taking Clint, giving

him the works, shampoo, plucking, nails. You got a problem with that?"

Alice shrugged, pulled out a cigarette, fired it up with an expensive-looking lighter. "You got money for stuff like that, I got no problem with it. But I'm not the one you got to worry about, girl. Am I?"

"You shut up," Chi Chi told her. "You don't know as much as you think you do."

She made a big production about kissing Clint good-bye.

"Other one's Grace," she whispered, her face half buried in the dog's fur. "She new." Then she turned her attention to Clint. "You be good," she told him. "Don't you bark and get her into trouble, you hear me?" Then, quietly: "Alice, she thinks she's better than me, she on her own." One look at my face, and she added, "She don't have a pimp, out there with no one to watch her back, make sure she's okay." She shook her head, feeling sorry for poor Alice, then flapped the back of her hand at me, letting me know it was time for me to go. But I didn't take her suggestion. I had something else in mind.

10

I'm Saving Up, Grace Said

WHAT you get for doing that?" Alice asked. "I'm think-ing, down the road a few years, I'll quit the life, do something else. It's not that I don't like the stroll. It's fast and easy." She put her arms out and shook her tits. "Nothing to it. But my counselor, he says I should think ahead, invest in my future. He suggested I consider selling beauty products, you know, door to door, like the Avon lady. I told him, I don't know, I'm going to be on my feet all day, I might as well keep doing what I'm doing." She poked at her hair, a puffy nest reaching skyward. "He says I need to get some job training, upgrade my skills." This time she shook her ass and made obscene sounds with her mouth. "My skills among the best, I tell him. Don't need no upgrading. You don't believe me, try me out, I told him. If you think you can afford me on *your* salary."

Chi Chi leaned close. "Once she gets started, she never shuts up."

"That pay good, what you do?" Alice asked. "Shampooing dogs, plucking?" She looked at Grace for approval, but Grace was on another planet. Grace was on fucking Mars. So Alice turned to Dashiell, staring, not the best idea in the world with a dog you've barely said howdy-do to, especially if it's a male, all the more so if he's a big one, and definitely if he's sporting all the equipment the good Lord gave him in the first place.

"He bite?" She looked as if she'd been in more cars than Mario Andretti. "What you doing with him? He look pretty clean to me. He don't need no plucking, do he?" She turned to Grace, who was picking at the skin around her press-on nails. "He don't, don't mean you don't," she said. "Look at your eyebrows, girlfriend, you growing a forest there, or what, the way they tryin' to meet in the middle? You never heard of no electrolysis?" She turned to me now. Her eyebrows, I now noticed, were thin and arched, and she had no blue shadow of a beard. "You do that, too?" Then back to Grace: "They take that out, right up the middle, it never comes back." She shook her head. "Least that's what they tol' me, and for the kind of money they charge, shit, that better be the truth, no way I'm doing that twice, all that pain, and goin' without food sometimes to pay her bill."

"I'm saving up," Grace said. "What you think, I'm out here for my health? My boyfrien', every time I have two dimes saved, I find they gone. Gotta find a whole 'nother place to put my money, it stays put." She stretched, and when her boa fell away, I saw an Adam's apple the size of an apricot pit and just as hard looking. She apparently hadn't had the money to take care of that, either. " 'I gots expenses,' he tells me. 'Don't you go nagging me now, bitch, or you live to regret it.'" She had a tattoo circling her biceps, a blue-black chain, more on her fingers, but I couldn't make out the letters against her smoky gray skin in the dim light of evening.

"Where Devon?" Alice said, pronouncing it D-*von*. "He late." She pulled out a cell phone and tried to make a call. "Shit, it dead. You lucky you get two days before they reports it's gone, then, boom, finished." She shook it, banged it against her other hand, and tried once more, then tossed it into the street.

A patrol car, cruising under the speed limit, coming toward us the way it would in a dream, no one in a rush, caught everyone's attention, bam, bam, bam, Alice, Grace, me, Chi Chi. Alice and Grace, going in opposite directions, split faster than roaches when you snap on the kitchen light at three in the morning. I'd wanted to mention Rosalinda, see what I got for my trouble, but that would have to wait for another time.

"Go home," Chi Chi said. "Do whatever you have to with Clint so you can get him back to me." She was shaking. I thought it might have had more to do with D-*von*'s failure to show than Clint's departure, but I couldn't be sure. I'd long ago ceased to be surprised by the way people loved their dogs.

"I'm sorry I have to take him. I know you'll miss him."

"I call Kenya tonight, have a talk with him."

"Kenya?"

"She my animal communicator. She's real good, honest. You want her number?"

"How's she going to communicate with him when he's with me?"

"She don't need to be *with* him. I calls her up and tell her what I want to ask Clint, and she communicates with him *telepathically*. Then she tells me what his answer is. Simple. So you better be good to my little boy, Rachel, 'cause I'm going to be asking Kenya to contact him, ask him what he have for dinner, if he gets to sleep in the bed like he was your own dog, if you nice to him, nice as you is to him." Pointing to Dashiell. Then peering both ways, looking for Devon.

A block away, I put the dachshund down. If he was going to learn to work like a dog, he had to start to be treated like one, the sooner the better. After lifting his leg on the nearest upright object, the building we were passing, he balked, waiting for me to pick him up again.

"Not tonight, little boy," I said. "And don't even think about ratting me out to Kenya."

He seemed to get that all right, because no sooner had I said it than he took off ahead of me, getting quickly to the end of the leash, then rushing around behind me, looping the leash around my legs and barking when there was no more slack and he was forced to stop. Whoever had helped Chi Chi housebreak him obviously hadn't taught him how to walk on a leash. I let Clint get twisted up, pull, balk, do whatever he felt like, for two blocks, then brought him around to my left side, asked Dash to heel, and made sure Clint was between us. With his view to both sides blocked off, Clint began to keep pace.

That's when the car door opened down the block, a big black guy in a long fur coat, a big hat with a yellow feather in the band, spit-shined shoes, a classic, stepped out. He bebopped our way, staring at Clint in his little red coat as he approached us but not saying a word. I kept right on going, giving Clint a pop on the leash when he began to growl.

"Must be D-*von*," I told the dogs when we were a block away and I was sure I couldn't be heard, "unless someone's making a film in the Village for a change." Clint looked up at me and wagged his tail. "Maybe Woody Allen's right behind us," I told him. "Or Quentin Tarantino. Around here, anything can happen."

My sudden good mood must have been infectious. Dashiell sneezed first, Clint a moment later. I sneezed back. If I wanted the little boy to respond to me well enough to learn a complicated series of behaviors, execute them in order, and do them in a place he'd never been, I knew I had to respond to him, too. When I looked down at him, he was looking up and smiling. It was a look I'd seen in dogs a thousand times. Thank God, it said, someone's finally addressing my brain.

As we passed Da Andrea, it started to rain. I looked inside and thought of how much I'd like to be there, a glass of wine in my hand, some rigatoni with meat sauce in front of me, my sweetie across the table telling me about the borzoi who turned on the kitchen faucet when his owners left for work, or the Chihuahua he taught to pick up socks and underwear and drop them in front of the washing machine.

I longed to be normal, to be trusting, to be entertained. But who was I to complain? Chi Chi was out in the rain, missing her dog, picking up strangers. I had work to do, too. At least I could do mine indoors where it was warm and safe. Or so I thought. The light was green. I scooped up Clint and ran across the street.

Back at the cottage, I began Clint on the sit. Dashiell sat, too, his look full of meaning. You want to see training, it said, watch this.

I told Clint he could break, moved to another spot, and once again held a ball over his head. In order to look at the ball, he had to sit. As soon as he did, I tossed the ball and let him retrieve it. He dropped it at my feet, eyes glowing. For the next ten minutes, we went back and forth, giving each other something each time, Clint having so much fun that he didn't notice he was learning commands, me bypassing the natural stubbornness of the breed by making work a game. Once he was steady on the sit-stay, I called him to me, told him he was brilliant, and went upstairs to boot up the computer.

11

I Thought I Was So Clever

WHILE my laptop clicked and chugged, I had another idea. I didn't know if all families were microcosms of the world at large, but mine surely was. We had a rags-to-riches story, my grandfather Meyer who came here from Russia without a penny and did very well for himself in the clothing business until his death at fifty-eight of a heart attack. We had a stay-at-home mom in the suburbs, my sister Lillian. And a cheating husband, hers. We had a musician, my father's mother, Gertrude, who played the flute, and a suicide, Gertrude's father, Samuel. We had an ex–dog trainer, me, a private investigator, me, and a divorcée, me. And we had a transvestite, my cousin Richie.

I checked the clock, not quite eleven. My aunt Ceil would still be up, getting ready to watch the late news. I dialed her number and waited.

"Yes. Who is it?" Living proof the voice is the last thing to go.

"Aunt Ceil, it's me, Rachel."

"Ruchela, darling. Is something wrong?"

"No, no. I'm sorry to call so late, but I knew you'd be up."

"You can call me anytime, sweetheart. I tell Richie the same thing. You're like my child, too, darling. So, what is it, then? Good news, I hope."

"Actually, I need to talk to Richie, and I don't have his number."

She repeated it twice. "Rachel, dear."

"Yes?"

"Don't call him so early. Call around three. That's when he gets home from work and he's all revved up. He'll be happy to have someone to talk to. Unless, of course, he has someone to talk to already, in which case he'll blow you off and call you back tomorrow. It's urgent?"

I filled her in. "I thought he might be able to help me understand these women," I said.

"Rachel, my Richie's a female impersonator, an entertainer. You should see him, darling, how clever he is with the lip-synching, you'd never know in a million years he wasn't doing it himself, and the hair, the makeup, the costumes, he's wonderful, so sensitive and funny. He's an artist, darling. What would he know about streetwalkers? Nothing. Nothing. He's a refined person. He—"

"Oh, I know, I know. But it's not his own experience, it's—"

"Hookers? He doesn't know hookers. What are you thinking? He knows makeup, hair. Ma, he says to me, cucumbers. Lie down on the bed, place a slice over each eye. It's like an eye job, he tells me. You'll look five years younger. You'll be able to pass for seventy-five again. So I said, what about tea bags? Last year, he told me tea bags, even what kind. Not Lipton, he said, green tea. And be sure it's organic. Now he tells me cucumbers. Tea bags, he says. That's so yesterday, Ma. He tells me when to color my hair, what shade to use. He sends me aloe for my skin. This is what he knows. Hookers? What would he know about hookers? Aren't they all drug addicts?"

She waited, but I didn't answer.

"This is necessary, Rachel, to talk to Richie, in order to solve the case?"

"Well, no, it's not necessary. The obvious thing I need to do is to get inside that meat market and see if the two murders are connected. And I plan to do that very soon." I decided to skip those details, suddenly wishing I had call-waiting or that the doorbell would ring, anything to get out of what I'd just gotten myself into. "It's just that it's not possible for me to be around these women and not—"

"But why upset Richie?" Ceil blew her nose. "He has a wonderful life, my Richie."

I thought I might skip talking to her about gender dysphoria for the time being. "I know that their lives are a world apart from his, and I know how supportive and loving you are as a mom, and how close you two are. I understand all that. But I want to understand what it's like when someone doesn't have that. I thought he might have some friends who weren't as lucky as he was."

"Well, there was a boy he brought home once, so shy he couldn't look me in the eye. Richie said when his father found out he was gay, he tried to beat it out of him, to beat him into being a man, he told him."

I looked at the dogs, both up on the spare bed and sleeping.

"I heard that some fathers had a difficult time accepting that a son was gay." I coughed and cleared my throat. Twice. "You never said how Uncle Isaac reacted."

"Isaac?"

"Yes. When he found out that Richie was gay."

"Oh, he adored him. What difference would it make to him, straight or gay? He loved his son."

Hadn't my mother told me, so many years ago, me only half listening because I was too wrapped up in myself to care, that Richie had run away from home when he was eleven or twelve? She'd found it funny, just something boys do if they don't get their way. Better still, it gave her a reason to lord it over Ceil because she had girls, ignoring the fact that one of her girls was a constant disappointment. "So they were close, Isaac and Richie?"

"Like peas in a pod. And Richie, he loved his father with all his heart. That's how little boys are, they worship their daddies. When I called Richie to tell him his father had died, it was so sudden, like your papa, he sobbed. 'Mom,' he said, 'it's a good thing no one's here. My mascara's running down my face. I look like shit.' He flew home the next day for the funeral, and when he went back to Florida, he took so many things that belonged to his father, even sweaters, socks, handkerchiefs. Take anything you want, darling, I told him. I knew he wanted his father with him, to feel his presence."

I glanced at the pad where I'd written Richie's number. "It's Rich Allen now, is that right?"

"Yes. A stage name. Kaminsky is, well—"

"Too long?" I suggested.

"Yes. People can't spell it. He wanted something more—"

"Memorable?"

"Exactly, darling."

"Well, I better get back to work now. Thanks so much for all your help."

When I hung up, I walked out into the garden. The rain had stopped. Standing under the black sky and looking up at the stars, I spoke out loud, both dogs looking up at me to see what I wanted. Like peas in a pod, I told them. I checked my watch. Still three hours before I could call.

Back upstairs, I started to do a search on drugs, but stopped after an hour. It wouldn't tell me what the girls were on, but I was pretty sure it was crack. The designer drugs, the ones my cousin Richie probably used, were too expensive, especially since most of the girls only got to keep a small percentage of what they earned, a much smaller portion than they would net if they were merely paying taxes. As for the effects of their drug use, some were visible, some weren't. What you couldn't see, that was the worst part. They might as well be playing Russian roulette. If the drugs didn't kill them, they surely kept them broke and kept them hooking. With their habit, their profession, the risk of disease, and the mood of their pimp, survival was an iffy proposition. Shivering in the damp, cold yard, I thought I was so clever. I didn't know the half of it.

12

His Nose Twitched

I WENT down to the basement, both dogs following me, Clint, with his long body and short legs, tacking as if he were a sailboat running obliquely against the wind. I needed to fashion a flap, something to approximate the cat door at Keller's, so that I could teach Clint to go through it. I needed to teach him to open a hook-and-eye lock, follow a path from the cat door up to the bathroom, and thanks to Chi Chi's eye for details, put down the seat and lid on the toilet so that he could stand on it and reach the windowsill. And I had to do it fast, before anyone else got killed.

I found a roll of felt I'd used years earlier to make hand puppets for my sister's kids. I cut a rectangular piece, about six by six. Now I needed someplace to hang it that wouldn't let Clint go around it. I had some boxes of books I'd never unpacked. I unpacked one, stacking the books along the wall, getting lost for a while rereading the beginning of *My Dog Tulip*. Then I cut a hole in the box the size of the felt flap, stapled the flap over the opening, and cut off the opposite side of the box so that when Clint pushed the felt with his nose and went through, he wouldn't be stuck inside the box; he'd be able to go right through it, to the room behind it.

While I worked, Dashiell stretched out near the stairs and slept. Clint ran around, stopping frequently to bark at me, unhappy that my attention was on something other than him. It was a good opportunity to deal with that, because once he knew the drill and was ready for Keller's, his safety might depend on his ability to become a stealth dachshund. Barking could attract attention to something I didn't want anyone to notice, and once I was in the building, too, our lives would depend on my speed and his silence.

So as I got the practice dog door ready, I got Clint to practice his newly acquired skills—sitting and paying attention. With my attention on him and with something new to do, he stopped barking and didn't resume it again until I released him and he'd wound himself up again, doing circles around the basement. It was all a game to him, and he was having the time of his life. For my part, I was encouraging both the control and the wildness, getting him to slip back and forth between those two modes, getting the job done faster than I thought I would. Clint was a quick study, but had I merely pushed him to be quiet, I would have seen how stubborn a dachshund could be, how much determination per pound these little dogs had.

I even sent Dashiell to find a ball. He disappeared up the stairs, Clint standing near me, his head cocked, waiting. When I heard Dashiell at the top of the stairs, I told him, "Out," and watched Clint back up and bark as the ball bounced down the wooden steps and rolled onto the basement floor. When he got it, I sent Dash for another, so that both dogs could retrieve while I shuffled work and play for Clint, getting longer and longer periods where he'd sit quietly and watch me, waiting for the signal to cut loose again.

When the box was ready I carried it upstairs, both dogs rushing on ahead of me, each with a ball in his mouth. I set the box in the doorway to my bedroom, blocking the space on either side of it with books so that Clint couldn't simply go around it, piling more books on top so that it wouldn't move and he couldn't see over the top. Then I took his ball, put it on the other side of the box, in the bedroom, and held the flap up and out of the way so that he could see it and get to it unhindered. Nothing like easy success to build confidence. In minutes Clint was playing the new game, tearing through the tunnel into the bedroom, snagging the ball, and waiting to be called back, my little Einstein.

I gave the dogs a yard break, grabbed a soda, and stood outside huddled in my jacket while I drank it and watched them play. Then I called them back upstairs. Putting Dashiell on a down, lowering the piece of felt, and dropping the ball with an audible thump on the far side of the box, I sent Clint through. His nose twitched. He lowered his head. He poked his nose under the felt, hesitated, and pushed through. This time, I didn't call him back. I wanted him to figure it out for himself, that when the job was done, he needed to get his butt back to me as fast as possible. I closed my eyes and began to count silently. By the time I'd mouthed "two," there he was. He dropped the ball in my lap, backed up, and barked. I sent it down the hall and listened to it thumping down the stairs, Clint after it as fast as he could go, wondering how much Chi Chi played with him, or if instead he just got to sit and watch her nod off on ketamine after a hard night's work.

I padded downstairs, coming in third in a field of three, filled the water bowl, and gave each dog a biscuit. Then I went back up to my office and called my cousin Richie, trying hard to figure out, as I listened to the phone ring and then his outgoing message, Streisand singing "People," why I had no recollection of his father's funeral.

"Richie, it's Rachel Kaminsky," I said, not sure he'd know the name I'd earned the old-fashioned way, by marrying and divorcing a Jewish dentist. "I got your number from your mom, and—"

"Rachel fucking Kaminsky? Be still my heart."

I laughed. "I didn't know if you'd know—"

"My mother talks about you a lot, Rachel. She says you're like the daughter she never had."

"Oh. Sorry about that."

"I know what you mean. I assumed *I* was the daughter she never had. At least, I've been trying to be. But what's a girl to do? You know you can never please these Jewish women. Speaking of which—"

"Yeah. A dentist," I said. "I wasn't able to score a doctor."

"Me, neither. Well, better luck next time. I lived with an accountant for eight months. I thought that would please the old bitch. After all, he did her taxes free."

"And?"

"Saved her four hundred and thirty dollars."

I whistled. "Impressive."

"In more ways than one."

I waited for more. A remark like that, there's bound to be more.

"Your dentist fool around on you?"

"Oh," I said.

"Well?"

"Not that I know of."

"He smack you around?"

"No."

"Oh, I've got it, he was a heavy drinker, am I right? Spent his time in bars, or in front of the TV with a scotch and soda in his hand, growing meaner by the minute?"

"No. Not that either."

"How curious. But you dumped him anyway, an income like that? Shame, shame. Come on now, tell your cousin, what *did* he do?"

"He wanted me to cook dinner."

"The filthy beast!"

"It was a little more complicated than that."

Richie laughed. "It always is. So, is this a social call? Let's see, we haven't spoken since we were seven, I think. Didn't we play doctor on the back porch that summer, or was that some other slut?"

"Rich, I called to ask you something to help me with the work I'm doing now. I've been hired by three transvestite hookers after one of their friends got her throat slit." There was silence on the line. I had a feeling the light banter was over for now. "I'm trying to understand—"

"Why transvestites get themselves killed? That's easy. No one likes them. Not even their own parents."

"But Ceil said—" This time he didn't have to interrupt. This time I stopped myself.

I heard ice cubes dropping into a glass. "The lady doth protest too much. You know what I mean? She's a little too loud, a little too effusive. But she tries. She can't help who she is." There was a silence on the line, then Richie was back. "How about dear old Auntie Beatrice? Did she nurture your sense of self-esteem, Rachel?"

"Not exactly."

"Well, what exactly?"

I took a deep breath. "I failed to live up to her high standards, Rich. Right up to the very end."

"But Lillian did?"

"Lillian? Are you in touch with Lillian?"

"She's in touch with me. She sends birthday and Hannukah cards. Never missed one in all these years."

"Well, yeah, she's like that."

"But not you?"

"No. Not me."

"So it wasn't personal, you ignoring my birthday all these years? Silly me, I do let my neediness get the best of me sometimes."

"Rich," I said, "what about your dad?"

"Ceil didn't tell you that either?"

"She said the two of you were very close."

The sound he made was barely human, the final protest of an animal being brought down by a pack of hungry wolves.

"Close to murdering each other, she must have meant. He found out when I was eleven. He came home from work early. I was wearing one of Ceil's half slips, pulled up like a strapless gown. And her silver ankle straps. Open toe. I wish I could find those now in my size."

I knew where he could, but I kept it to myself.

"What did he say?" I asked.

"Say? Nothing. Nothing at all. At least, not to me. He closed the door, rather quietly, and went downstairs. I opened it, also quietly, and went to the top of the stairs and listened.

"'Ceil,' he said, 'there's something wrong with your son.'"

I waited, but there was only silence on the line.

"I'm sorry. I didn't mean to rake this up."

"Where do you think it is, Rachel, locked away in a vault for safekeeping? It's with me every day. Even after fourteen years of therapy. Your clients, it's even worse for them. At least I have friends and legitimate work. Well, if you call wearing panty hose and lip-synching legitimate. At least my life's not in peril every day, not since I got out of my parents' home. But tranny hookers, they've got nothing. Every day of their lives, that could be one of them, found with a slashed throat and no one giving a shit."

Not no one, I thought. But I couldn't get the words past the lump in my throat.

"Your mom talked about your dad's funeral," I said after a moment.

"Oh. Was there one?"

I opened my mouth, but Richie spoke before I got the chance.

"Ceil called. I do recall that. She asked if I was coming up. I said, 'The king is dead. Long live the queen.' Was I fucking coming up! Oops. There's my other line. Wanna hold?"

"No, it's late. I better go."

"But you'll call again in another twenty years, won't you?"

"I—"

"That's my good girl. You take care now."

The dogs were on the spare bed, back to back, asleep. But there was more work to do, and that's what I had to concentrate on, at least for now. I needed to start Clint on opening hook-and-eye locks if I was going to get into Keller's soon and get him back to where he belonged. I hated the idea of keeping him away from Chi Chi, all the more after listening to my cousin's story.

I went back to the basement and looked in the toolbox for some cord, knotted one end, then woke Clint and began a game of tug-of-war. We worked for another hour, going back and forth between commands, everything fun for him, deadly serious for me. When the birds started their day, I finally finished mine, Dashiell across the foot of the bed, Clint with his head on the pillow, right behind mine.

13

The Sound Was Getting Closer

THERE was a lot of construction going on in the neighborhood, people trying to cash in on the strong real estate market while it lasted. Earthmovers were parked along the curb or behind makeshift plywood barricades, quiet until dawn when, like it or not, the onslaught of noise would be your alarm clock. But there wasn't any work in progress on West Tenth Street, and I'd been able to sleep most of the day, the shutters closed, the room almost as dark as if it were night. After breakfast, which would hold me until I got back home for a combination lunch and dinner, I'd walked the dogs, then worked on the rest of Clint's commands. Now we were going to seam them together. With luck, he'd learn the routine he had to perform as quickly as he'd learned the individual pieces.

I left the cottage just after dark, heading for Little West Twelfth Street with Clint, who for a change was walking instead of being carried and who was not wearing his red leather coat. We moved quickly, going straight to Washington Street, avoiding the people walking their dogs or out to meet friends at the White Horse Tavern for a beer, soak up atmosphere, breathe in smoke, tell the story of their lives.

Passing Keller's, I stopped to scoop Clint up and stuff him into my leather jacket, closing the zipper just enough to keep him from slipping out. I had his ball in one pocket, a flashlight in the other, the knotted string tied around my wrist, my knife in the waistband of my leggings. All in black, like a cat burglar, I climbed the tree I'd climbed before, walked gingerly across the roof, ape-style, talking to Clint as I went, approaching the skylight, then opening the knife and slipping the blade once again under the rusty metal rim until I could lift it and drop down inside. Once I was in, I took Clint out of my jacket, unhooked his leash, turned on the flashlight, and got to work.

We started at the farthest place he'd have to go, and with one of the toughest jobs, the lock. I attached the string to the hook, closed the toilet lid, and tapped it. Clint hopped up. There was already a hole in my great plan. I could wiggle the string and Clint would pull it. But from where he stood, he would be pulling the string down, forcing the hook tighter into the eye instead of loosening it. This project needed work and needed it fast. I took a good look at his body, measured the ledge with my eyes, and decided that if this was going to work, I'd have to take the chance of having him on the sill.

I called him off the toilet seat and watched him bounce down to the floor. Then I tore out of the bathroom, calling him to chase me around the upstairs offices of the empty building. That done, I started all over again.

This time, I lifted him up and put him on the sill. For a moment, he leaned against the dirty, frosted window and didn't move. But when I told him to tug, he immediately picked up the string and yanked. However, instead of pulling up, he shook his head back and forth, as if he were trying to snap the neck of a small rodent. I praised him and called him off. This time he jumped from the sill to the closed toilet seat, then down to the floor, ready for another chase game. Instead, I tapped the seat, and once he'd backed up and made that jump, I tapped the sill. Clint put his paws on the sill and whined, but he was a game little dog. I tapped again; he barked once and made the jump.

This time I held the string so that the piece sticking out of my hand was over the hook. Clint cocked his head. The only way he could reach the end of the string was to stand on his hind legs. "Take it," I told him, an urgent whisper. "Take it."

He stood. He pulled. On the third yank, the hook popped free and we ran around the old building until I could no longer breathe.

So far, so good. But once he got to Keller's, there'd be no string, only the hook.

Clint was practically manic now. I tapped the seat, tapped the sill, and twice more he opened the hook that kept the window locked by tugging the knotted string up. Twice more I raved about his mental capacity, dazzling good looks, and re-markable courage, and twice more we raced through the dark, empty offices, me stopping and turning at the last min-ute so that he could catch me.

This time I untied the string, clicked the hook back into the eye, and with Clint on the floor, pointed at the hook and told him, "Take it."

He hopped up on the seat, then onto the sill, and stood on his hind legs. He looked for the string and, not seeing it, turned back toward me, his head cocked. I lifted my right pointer, moved it toward the window, and tapped the center of the hook with my fingernail.

"Take it."

Clint froze. I tapped once more, then withdrew my hand. For what seemed like ages, we stayed still in the dark bath-room, the flashlight sitting on the back of the john now, its beam shining on the hook and eye. Then Clint bent his head, grasped the hook with his teeth, and gave a pull, nearly falling off the sill when it popped up.

That's when I heard it, a low scratching sound.

It stopped, then started again.

Mice in the walls?

Clint heard it, too. He let go of the hook and put his front paws down on the sill. I scratched his head; "Good boy," I told him, tapping the open hook. But my concentration was elsewhere. So was his. The sound was getting closer.

Clint made a rumbling sound in his throat, and he was off. He hit the toilet seat with a loud thump and pushed off again immediately. I caught him in midair, pulling him close to my chest, zipping my jacket around him. I didn't want him barking until I was absolutely sure what species was making the noise.

There it was again. Louder. Clint's motor started, prelude to a bark. It felt like a vibrator against my chest. I put one finger over his muzzle to calm him, shut off the flashlight, and backed into the corner, holding my breath and listening.

For a moment there was nothing. Then it was back. Only, it wasn't coming from inside the walls. It was coming from above. Someone was walking across the roof.

14

We Needed Time, and There Wasn't Any

OLDING on to Clint, I waited, listening to the creaking of the roof, realizing with a flash of heat in my gut that the skylight was propped up because I'd seen no reason to close it. No one could see it from inside the building, since I was the only one here. And it wasn't visible from the street. Nonetheless, someone was up on the roof, and from that vantage point, you couldn't miss it.

The creaking sound was heading across the roof, from front to back, the exact route I'd taken with Clint. And now, added to that, there was the sound of air coming out of a person more rapidly than normal, the way it does when you get socked in the stomach, or you fall, which is what had happened above me, since the *oof* was accompanied by a thump. And then a creaking sound moving toward where the thump came from. Two people on the roof. I zipped my jacket higher, hoping it would keep Clint from barking.

The creaking continued, a subtle sound. The people on the roof had taken off their shoes so that they wouldn't be heard. Did that mean they knew someone was already in the building? As if they could miss that fact with the skylight gaping open.

Clint began to whine, his feet pushing against me as he tried to get free. The sound kept moving toward the back of the roof. I wondered if there was a closet I could hide in, or if I should go downstairs, if whoever was coming wouldn't think to look in what used to be a refrigerator.

Didn't that depend on who they were? And on why they'd come?

And then I heard something else, something familiar.

"Yoo-hoo, Rachel. You down there?" Loud.

And then not as loud, but certainly audible: "Shit, I ripped my panty hose. This no place for a lady to be crawling around. Where is that bitch? Chi Chi said she wasn't home, she'd be here."

Then loud: "Rachel, honey, it's LaDonna and Jazzy. You down there? I ain't jumping down there in the dark, you don't say somethin'." And more quietly: "What she doing in this hole, anyway? She lost her mind?"

"I'm here," I shouted. I let Clint out of my jacket, turned on the flashlight, and walked to the back of the building, standing under the open skylight. "What are you doing here?"

"It's Chi Chi," Jasmine said, her dark hair falling over her face as she leaned down into the hole.

"What about Chi Chi?"

"Devon beat the shit out of her is what," LaDonna said. "She home, and she need her dog."

"How bad is it?"

"Bad. She need that dog now. He cut her off, she not getting much else."

"Shit. He's almost ready to get me into Keller's. Can't she manage without him for one more day?"

Jasmine rolled her eyes. "You wouldn't even ask if you saw her, honey."

"Yes," I said. "I would."

She exhaled now, looking back at LaDonna.

"Back up, bitch. I'm coming down." LaDonna swung her long legs over the side, her big feet shoeless, her stockings black and torn. I did as I was told, and there she was, looming over me, Clint at my side, barking.

"She way bad. Don't you go giving me no lip, woman. She need her dog." She bent to scoop up Clint, but he slipped away, barking at her from behind me now.

"She's alive, isn't she?" Me barking back, too.

"Shit." From above. We both looked up.

"Our fault. Hire some wiseass, bigmouth private eye, thinks she knows everything, what'd we expect?"

"No. I don't know nearly enough. That's why I need Clint. Didn't Chi Chi tell you what I'm doing with him?"

LaDonna shook her head. "She just said you took him and ran into Devon or something, then he comes and beats the crap out of her because you had the dog."

"Why? Didn't she tell him I was going to groom him?"

"You a groomer now?" LaDonna said. "What all don't you do, girl?"

"No—that's what Chi Chi told the other hookers. That was the cover story."

"You don't do no cover story with Devon. Devon don't want no stories. He wants money."

"Money? What does this have to do with money? You mean he thinks she gave me what should have been his to groom Clint?"

Jasmine sighed. "You slow as some of these old guys, come to the stroll because they can't get it up at home, expect us to wave a wand, make them as hard as a sixteen-year-old again. They think my name is Vi-agra. Shit. Didn't you look in his coat pocket? I thought you were a de-tec-tive." She was pointing down at Clint with nails so long they curled back toward her palm.

Now it was my turn. "Shit." I'd pulled the coat off him and tossed it onto a chair or the couch. I'd never even thought about checking the pocket.

"You can say that again, and not only that, Devon don't want us talking to no outsiders." Jasmine pointed down at me for emphasis, in case I hadn't figured out exactly which outsider Devon was referring to. "He don't want us getting any ideas. This girl Opal, she got her teeth knocked out for talking to a counselor."

"It's for our own good," LaDonna said. "He take care of us. We listen to you, you going to see to our needs?"

I shook my head. "Look, can we call Chi Chi? I need two more days."

"Impossible."

"Okay," I told Jasmine, "one more day. I'll go in tomorrow night."

"I mean impossible to call her. Her cell phone's dead."

"You mean another stolen cell phone got shut off?"

Jasmine swung her legs over the side. LaDonna reached up and helped her down. "You have no call to talk like that." She stood on her toes so that her face was close enough to mine that I could smell what she ate two weeks ago. Then she turned to LaDonna. "I told you we shouldn't be hiring a *white* bitch. But you wouldn't listen." Hands on hips. "Not *her* fault. She just grew up that way, feeling entitled to talk down to people of color, because she is a superior being and we are nothing, zero, nada."

"Oh, cut the—"

"Devon gives us phones so he can call us, make sure we're okay." In my face.

"Impressive," I said. "A regular Mother Teresa. Now, will you two get the hell out of here so that I can finish training this dog? If I have to go in tomorrow, I have lots to do."

"She say she want—"

"No. Tell her I said no. I'm trying to keep you three alive, do you understand? I'm trying to find out what you asked me to, who killed your friend Rosalinda, and in order to do my job, I have to get into Keller's when they're closed and see if I can find a connection between the two murders, Rosalinda and the butcher who was killed the same night."

"Mulrooney," LaDonna said.

"Yes."

"You think that'll help, finding out who killed him?"

"It might."

"You think it's the same person, killed Rosalinda and this Mulrooney?"

"It's a good possibility."

Jasmine reached down for Clint. LaDonna put her big hand in the way.

"Thank you. And be sure to tell Chi Chi I understand completely and I'll work as fast as I can."

LaDonna had turned the other way, but Jasmine was staring at me. Neither of them said a word.

"Unless you've changed your minds. Unless you want your money back. Unless you want to take your chances, bank on the fact that the two deaths were unconnected and that Rosalinda's murder was something random, something that won't happen again, not for maybe weeks, or even months."

LaDonna opened her mouth, but it was Jasmine's voice I heard.

"We didn't say that. A deal's a deal."

"Can she get around?" I asked.

LaDonna nodded. "But she in pain."

"Suppose we take Clint to her for an hour or two, bring him back to you?" Jasmine said.

I shook my head. "If he sees her now, all this work might go right down the drain. Chi Chi asks different things of him, and he could fall back into that pattern too easily. You understand? I'd be back to square one. Or worse."

Jasmine pointed to Clint. "He helps her," she whispered. "He knows when she's hurting."

"I understand. I really do. But she's going to have to give me one more day."

"I don't know."

LaDonna pulled the chair I'd used to climb back out into position and stood on it, hoisting herself back up to the roof, a powerhouse of a woman. "Get up there, Jazz," she said. "We hire this woman to do a job, let's get out of here and let her do it."

"Thank you."

Jasmine stood on the chair, and LaDonna reached for her with her long arm, grasping her wrist and pulling. I stood and watched as Jasmine disappeared up into the dark, like a circus act, costumes and all.

"So you going into Keller's," LaDonna said, leaning back down the hole, "have yourself a look-see?"

I nodded, but in the dark, the flashlight pointed away from me, I don't know if she saw me. "I am," I said.

"Good. I tell Chi Chi you doing the right thing. I get her something to tide her over."

I waited, listening to them make their way over the roof in their stocking feet, waited while they climbed down the tree, retrieved their shoes, and went to work. Clint and I did, too. We needed time, and there wasn't any. I didn't know if I could string all the commands together in only one night, but one night was all I had.

15

I Still Had a Couple of Hours

'D slept all day, waking up when most people are getting home from work. About fourteen hours earlier, during that cusp of time after the knackers have picked up the bones set out in oversize trash cans along the dark, greasy streets of the meat district and the hookers, denuded of most of their night's earnings, have headed home to doze in front of their TV sets, but before the butchers arrive to don their white coats, hairnets, and hard hats and the refrigerated trucks turn south on Fourteenth Street and roar into the market, I led Clint to the approximate place in the closed market where he'd be when he went through the port at Keller's, whispered, "Take it," and waited in the old refrigerator, wishing I could actually hear the hook that locked the bathroom window being pulled out of the old rusty eye, a soft, scraping sound, knowing I couldn't, which is why I'd added one more link to the chain, a single, small bark indicating that the job had been successfully completed.

He only did it once, but we'd run out of time. If I tried even one more run, I might be climbing down the tree out front with trucks of pork pulling up next door, with butchers arriving, carrying take-out coffee, unlocking their shops, ready to begin work. We'd done it all, the run through the once-refrigerated first floor, the stainless-steel walls creating eerie pictures of the little dog, as if they were fun-house mirrors. He'd poked his way past the ribbons of translucent plastic, thick and wide, that separated the cold downstairs from the offices above. He'd gone up the worn, wooden steps, game and eager, pleased finally to have a job. This last time, I didn't run along behind him, repeating his command. This time he did his run alone. It was good, he got the job done, but it wasn't great, he took too long. And until the real trial, I wouldn't know two things: if Clint could do it in the strange building, in a place where the room he entered would be cold as a killer's heart; and, an even bigger question, if I could get into the bathroom from the roof, given the distance between the two and my inconvenient fear of heights.

I'd been worried there might be a padded, swinging door separating the downstairs, where the meat hung, from the staircase to the offices, a door the butchers could open with their shoulders when their arms were full. Clint was a very small dog. Even with the grit and stubbornness the breed is famous for, no way could a ten-pound dog nose open a door that heavy. But Chi Chi had described Keller's in detail. And Keller's, too, used strips of plastic to contain the cold. There was no door at the foot of the stairs. But there was a problem all the same. I'd counted on Chi Chi to be there the night before, which was out of the question now. It *was* the night before, and Chi Chi was home, in pain. I had hoped she would be able to push a nail partway into the worn wooden floor right in front of the bathroom door so that it couldn't close all the way, but would close enough so that no one would be apt to notice the difference. But Chi Chi couldn't help me, and it was now or never.

On my way to Keller's with Clint for our one go at getting in there, I knew there was a chance the bathroom door would be closed, and all our work would be for nothing. If that happened, if he didn't show in ten minutes, more than enough time for him to make the trip and open the lock, I'd have to get back off the roof, go down the tree next door, push open the port, and whistle him back. This we'd never practiced. Nor had I practiced getting from the roof into the small window he was supposed to open for me. Necessity was once again going to have to be the mother of invention, but all I could think as we approached Little West Twelfth Street was that, more often than not, necessity was simply a mutha.

It was nearly ten. The markets were closed, the hookers in their customary places. Like family members at the dinner table, they returned to the same spots every night. A few cars were cruising by, checking out the merchandise. Some would go around the block three times before stopping. Newbies. Or old pros, afraid the cops were nearby.

We went under the sidewalk bridge, the moon no longer lighting our way, then out into Keller's courtyard. When we got to the port, I put Clint down and unhooked the leash, crouching right next to him.

"This is it, kid," I told him. "I'm counting on you."

His eyes were bright. He wagged his tail.

I didn't push the port open for him, in case he had to come out this way. I pointed, my heart racing. "Go," I told him, "take it," and before he'd disappeared, I was running, too, out of Keller's courtyard and into the one next door, climbing up the tree, running over the old roof, crouching low, as if I weren't a modern ape at all but one of my distant ancestors, going over the parapet and onto Keller's roof, then, belly down, leaning over the edge and waiting for the pop and the single bark that would tell me the window was unlocked.

I tried not to look down, and when I failed, and my stomach had spun out of control, I told myself that falling off the roof was the least of my problems. With that cold comfort, I closed my eyes and pictured Clint coming out of the port on the inside of the refrigerator, passing sides of pork hanging in rows, going straight back, then to the right, nosing his way through the plastic ribbons, just enough for him to skinny by. Instead of looking down into the parking area in front of Keller's, the place where I'd first noticed the cat port, I imagined Clint tacking up the stairs, heading left, then right, those short legs propelling him forward.

Then there was the short distance to the bathroom, nosing open the door, putting his whiskered face behind the toilet seat, then behind the lid, jumping back when each slammed closed, a politically correct male if ever there was one. Then he'd back up and dash forward, hopping up onto the lid and once more onto the sill.

But there was no pop, no movement, no bark, no little dog making things ready for my own test of courage.

Had he stopped to taste a side of pork? Was the bathroom door closed, the place he had to go impenetrable? Or had Clint met the cat? Helpless, I wondered if there was a standoff on the staircase, kitty's back arched, her fangs bared, Clint unable to get by.

Hanging over the edge in the dark, I waited and waited, the fear in my throat now, thick and sour. Had I expected too much? Should I have waited for Chi Chi's help? What if nothing happened? How long would I wait before trying to get Clint back out safely? And what if I couldn't?

And then it happened. There was an almost inaudible sound, metal on metal, a nearly imperceptible movement of the window, a single bark. I whistled, Clint's signal to jump back down. He had done his part. Now I had to do mine, the part I hadn't let myself think about. I had to hang off the roof over the cobblestone courtyard and somehow get my body into the window before I lost my grip, literally and figuratively, and fell to my death in the rat-infested hellhole below me.

Hey. No problem. I was an experienced, highly paid professional, wasn't I?

I decided to go backward so that I wouldn't have to look.

The parapet was low. This roof was not cocktail-party ready. Though the view was spectacular, the lights from the Jersey side shimmering in long wavy lines across the Hudson River, the roof was unimproved, no decking, no fancy railing, no chairs, no plants. Just the parapet to grasp. I swung one leg over, then the other. Then, holding tight to the lip of the low wall, I lowered myself until I was hanging straight down, which, if I was really lucky, would put my legs parallel to the window Clint had unlocked for me.

Feeling around with my feet, I found the opening. I sneaked a peak, but closed my eyes tight when my knife fell out of my pocket, hitting the building, then bouncing far out into the courtyard. The sound it made on the stones below let me know what my body would do if I failed to hold on, how I'd be smashed against the building on my way down to becoming a corpse.

It was instantly clear that the only way I could get inside would be to let go of the edge of the parapet and hope I could grab the top of the window as I fell. This meant I had to pull the window open with my foot. I began to scan my memory for ideas for other ways to earn a living, but the image of Rosalinda in her white dress, the bodice covered with blood, stopped that in a hurry.

I was able to find purchase on top of the window where it had popped open about an inch when Clint had released the latch. Carefully, using the toe of one sneaker, I was able to pull the window open, then with the side of my foot push it out all the way. Then I reached with one hand, barely touching the top of the window. Once I let go, I'd have to move with speed and grace. I didn't know if either was my forte, but at this point I was really out of choices. I doubted I could hoist myself back up from my stretched-out position hanging like a rope down the side of the building anyway. And time was ticking by while I hesitated.

I took a breath and opened the hand that was on the ledge. As I dropped, I grasped the open window, heard a terrifying crack as it pulled away from the frame. With no time to think, I grabbed the frame with one hand, swung my legs inside and pushed myself feet first into Keller's, my ass grazing the sill, awkwardly twisted around so that my knees were on the closed toilet lid, and finally I was standing on the floor, safe. I turned on the flashlight and looked around. Chi Chi was right. The place was a dump. Then Clint was all over me, jumping up and whining with delight, and, ingrate that I was, instead of being happy I wasn't crumpled like a marionette without strings in Keller's courtyard, I stood there wondering how I'd get back out, one of the many things I hadn't thought about. But I figured I'd take things a step at a time. For now, there was important work to do.

Flashlight on, the bar of light circling the dark bathroom, Clint following right at my heels, I found the office with the file cabinets and got to work. The file was unlocked, which was lucky, since my knife was now in the land of lost tools. The personnel files were in the bottom drawer. I found Vinnie's file, and Mulrooney's, faxing the pages that looked useful to my home. While that was happening, I began to check the contracts with haulers. The going thinking was that Mulrooney had been killed because he'd changed trash companies, perhaps as a lesson to the rest of the markets despite the new law that theoretically did not allow for a wise-guy monopoly of the carting business, you put out for bids and one comes in, take it or leave it. But there'd never been a law passed you couldn't get around.

I faxed those pages home, too, carefully putting everything back where I'd found it. Then, checking the time, and knowing better, I looked through the rest of the file drawers. I knew it must be time to go. Chi Chi never said just how early Vinnie came in when he wasn't meeting her, but it was only an hour to the time when he'd be there if they had a date. Still, this was a one-shot deal, and I didn't want to kick myself later for not looking further. I checked my watch again and went back to work.

My hands pulling file folders forward as I scanned each one, Clint asleep now on the beat-up couch on the other side of the room, I found mostly orders coming in and orders going out, the names of the slaughterhouses and names of restaurants and hotels. I checked everything, even looking for small scraps of paper in the bottom of each folder, a memo, a note, a scribbled cell phone number, something that would give me a reason to shout Eureka, albeit softly in case, against all odds, someone was passing by. After all, there was an open window. But before I had the chance to do something about that, something caught my eye, something that had been hastily stuffed in the front of one of the file drawers, as if someone was coming and whoever was reading what I found didn't want to be seen doing so. It was a page ripped out of the *Times*. Working the way I was, obsessed with the case, I hadn't read the paper or watched the news on TV. The article was short, on the bottom of page 32. It wasn't major news to the *Times*, but it was to me, and to whoever had torn this page out and hidden it in the file drawer. It was about Keller's, about the murder of their manager. The police, it said, had released both suspects. It seemed that both Capelli and Maraccio had airtight alibis for Halloween night. No one else, the article said, was in custody, but a vigorous investigation was going on.

I went back into the bathroom, pulled the window closed, and latched it. No harm in being careful. That in mind, I aimed the flashlight at my watch again, and froze. It was the same time it had been when I'd last looked.

When the hinges had started to give way under my weight, making that awful cracking that made my stomach feel as if it were filled with cold water, there'd been another sound, one too low to hear over the sound of the hinges and the sound of my own ragged breathing. I'd smacked and broken my watch. I looked around frantically for a clock, finally finding one on the thermostat in the hall. It was later, much later than I'd planned to leave, but I could still get out in plenty of time.

Against my better judgment, I took one more look around the office, finding a thin file under some papers on the desk. I took Timothy McCoy's file and stuck it into the fax machine, pressing redial, waiting impatiently for them to slide through the machine so that I could put them back where they'd been. I looked around to see if everything else was as I'd found it. Now it really was time to go.

It wasn't until that moment that I gave serious thought to how I'd get out. It wasn't until then that I remembered the padlock on the front door.

There was no way on earth I could get Clint and myself back up on the roof. Nor could I fit through the cat port. I'd gotten so involved in my crusade, in helping these women that no one seemed to care about, I'd been sloppy.

Now I was going to have to hide until Vinnie opened up, then try to sneak out without being seen before the rest of the butchers arrived. And I was going to have to keep Clint quiet when the time came, until we were safely back on Little West Twelfth Street. This time, even though the heat was off upstairs and the bathroom and offices were almost as cold as it must have been downstairs, I was sweating. I'd made mistakes before. Plenty of them. But this one was a whopper. This one could cost me my life.

When I headed for the stairs, Clint tried to go first, but his side-to-side method was slow and clumsy. Besides, he had no idea what I was thinking, lucky dog. I pointed to the ribbon curtain and let Clint open it. Keeping him in a work mode was the best bet I had of keeping him silent when he heard the padlock coming off the front door.

Standing at the back corner of the refrigerated ground floor, I looked for a place to hide. Hiding there would mean I could get out minutes after Vinnie showed, minimizing the time I'd have to keep Clint quiet. But unless I wanted to crawl inside a dead pig, or jimmy open the trapdoor that led to the underground refrigeration system, and probably the home of hundreds of rats, there was nowhere to secrete myself and Chi

Chi's dog. Forgetting my watch was broken, I checked the time again, thinking if Vinnie wasn't coming early to meet Chi Chi, it would also be much too long to be in a refrigerator.

I turned and pointed to the plastic curtain. Clint pushed his nose into the middle, and with me right behind him, we started back up the stairs, and were still there, halfway to the top, when I heard it, metal against metal. Someone was unlocking the padlock.

I scooped Clint up and ran up the stairs, not knowing which way to turn. There were two offices, a small room with a coffee machine, a beat-up round table and unmatching chairs, and a small sink with three or four dirty mugs in it. Whoever was coming might go there first to make coffee. I was pretty sure which office Vinnie used. The one I'd been in. The smaller office looked as if it was rarely used, but maybe supplies were kept in there. It must have been used for something.

There was always the bathroom. Of course, if whoever was coming had to use it, there was no place to hide in there.

At the top of the stairs, I noticed two other doors. One was to the back area, the room under the skylight. I tried the door, but it was locked. The other, my last chance, was a closet. There were five empty, bent wire hangers in it, and six other hangers with white coats hanging on them. The shelf was full of hard hats, the floor lined with high rubber boots. Whoever was coming would certainly open that door. But they might not do it right away. They might not do it until the market was about to open, and all I needed was five minutes' grace to get myself and Clint out of harm's way. If my luck held out.

I ducked inside, wedged myself into a recess on the right, and pulled the white coats closer so that if someone opened the door and reached in without really looking, they might not see me, assuming, of course, that the barky little dog I was stuffing into my jacket kept his yap shut.

That's when I realized I hadn't heard anyone coming up the creaky wooden steps.

Nor had I heard the big front door open or close.

Breathing shallowly, opening the closet door a crack, I tried my best to listen now, but there was a long way between me and the downstairs. With the sound of the compressors, it was impossible to know what was going on down there. Something not as small as I would have liked brushed by my ankle. I bit my lip to keep quiet, someone playing bongo drums inside my chest. When I finally heard voices, they were at the top of the stairs.

"What made you just show up like this, without no call? Are you crazy? Could have been someone here."

"I missed you, honey. I thought you might be missing me." Chi Chi. What the hell was she doing here?

I looked down at Clint, then reached into my pocket for one of my gloves, teasing him with it and then giving it to him to chew on.

"What you doing here so early? You hoping I'd show?"

"I have some work to catch up on, in private."

"I could do you real quick, you'll feel like a million, get your work done in half the time. I could—"

"Jesus. Chi Chi. What happened to you?"

No answer.

"Who did that to you?"

"I fell."

I heard his boots on the floor, her heels scraping as if he was dragging her, maybe to get a better look under the light.

Clint's tail was banging my side. I tugged at the glove to keep him interested.

"Shit. You see a doctor?"

"It's nothing. It looks much worse than it is. Come on, baby. I been missing you so much. You don't even have to pay. You know what I mean? I'm thinking, how many more times you going to see Vinnie before he marry his sweetheart and you never see him again?" Her voice was muffled, as if her mouth was swollen. "No, no, no, I don't want your money, I just want to make you feel goood," the last word loud and stretched as long as the gay pride parade.

With that, and one powerful push with his hind legs, Clint kicked off my chest and hit the ground running.

They both squealed at the same time.

"Where the hell did he come from?"

The closet was now open nearly a foot instead of two inches, the light from the office pouring into the hallway.

"He was with me all along," she said. "I put him down to go. Didn't you see him when we was in the courtyard? He must of slipped in with us." A false laugh. Loud. "You was that busy looking at Chi Chi, thinking of what I'm going to do, real good, the best, and then I'm going to *get out of here* so fast, you'll get all your work done, no problem."

I heard the office door click shut.

"Why'd you do that?" he asked, his voice muffled now.

"Shut out the world, baby. Who needs it? Oooo, look at that fine, big prick, and you saying you not happy to see Chi Chi."

I heard a guttural laugh, and then, as fast as Clint, I was out in the hall, tiptoeing across to the stairs, stepping on the outsides of the treads so that they wouldn't creak, racing through the plastic strips and by all that cold pink flesh, past the huge black cat crouched at that trapdoor near the middle of that ice-cold room, his tail swishing, and out the front door, slipping to the side of the courtyard and out onto the street.

16

What Happened in There?

I was feeling almost smug, standing across the street from Keller's, knowing all the papers I needed were waiting for me at home. I hardly noticed the time passing, until the ambient sound on Little West Twelfth Street changed. I heard a bird singing.

The sky was still dark, but no longer inky. It was more of a blue gray now. I looked west, out at the river, but that wasn't going to help. The sun hadn't risen in the west as far as I could remember. I must have been more tired than I realized, or now that I was safely out of the building, the adrenaline no longer pumping triple time, I was due for a crash.

Two birds now. A pair. I looked toward the old chicken market to see if they were in the tree I'd climbed, but these were city birds. They didn't need a tree. They might have been on the sidewalk bridge, or on a tiny lip over a doorway. They might have been on a windowsill, the very one I'd slipped through so gracefully, surprising the hell out of Chi Chi's dog.

I heard a truck, the meat market coming to life. So where the hell was Chi Chi?

I looked at my watch, forgetting it was broken. But I didn't need it to tell me it was too late for Chi Chi to be at Keller's. What the hell was going on?

And then a car turned the corner, a tan Toyota. Whoever was driving pulled into the parking area at Jeffrey's Poultry Market, cut the engine, and sat behind the wheel for another minute, just waiting. He was taking something out of the glove compartment. Or putting something into it. I saw the tiny flame of a match. Then the door opened, and a foot came out, clad in steel-toed work boots.

He locked the car door and walked quickly toward the street. I turned my back, the way I'd seen so many hookers do, like children closing their eyes so the boogey man wouldn't see them. I expected a hand on my shoulder, a voice behind my back, but neither happened—something worse did. I waited, counting to twenty, then turned in time to see the door of Keller's closing behind him.

The next ten minutes seemed like hours, waiting to see if Chi Chi would come out the door, or out the window. Or if she'd show up at all.

Another ten passed. I was about to head for Washington Street, see if I could find LaDonna and Jasmine, when the door opened and Chi Chi slipped out into the courtyard and, bare legs moving, made her way out to the street, then across to where I was standing.

"What happened in there?"

"What you *think* happened in there?"

"I don't mean that. What kept you so long?"

"Wasn't longer than usual," she said, her eyes on nothing in particular. "He come in early, the manager. He surprise Vinnie."

"McCoy? You mean he walked in on you?"

She shook her head. "Clint heard him and began to growl. I could feel it against my chest."

"He's in your jacket when you—"

That just got me a dirty look.

"How'd you get out? Where'd you hide?"

"Bathroom. All three of us. Then Vinnie went into the office and closed the door, the way I done."

I nodded.

"That ever happen before?"

She shrugged.

"That ever happen, you think, when Rosalinda was there?"

Chi Chi ignored me. Whatever happened, she was used to it. If she'd been in danger, it was just part of her life, nothing worth talking about. Chi Chi, in fact, had other things on her mind. The left side of her mouth was cut and bruised, a tooth missing, maybe two. It was too dark to tell. One eye was swollen half shut, and her wrist was wrapped with an Ace bandage. God only knows how many bruises there were that I couldn't see.

"I thought you couldn't work. I was told you were messed up real bad, in pain. You are, aren't you? You look like hell," I told her. What was I thinking, that she didn't know? That she hadn't looked into the mirror a hundred times by now, cried over what she saw, over what she felt?

"You don't look so hot yourself." Hands on hips now. Head high.

"How'd you know I'd be here?"

Again, Chi Chi didn't answer me.

"Well, I'm glad you came," I said. "If you hadn't, he might have seen me. Vinnie. I wasn't sure how I was going to get out of the closet and down the stairs with the office door open and a chance of the compressor going off just when I needed cover. I was hoping he'd go to the john, but then I thought, Schmuck, no one's here, not that he knows of. He's not going to close that door either. So it's a damn good thing you came for Clint."

Chi Chi looked stung. She dug her hand into her jacket pocket, winced, fished around, and came out with a folded tissue. Then she opened it carefully and held it out for me to inspect. It was a brad.

I reached for her arm, but she pulled away.

"Is it jus' me," she asked, "or don't you trust nobody?" When I opened my mouth to answer her, she put her hands over her ears. "Don't tell me," she said. "I don't want to know. I'm already hurting enough. Anyways, whatever you tell me, it's going to be a lie, so save your breath." She lifted Clint's face and bent toward him. I thought she was going to kiss him, let me know she knew who her real friends were, but she didn't. She closed her eyes and inhaled deeply. Then she looked at me again, nodding. "He did it," she said.

"Devon?"

She waved her good hand at me. "Clint. He did it. He got you in there."

"Chi Chi, I'm sorry."

"I tol' you I'd help you out."

"You did."

"But you didn't believe in me."

"I heard you were hurt. I didn't think you'd be able—"

She looked away for a moment, toward the river, the water still dark as death.

"Yeah, sure," she said. "You wouldn't be the first one. But you had faith in him."

I nodded.

"And he did it, right? He came through for you."

I nodded. "He was unbelievable. I wish you could have seen him. I taught him at least a dozen separate tasks and strung them all together. After Jasmine and LaDonna came to tell me you needed him back, I telescoped everything into one work session, last night, and we only had time for one complete run-through."

Her eyes rolled up, and the sweat was pouring down the side of her face.

"Let's get you something to eat."

"Can't." She pointed to her mouth. This time I winced, at the thought of what she'd just done to help me.

"Come on." I took her by her good arm and headed for Washington Street.

She shook her head.

"Be real danger there."

I looked around. "What?"

"I be seen with you, someone tell Devon, he kill me this time. Devon, he see us hisself, we both dead." She started walking the other way, toward the river. "Hurry up," she said. "You dragging your feet."

I don't know who started it, but the two of us were running, Chi Chi in bare legs and platform stilettos, the dog bouncing around in her jacket, the wind whipping at our faces, sharp and cold, the market opening slowly behind us, like a bear waking up from hibernation.

When we got to West and Jane, the side of the Riverview Hotel, we slowed down.

"He didn't give me nothin'."

"Who? Vinnie?"

She nodded.

"He didn't pay you? But you told him he didn't have to. I heard you."

Chi Chi looked at me, then looked away. "You get the stuff you was after?"

"It's all home. I don't really know yet."

"What you mean, it's all home?"

"I faxed it. I couldn't just steal it, could I?"

"Not someone like you, someone with high moral principles, no way. You could break in, but you can't steal. You telling me you didn't even snag a roast on your way out?"

"Look, I don't have time for this."

Chi Chi sighed. "That's what they all say eventually. Sometimes they say it you ask if they want to party. Sometimes they say it after, you asking for your money. One day, Devon say it. That'll be the last day of my life."

"No," I said. "We're going to get the money for him. You'll be fine." Rachel, the enabler.

"What you mean? Where we goin'?"

"My house."

Chi Chi stopped walking. I'd never seen anyone look quite so scared. She began to shake her head.

"It's okay," I told her. "Come on. I'm going to make you something in the blender. You like chocolate?"

She shook her head again.

What was wrong with me, thinking a shake would fix her up when what she needed was crack?

"Okay, okay. We'll just get Clint's coat."

"Don't want that coat no more."

"That's fine. I'll hold it for you, in case you change your mind. I'll just give you the money, from the pocket."

She was shaking badly, trying to nod, her teeth, or what was left of them, chattering.

"I give him the money, he know I seen you. I don't give him the money, maybe he finish what he started."

I stopped and took her by the arms, careful of her bandaged wrist.

"What should we do?" I said.

Her head was down, her knees bent. She looked like a rag doll, being held up by God knows what.

"I tell him all the money is from tonight. I say I had a great night. Do you think that might work?"

"I do," I said.

"I tell him, See, you didn't hurt Chi Chi so bad. I always tell him that. He don't mean nothin' by it, Rachel. It's just his way. He say if he don't remind us girls to be respectful, some of us will walk all over him. He says he don't put his foot down, there be chaos."

I nodded, as if I understood.

"I tell him, Chi Chi know you love her." Then to me: "Chi Chi know that. Devon take care of me. Without Devon, don't know what would happen to me. That's why I goes out and does my job, show him some respect." Now she was nodding. She reached into her top and pulled out a twenty, held it up for me to inspect, in case I wasn't clear on how you show respect to a pimp, in case her message had been lost on me. That's when I noticed she was crying.

I put my arm around her shoulder and we began to walk again. "You going to be okay?"

"I catch up with one of the other girls. Someone bound to have something for me."

"Can you eat anything at all?"

She shook her head. "I can't eat when I'm nervous," she said. And then she saw where we were and froze.

"Why we here? You said you was going to give me my money, and you bring me to the police? You tricked me."

"No, Chi Chi, I live here, behind that gate."

But she was looking the other way, at the Sixth Precinct across the street, a place she must have been too many times already, a place she didn't want to go again.

"I can't go in."

"We're not going there, we're going here."

But she turned away, facing the brick wall to the right of the gate, and there was no moving her.

"Okay. Don't move. Wait here. I'll be back in a minute with your money." And then I was running again, through the tunnel, into the garden, opening the door, greeting Dashiell without really stopping, not stopping until I'd grabbed Clint's red coat from the arm of the sofa. How could I have missed the bulge? Or had I thought it was a bunch of pickup bags, a totally stoned hooker was prepared to scoop, any time of the day or night?

Standing there for a moment, Chi Chi's money in my hand, crumpled tens and twenties, I wondered what I was doing on this case, and what would happen to me, to all of us, by the time it was over.

17

More Than I Need to Know, I Told Her

AFTER giving Chi Chi the money and watching her pick her way down the block, as if she were walking through a pit of vipers, I took Dashiell around the block, fed him, and then, not bothering to eat or even look at the papers I'd faxed home, lay down across my bed, fully dressed. I remember thinking I'd rest a minute before reading the files I'd stolen from Keller's. Instead, I fell into a deep sleep.

Even when I woke up at five in the afternoon, showered, ate, walked Dashiell, and started to read the papers my fax machine had spit all over the office floor, it didn't occur to me that I was now working the same hours as my clients, falling into a coma near dawn, getting up when it was already dark. There was too much to do to think about myself. Or perhaps it was something else, what I'd thought about before going to sleep, that I was involved in something so deeply ugly, I didn't want to understand it. If I let myself think, I might think my way back to dog training. For the time being, I had another commitment, and the less I thought about *my* life and the more I thought about *the* life, the faster I'd get to where I was going.

I had some papers now that showed the history of the private carting companies Keller's had used over the past few years. It was true, as the *Times* had reported; only a little over a month after Mulrooney had been hired to manage the plant, he'd changed carting companies. But that had been the third change in two years.

I remembered the stink in the paper when Giuliani took on the corruption at the Fulton Fish Market, requiring all businesses seeking to operate within the market to register with the Department of Business Services and for all their employees to undergo background checks and then be issued identification cards before they could work there.

Giuliani had cleaned up the fish market and had moved on to do the same at Hunts Point. Next on his agenda was the Gansevoort Meat Market and the Brooklyn Terminal Market. Hadn't there been some sort of law passed that would cover the industry citywide, as it were? Still, there wasn't any law enacted that couldn't be gotten around. Wasn't this just a case of the more things changed, the more they stayed the same?

CityWide Carting had been getting Keller's business for only eight months. And now the two men who had been arrested in connection with Mulrooney's execution, both of whom were employed by CityWide, had been released. What was that all about? After all, Mulrooney had been killed a week after Keller's switched to a new carting company, cutting CityWide out of the loop. I wasn't ready to accept Capelli and Maraccio's airtight alibis, even if the court was. I was still wondering how many times in that week Mulrooney had been threatened before someone actually got the job done.

I pulled out his personnel file. Until his untimely death, one of my all-time favorite phrases, Mulrooney had lived in Rego Park, Queens, with his wife, Frances. He took only one dependent on his paycheck. That meant their kid must have been grown and out of the house by then. I set that page aside, thinking I ought to pay Frances a visit, wondering whether or not I should lay things on the line for her or make up a story that would get what I needed to know but not give her any information at all. Then I started reading the rest of the papers, looking for the smallest clue that the death of Kevin Mulrooney was somehow connected to the death of Rosalinda, whose untimely demise was what I had been paid to investigate in the first place.

I had the notes from Vinnie Esposito's file in my hand when the bell on the wrought-iron gate rang. I glanced at the clock. It was eight-thirty. I was wearing the clothes I'd put on yesterday, clothes I'd crawled around a filthy roof in, clothes I'd slept in. I put the papers back on the pile, opened the top drawer and shoved them in, then took the steps two at a time and headed for the gate to see who was there.

I could see the bronze hair before I saw anything else. And two big hands holding on to the gate, as if she were in jail, holding on to the bars, watching for her attorney to show, waiting for something to happen.

"LaDonna. What a surprise."

She waited for me to unlock the gate.

"You don't know the half of it." She swept by me like the Queen of Sheba, sashaying down the tunnel into the yard, stopping, hands on her nonexistent hips, to observe my digs. The outside lights were on. It had just started to snow.

"The weather's gone nuts," she said, holding out a big paw to catch the tiny flakes. "You going to invite me in, or we going to stand out here while the snow piles up to our privates?"

"It's not going to stick," I said. "Door's unlocked." I pointed, ever the gracious hostess. Just what is this about? I wondered, following LaDonna through the yard and up the steps to my front door.

But before we got the chance to go inside, the bell rang again, the muffled sound coming through the closed door.

LaDonna turned and put a finger on her cheek. "Now, who could that be? Oh, I know. I bet it's Jasmine. I told her, 'Meet me at Rachel's at eight-thirty.' Bitch never showed up on time once in her whole life."

She stood where she was while I went to open the gate a second time. I doubted it was a social call. I wondered if they were here to ask for a refund. After all, I was no closer to the answer they needed now than I'd been the night they hired me. I sure had expected Chi Chi to finish with Vinnie faster than she did. Maybe they thought I should be faster, that I could solve the case, get them the name they wanted, one, two, three.

Jasmine passed me without a word, as if I were her butler. When I turned to follow her, I noticed her ass. It was difficult to miss, bare and sticking out of her short shorts the way it was.

"You'll catch your death," my mother would have said, and for once, she might have hit the nail right on the head.

I opened the door; Dash sniffed the girls and then followed us to the living room.

I pointed to the couch, a real Emily Post. "What's up?" I asked.

"That's what we came to ask you," Jasmine said. There seemed to be a bruise on the outside of her left eye, but her hair was falling forward onto her face, and I couldn't tell for sure.

"Oh, you came for a progress report?"

"We did," she said.

I looked at LaDonna, but she didn't say a word.

"I got into Keller's."

"We already know that." Jasmine pulled at her hair so that it covered more of her face.

"I was just going over the paperwork when you showed up."

"And?"

"Well, I don't have an answer for you yet, if that's what you're asking."

"When will you?"

"I don't know."

Now all three of us were mute and staring, me at Jasmine and LaDonna, the two of them at me.

"Too slow," LaDonna said.

"We could be killed while you're crawling around looking for a connection. We don't care about that. We only want to know who did Rosalinda."

LaDonna frowned. I didn't give her a chance to speak.

"I know that. I really do. I'm looking for the connection only to see if that will be the route to finding out the name you want. I'll tell you this—"

LaDonna raised one huge hand, a silver ring on every finger, including her thumb. "Just one thing you need to tell us. The name of who killed them. We don't want to hear how you swung through the window like Errol Flynn. It's beside the point. It don't help us one damn bit."

"I'm working as fast as I can."

"We want you to work faster," LaDonna said, standing. Dashiell stood, too. I didn't take that as a good sign, and suddenly all the things I'd ever heard about tranny hookers came crashing into my head, especially the stuff about how crazed on drugs they all are, how desperate and violent, how they all carry razor blades, just in case they need to protect themselves. I stood, too. Now only Jasmine was sitting, leaning forward, her elbows on her knees.

"We need to see your stuff," she said.

"My stuff? What stuff are you talking about? You mean the papers from Keller's?"

She gave LaDonna a look. "Your *clothes*, girlfriend. We think the answer's out where we are. We think that's where you need to be to find it."

I sat.

Jasmine got up.

"No," I said, shaking my head. "No way. I never told you—"

"No. You're not telling us. We're telling you. I'm going to watch you. You're not going to be in danger. It's just—" LaDonna looked toward the kitchen, then back at me. "You got anything to drink?"

"What'd you have in mind?"

"Orange juice. Soda. Scotch. Beer. I'm real parched."

I got up and brought the juice container and two glasses, setting them on the glass top that sat on the little red wagon and served as a coffee table.

LaDonna picked up the juice and just held the container. "We out there. But we don't know what to look for, the way you do." She filled a glass for Jasmine, then drank from the container. "Got anything to eat?"

"You want me to order a pizza?"

LaDonna nodded. Jasmine didn't move. I sent Dashiell for the phone.

When the pie arrived, LaDonna went poking around in the kitchen and came out with a bottle of Chianti, a corkscrew, and a shit-eating grin. "You neat," she said. "I can find everything I need in that sweet little kitchen of yours. I could live here in a second, 'cept for what's across the street."

"There is that," I said.

We moved to the small marble table outside the kitchen.

Jasmine said she understood if I didn't want to do any of the johns, she really did. "'Course, you could make a couple a hundred a night," she said, "in addition to what we paid you, if you change your mind." She waited. I chewed. Jasmine shrugged.

I thanked her for her understanding.

She said she wouldn't know how to do my job any better than I'd know how to do hers.

I thanked her again.

When she started to explain how to put a condom on a john without using your hands, so he wouldn't even know you were doing it, I put down the piece of pizza I'd been eating and held up my hand like a stop sign. "More than I need to know," I told her.

Jasmine nodded. She was pretty understanding. You had to give her that.

"Truth is, we only want to dress you for the part," said LaDonna, grinning again.

"You mean you're in a big rush for me to solve this, get you the name you're after, but you have the time to play with me?"

They both nodded. LaDonna picked up the piece of pizza I'd started and finished it in one bite. "You only ordered one pie?" she asked with her mouth full. "How'm I going to keep my strength up?"

I shrugged. Who knew, with all that cleavage, they'd eat like truck drivers?

"Ready for us to get serious?"

"Sure. What the hell."

"We want you to come out this weekend, Friday night and Saturday night. One of us will stick with you. You just have to keep your ears open."

"And your mouth shut." That Jasmine, ever the comedienne.

"Count on it," I told her. This time I was the one who got up, went to the kitchen, and came back with a bottle of Chianti. LaDonna stood and took out the cork, filling our glasses without waiting for the wine to breathe.

"We want you to see what's out there, maybe get some ideas about the case when you see who shows up, what their attitude is, what they say, all that. Because it could be, it's a customer done her. It happens."

I nodded.

"One time, this john's wife comes out, in his car and in his clothes. He was doing her one night and he says another name, then starts to cry, confesses that once in a blue moon he comes to the meat market, which could or could not be the true story. So what does she do? She shows up in fucking drag. She's asking for Monica, which one's Monica, so she can warn her off, tell her she ever does her husband again, she'll be hanging on one of those hooks, like he told her the real story in the first place, like there's a Monica out there who did her old man." Jasmine shook her head. "So you see a john without a dick in his pants—"

"Jesus, ladies." I covered my face.

"What?" Jasmine was looking from me to LaDonna.

"She delicate," LaDonna said, serious as an oncologist.

"Just can it," Jasmine said to me. "We heard you had balls, so don't go crapping out on us now when we got this funny feeling about the stroll."

"What funny feeling?"

"That something bad's going to happen again." LaDonna stuck two long fingers into that nest of teased, sprayed hair and scratched. "Soon."

"What do you mean?"

"Ebony, she said she was thinking of moving over to Madison Square Park again, even Hunts Point. She got a sick sense about these things. She been saying to watch out. It don't feel right out there. Things happen in threes, she said, and there's been two murders already."

Jasmine leaned across the table. "We gave you our whole stash," she said. "Every dime we'd put away. It'll take me an extra year to cross now. But without you finding out who did Rosalinda, I might not be here to do it. At all. We need you, Rachel. We're counting on you."

LaDonna flipped the lip of the pizza box closed and drank the rest of her wine as if it were water and she'd just run a marathon. Then she stood and reached for my hand. "Time to look in your closet, bitch."

I'd had too much wine and not enough pizza. I gave her my hand, stood, and nodded. That's when the phone rang. I was going to let it go, but Dashiell picked it up, brought it over, and poked me in the leg with it.

"Hello?"

"Rachel, it's me," he said.

"Oh, hi."

"Why do you sound so funny? Is something wrong?"

I looked at Jasmine and LaDonna and pointed to the stairs. Start without me, I mouthed, vaguely thinking about all the stories I'd heard about transvestite hookers stealing anything they could get their hands on. I watched them take the first few steps in their high heels.

"It's difficult to say," I said into the phone.

"You're not alone?"

"Not hardly."

"Rachel?"

"It's just a night in with the girls, you know, nails, hair, fashion." I reached for my glass and finished what was in it. "You know something," I whispered into the phone, "if not for their hard-core drug addiction, really strange appearance, lack of education and experience, and dysfunctional behavior patterns, these girls could really be something."

I heard Betty bark.

"I mean, think about it. The strength of a man and the determination of a woman."

I heard a huge crash coming from upstairs.

"Why are they there?" he asked. "What's up?"

I looked toward the stairs and wondered that myself.

"They stopped by to give me some advice, about the job. No big deal."

"Be careful, Rachel. No matter what they say, these women, they don't know dick about anything. They did, they wouldn't be leading the lives they do."

"Right you are." I thought dick was *exactly* what they knew, but I didn't feel like arguing over semantics when I had guests waiting.

"Listen, Rach. I have some bad news. I spoke to the boys today, and they really want me out there for Thanksgiving. I know we talked about spending it together, but—"

"No, no, it's okay. Hey, they're kids. They miss their dad." I picked up the empty wine bottle, held it over my glass, and gave it a shake. "Don't give it a second thought."

Another crash, a smaller one this time, as if someone had thrown a shoe and the other party had failed to catch it. Theirs or mine? I wondered.

"I can always spend the holiday with my girlfriends," I said into the phone. Of course, at the time, it was just a private joke. I had no idea that what I was saying would turn out to be the naked truth.

"I've got to go," he said. "I just pulled into my client's driveway, and she's standing in the doorway. I'll call you as soon as I'm finished here. Just be careful."

"Promise," I whispered, putting down the phone and heading upstairs to where the laughter was.

18

It's for a Date, I Confessed

For the second day in a row, I was on the main floor at Saks Fifth Avenue, pretending to select a handbag because the leather goods department offered me a decent view of the perfume counter. Yesterday I'd chosen a tiny lime green Prada bag, something I definitely couldn't afford and would have absolutely no use for were it given to me. What did women put in these mini bags—what my mother's mother used to call "mad money" and a set of house keys? You couldn't get your cell phone in here, your PalmPilot, or even some makeup for a quick touch-up, and the only way you could have an extra tampon with you is if you were willing to let the whole world see it bulging out of your fifteen-hundred-dollar purse.

There'd been a work number for Frances Ann Mulrooney in her husband's file, and when I'd called, I knew I'd gotten lucky this one time. She worked at Saks, in the perfume department. No, they wouldn't call her to the phone unless it was an emergency, but yes, they'd take a message. I declined to leave one. They declined to mention she had Wednesdays off. At least, that's what I was hoping, that she hadn't been here all day because it was her day off. If she was down with the flu, this case was going to take even longer to solve, and my clients were getting impatient.

I would have been happy to take my chances with her imported virus, were that the case, had I only been able to think of a plausible story that would get me into her apartment. I couldn't. But I did have one prepared for Saks, and if I had to say so myself, it was a doozy. I was hoping she'd buy it; I really needed to be able to offer my clients some actual facts when I met them later in the day.

I was examining something more sporty and lots cheaper than the little green Prada bag this time, but still more than I'd spend. In fact, I thought, unzipping the Coach bucket, what was wrong with pockets? Sure, your stuff made unsightly bulges in all the wrong places, but that seemed a small price to pay compared to the price of a handbag at Saks, three-seventy-five for the one in my hand. But then there was a reason to check out the Chanel display, and my handbag shopping came prematurely to a halt.

I walked across the aisle and stood opposite her, waiting for her to notice me, the only saleslady I'd seen old enough to be Mulrooney's wife, her little brass name tag telling me I'd guessed correctly. She was a fair-skinned redhead, her large body packed so tightly into the staid black dress she wore and the foundation garment beneath it that she looked sausage-like. I couldn't see her legs, but I expected if I did, I'd see support hose and nun's shoes.

"Can I help you?" she asked, her smile changing nothing but her mouth.

"I don't know," I told her, already in my Improv 101 mode. "I was thinking . . ." I lowered my eyes.

"Of purchasing a scent?" she inquired. Her broad hand still held the bottle of perfume she'd been trying to put away, the nails short, neat, and shellacked with one of those clear polishes that just make them shine. Her wedding band, which probably hadn't been off since it had been placed on her hand some twenty years earlier, was a plain gold dome with a patina of scratches. Perhaps it had been passed down a generation or two.

"Yes. I was thinking of purchasing a scent." Eyes still down.

"Do you have a brand you prefer, something you usually wear, or will it be something new this time?" A slight lilt, as if she'd come over from the old country when she was still a girl.

I sighed. "It's for a date," I confessed, leaning ever so slightly forward. "My first."

"Well, surely you—"

I lifted my left hand and wiped at my right eye with my fingers, so that she could see my wedding band.

"I mean, my first since—"

"Oh, I *am* sorry."

"It's not that long, but some of my friends . . ." I shrugged. "Well, this one friend, she said she knows this really nice man, but I don't feel ready. I don't even know what people wear now, I mean, dating. I . . ."

I looked up, into her green eyes, displaying my strongest talent, lying to decent human beings who are going about their lives honestly and would never suspect such treachery from a perfectly normal-looking stranger.

"Well, scent is the ideal place to start." She patted my hand quickly and respectfully. "It's a real confidence booster." She reached under the glass counter, put the bottle she was holding down, and picked up another. "Chanel Number Five. You can't beat it in an emergency like this." Her smile was professional, like her outfit, but I was starting to see something else, something that encouraged me to rush even more quickly down the road to hell. She opened the bottle, tipped it enough to wet her finger, then ran her finger along the back of her other hand, offering me that hand to smell.

"It's lovely."

She smiled. "It's not for nothing that it stays so popular. Do you want to try it on your hand? Your own body chemistry will alter the scent of any perfume, though I've never met anyone who couldn't wear Chanel, not a single soul."

"What on earth should I wear?"

She looked stunned, then perplexed. I wondered if I'd gone too fast.

"Oh, well, there are so many designers represented here. I'm sure someone upstairs could help you with that."

"I'm terrified."

Frances touched my arm, and this time she let her hand stay for just a moment longer. "I know," she said. She looked around, then back at me. "It's difficult."

"It was very sudden. I mean, it was unexpected. There was no preparation, and I . . ."

She nodded.

"Do you have anyone to talk to? Anyone at all?"

I shook my head. "My friends, well, they mean well. But they don't know what it's like, so they don't really know what to say. And it seems to me, they don't want to hear anything, either. It just makes them frightened to realize that something so terrible could happen to anyone. One moment you're a have, the next a have-not."

"I lost my Patrick recently," she said.

"Oh, I'm so sorry. Now look what I've gone and done. I shouldn't have . . ." I looked down at my hands, both flat on the glass of the counter. "This is so inappropriate. I can't apologize enough. I'm usually in better control, but you're so easy to talk to that . . ."

"Well, and how were you to know that you'd found someone else who'd had the same misfortune? What are the chances?"

"Still, I'm so sorry I—"

Frances interrupted. "I go to this group, other women who have also . . ." She reached into her pocket and took out a white handkerchief with lace trim, but she didn't use it. She only held it tightly in her hand. "Other women in the same boat, as we say," sounding now as if she'd just gotten off one.

"And it helps?"

"That and the job. Without this, I don't know where I'd be." She looked around again and took out another perfume for me to try. "Are you working?"

I shook my head. "There was a little money, some insurance, but I absolutely need to find a job. I feel totally foolish for something else now." I pointed to the bottle of Chanel. "I'm sure I can't afford . . ."

Frances leaned forward. "Don't you worry about the purchase."

"But now I've wasted your time," I said.

"And do you think that everyone who stops by this counter buys a bottle of Chanel? Don't you give that a second thought. But the job, think about that, that's essential. The worst thing you can do is stay at home. The very worst."

"Might there be anything here?"

Frances nodded. She picked up a little pad and wrote down a woman's name, and where the personnel office was, tearing off the page, folding it in half, and handing it to me.

"They're hiring now for Christmas. It's temporary, of course, and it might even be part-time, but if you do well, there's always a chance for something permanent after the season. There's always a lot of movement among the younger employees."

"I don't know how to thank you."

"Never mind that. It'll do you a world of good."

I insisted on buying the smallest bottle of Chanel toilet water—an unfortunate description, but as Frances Ann said, it would give me confidence for my interview as well as my date. I promised I'd take her to lunch if I got a position at Saks, the only truthful thing I'd said to her so far. Her cheeks flushed a lovely pink. She told me she'd like that. Then she was all businesslike ringing up the sale, except for the part where she let her hand touch mine one last time when she handed me my change.

"I hope it all works out for you," she whispered, picking up the sample I'd tried and returning it to the cabinet below. I thanked her again and headed for the elevators.

19

She Wants Those,
and I Want These

I GOT to Jeffrey early and started browsing, wondering what LaDonna could have been thinking, asking me to meet her here so that she could outfit me for the stroll. I poked inside a red leather jacket, trying to find the price tag, doubling what I thought it would be and still being off by half. How would I possibly have any money left for drugs if I paid these prices?

I was in the shoe department, holding a little number made of two thin snakeskin straps, a feather, a thin sole, and a heel the height of the twin towers, when I heard LaDonna entering the store, her voice so loud that I wasn't the only one who turned to stare. To make things worse, when she spotted me from the entranceway, she gave a center-stage wave and a loud yoo-hoo. Now everyone turned to stare at me. I couldn't believe the number of people there to do it. With tiny leather skirts at eleven hundred dollars and shoes running five hundred and up, you'd think the place would be empty. Instead, it looked like Toys R Us two days before Christmas.

"Oh," she said, hand on her fake chests, "those are divine. Have you tried them on yet?"

"Please." I showed her the price tag.

"Never mind all that. I just need to know your size."

I screwed up my mouth to ask why, but got yanked by the arm instead and shoved onto a backless padded leather bench so that I could slip on the little number now in her hand. LaDonna was feeling no pain.

"I can't walk in shoes like that," I complained.

LaDonna flapped her hand at me. "You learn."

"Where are Chi Chi and Jasmine?"

"You just pay attention to what's in front of your nose, Miss Thing. Now, which of those there *could* you walk in? And don't go picking out your usual." She used the snakeskin shoe as if it were a pointer, aiming it at me, and then over her shoulder at God knows what. "No one's going to buy you're real, girl, you wearing jeans and Reeboks, one of your boyfriend's sweaters, and that long sheepskin coat covers all your ass-ets, no one can see what they're about to purchase."

I smiled and pointed to a pair of red platform ankle straps. I always wanted to try on a pair anyway. Suddenly, I felt walking wouldn't be a problem after all. Hell, I had to, I could do a triathlon in them. Having just been employed by Saks Fifth Avenue to sell socks through the holiday season, part-time, was making me feel as high as LaDonna apparently was.

"Guess what?"

LaDonna, sitting next to me, her long legs crossed, leaned closer.

"I found Mulrooney's wife. I made contact with her."

LaDonna looked as if she were going to speak, then changed her mind, holding up her huge paw and curling her pointer at the young clerk, a cute young guy in a pristine white shirt, his dark hair gelled so that it looked wet.

"We needs our feets measured up," she told him, her mind on the task at hand. "She wants those," she said, pointing to the red ones, "and I want these." She elevated the strappy one with the feather.

I turned out to be an eight. Still. And LaDonna was practically off the scale. The clerk apologized when he came back, handing me the platform number and saying he was so sorry, but he didn't have the snakeskin number in LaDonna's size. Would she like, perhaps, to see something else? He had, in fact, a box with him, one big enough you could bury a dwarf in it, assuming you had one you needed to bury. He said he'd found something for her, something in lizard. Lizard's cutting edge, he told her. It's very now. Could she use green? he wondered.

LaDonna feigned great disappointment, motioned for him to put the box down, said she'd "think on it," then asked for the ladies' room, and disappeared while I tried on the shoes of my choice, teetering toward the mirror, then back to my place.

When LaDonna returned, she tried on the green shoes, holding up one huge foot at a time, then walking over to the mirror to have another look. I looked at the side of the box. The green lizard shoes were going for six-fifty. I tried to get LaDonna's attention, tell her what the shoes cost, but she was studying her feet in the mirror, a very focused shopper.

She called the clerk with another hand gesture, palm in, four fingers vibrating. "They pinch my little toe," she said, motioning for me to put my sneakers back on. Then she led me back to where I'd been earlier, the rear of the store, where all the clothes looked so tiny, they might have been for Barbie dolls.

LaDonna proceeded to take things off the racks, hold them up against me, cock her head, click her tongue, and put them back. After about fifteen minutes, she said it was time to go. Since I hadn't argued with her before, I decided not to now and docilely followed her out the front door.

"So what'd she say?" she asked. "Mrs. Mulcahey."

"Mulrooney."

"Whatever."

"Not much. It was just a first meeting."

"You hoping for a second?"

"There'll definitely be a second."

She nodded thoughtfully, glad to see I was doing my job.

"So what was this all about?" I asked.

"You'll see. We supposed to wait for the others across from the Gay and Lesbian Center. Come on."

"What others? Were they in there?"

LaDonna shook her head. "You aks too many questions," she said. "Always did. Probably always will. I guess it's a good thing, too, considering your line of work. So, you going to ask this Mulrooney's wife what she knows?"

I nodded.

"She won't know nothin'."

"What makes you think that?"

"Beg pardon?"

"What makes—"

"She a wife, right?"

I nodded. "Well, a widow now."

"Same difference. They never know nothin'. They dependent on a man, makes them stupid. They invested in seeing nothin', hearing nothin', saying nothin', like the monkeys."

Was she talking about husbands and wives, or hookers and pimps?

"But you go aks your questions, it makes you happy. What about the johns? You'll aks them questions, too?"

This time I didn't nod. We were walking along Washington Street, too late for the meat markets, too early for the hookers. It was called a twenty-four-hour neighborhood, but it was actually only about a twenty-two-hour one, unless you counted Hogs and Heifers, the motorcycle bar. I didn't ever remember seeing that closed, even though I was sure it did.

Did LaDonna, Chi Chi, and Jasmine really expect to tart me up and have me out here pretending to be a hooker? Working in the hosiery department at Saks was one thing. This was quite another.

LaDonna began to count on her fingers as we turned onto Thirteenth Street.

"One, to start out, you say, 'Going out?'" She looked at me. "'Going out?' You got that?"

"Going out?"

"Right. Only more, what do you call it?"

"Sexy?"

"No. Your clothes take care of that. Your location takes care of that. That's why they come here."

"Blatant?"

"Wiseass."

"Suggestive?"

"That's the one. Some of them say, 'Do you want a date?'"

I repeated that, too. LaDonna smiled.

"'Course, you could say, 'Like a blow job or something?' instead. More to the point. But you're probably too delicate a person for that one."

My mother rolled over in her grave. In fact, my whole family, all the way back to the Garden of Eden, did.

"Two, the prices. You gonna be aksed. You gotta know."

I nodded.

"You say, 'It's forty for a blow job.' Got it?"

"Look, you said I wouldn't actually—"

"You gotta look real. You gotta sound real. You don't gotta do real. I'll take care of that part. Can I go on now?"

"Please do."

"Forty for a blow job, but late in the night, you got to be willing to bargain. Too high's no good. But don't go too low. That's no good either. Some of 'em, no matter what you aks, they's going to drive away. They's just looking. Or they gets scared. Or they don't like your type, they want darker, bigger, hairier, whatever."

I nodded.

"A straight fuck, aks fifty. Half-and-half, that's seventy."

"Whoa. A straight fuck? Half-and-half?"

"I figured, in case you change you mind." She patted her hair. "Things we can't do, you can. You can make hundreds in one night."

"Yeah? And how much do I get to keep?"

"I didn't say you wouldn't incur no expenses, did I?"

"No. You certainly didn't."

"No need to get your tits in a knot. You got expenses being an investigator, don' you, advertising, wardrobe, ve-hicles?"

"Yeah, right. So what expenses do I have here? Gotta know what to put down on my Schedule C."

"You out there, we going to have to give a little something to Devon."

"But I won't be making anything."

"You wanna tell Devon that?"

"Does everyone have a pimp?"

LaDonna shook her head. "You could come out on your own. Some do."

"But you don't?"

No answer.

"It's just a temporary thing, you being out there. Jasmine, she told Devon you from San Francisco, you on the run, something to do with some john, find himself dead. She told him you probably won't stay, you saving up now to go to Miami, you hate the cold, but you don't want no trouble while you're here, you'll pay him to take care of you for the time being. That's what she arranged."

"And where is this money coming from?"

"Not your problem."

"So why'd you even tell me?"

"Because he come, I want you to turn your back, like you don't want to be seen. You promise money, he'll respect that. You don't, or you stare at his face, look him in the eye, he beat the shit out of you."

"For taking up business on his turf?"

"For dissing him, girl. The way Chi Chi did, letting you take her dog without going and aksing him first could her dog be groomed by a professional."

I looked at LaDonna, who was looking straight ahead, her chin slightly up, a trickle of sweat sliding down her cheek.

When we got to Greenwich Street, she grabbed my hand and began to run across the street, dragging me along with her.

Jasmine was lighting a cigarette. Chi Chi had just put Clint down to let him pee. They each had a shopping bag, but not from Jeffrey. Chi Chi had one of those plain brown bags with a handle. Jasmine's bag was from D'Agostino's.

"You ready?" Jasmine asked me. She handed me the shopping bag. Chi Chi picked Clint up and motioned for me to take her bag, too. Her mouth was yellow now, and her eye was still very swollen.

"There's makeup, shoes, everything," Jasmine said. "We meet you here tomorrow night, nine o'clock, see what you can find out. I spoke to Devon. We cool."

"Yeah. That's what LaDonna told me."

"Okay. We'll watch out for you, but LaDonna, she'll be right with you, like you're going to do a two-fer. She might do the talking, but you might have to say something, too."

"Might be better, her mouth, I say she don't speak English," LaDonna said. "At least the first night."

"Whatever." Jasmine drew in hard on her cigarette, blew the smoke down toward her plastic, see-through, high-heeled mules. "Word is, someone in the life knows something, so you talk to the other girls, too. But be careful. Some of them are real weird."

"Weirder than us," LaDonna said, punching me in the arm and nearly knocking me over. "She'd be something, wouldn't she?" she said to Jasmine. "Good thing she's not going blond, or one of the others kill her for sure."

"I do okay," Jasmine said, "she don't scare me."

It went on like that for a while, the two of them talking about me as if I were across the street instead of inches away. I stayed, my mouth shut, watching and listening, thinking that if I did open my mouth, that's what I should sound like, voice deep, pride deeper, and eyes sad as hell. I remembered something my t'ai chi teacher used to say when someone was puff-puffing, all ego and nothing real. The bigger the front,

the bigger the back. He might as well have been talking about
the stroll.

I opened the D'Agostino's bag and looked in. There was a
kelly green leather miniskirt, a feather boa that might have
been white at one time, and what must have been a halter
top, what there was of it.

"From Jeffrey?"

"From Rosalinda," Chi Chi said, the first words she'd spoken since I got here. "She was about your size. Except for her
feet."

Everything got quiet for a moment, even the traffic. Or
maybe it only seemed that way. I opened the other bag. Red
platform shoes, the ones I'd tried on at Jeffrey. Then Chi Chi
held out her hand and slipped something into mine. "Tape it
to your hip," she whispered, "because you never know, you
might need it sometime."

I could feel it through the tissue paper she'd wrapped it
in.

"Look," Jasmine said. "She's so moved she's going to cry.
Do it now, you going to do it. You do it tomorrow, your mascara's going to run, ruin that boa. She had three. That one
was her favorite. She said it brought her luck."

"We got to go to work now," LaDonna said. Chi Chi
looked up but said nothing. Jasmine wiggled her fingers at
me.

"Okay, then I'll see you here at nine," I said, turning away
from them, the razor blade still in my hand, suddenly aching
to be with Dashiell. I missed him so desperately I thought my
knees would buckle when I tried to walk. But I didn't walk
away, not just yet. "I'm bringing Dash," I said, spinning back
around. "That's not up for discussion."

Jasmine shrugged. "Whatever gets you through the night,
honey. Same as for the rest of us."

She took a last puff on her cigarette and flicked it far out
into the street, the sparks flying up and out, bright in the dark

night, then disappearing. When I turned away again, I saw Devon headed our way. Head down, I crossed the street, and as soon as I'd passed the building line, I began to run and didn't stop until I was unlocking the gate, Dashiell's barks coming at me from inside the cottage, making me feel human again.

20

I See You Got My Message, He Said

I WAS standing in front of the full-length mirror dressed as a hooker when I heard the key in my front door. I teetered over to the top of the stairs, heard the refrigerator open, a soda can pop, the latch on the door lock, and there he was. He stopped as soon as he turned the bend of the staircase, as soon as he could see me standing taller than usual in my ankle-strap platform shoes with matching sheer red stockings, a kelly green miniskirt that covered some of my ass and wasn't exactly leather, as I'd thought at first glance, but some sort of leatherette, and my wowsa halter top, designed to make the most of cleavage. Rosalinda must have been on hormones. No way you could wear this top with a faux bosom. The boa was casually draped around my shoulders, devil-may-care style, hanging down to my knees. But it was probably the makeup that surprised Chip most, the false eyelashes, the green eye shadow, the glitter along my cheekbones, lipstick to match my shoes.

"Hi," I said, the mistress of understatement.

"I see you got my message," he said.

"What message?"

Dashiell went down the stairs, nearly knocking Chip over to get to Betty. Better late than never. Chip stayed where he was, shaking his head from side to side. "You look—"

"The outfit belonged to Rosalinda."

He screwed up his face.

"Angel Rodriguez."

"Ah. Then they're right," he said. "Clothes make the man."

I nodded. "The shoes are new." I held up one foot, holding on to the wall as I did. "Shoplifted from Jeffrey."

"You didn't."

"Right. They did. But knowing that, I'm sure I'm guilty of something."

He came up to the second floor, took my hand, and twirled me around.

"I have good news." I patted my hair, which I'd piled high on top of my head, the way LaDonna wore hers, wispy tendrils falling down along my forehead and cheeks as graceful as shoots of wisteria, a rhinestone comb on each side. "I got a job at Saks, part-time, through Christmas."

"Hence the outfit."

"I'm not supposed to say that."

"What?"

"Hence."

He looked puzzled.

"Mulrooney's wife works there. At Saks."

Nothing. He was simply staring.

"Tomorrow I get a couple of hours of training and my own locker. So I'll be really busy while you're in California. When do you leave?"

"You know something—" he said.

"What?"

"I could learn to like this."

"What?"

"You dressing up for me."

He swept me up in his arms and carried me to the bedroom.

"You forgot to ask how much," I said as he was unzipping my green plastic skirt.

"Be quiet, Rachel. This isn't the best time for conversation."

21

Dashiell Was on the Daybed, Snoring

WHEN Chip fell asleep, I slipped out of bed, put on his sweater, and went into my office. Dashiell came with me, sailing over Betty, who was asleep on the saddle of the bedroom door.

Sitting at my desk, I opened the top drawer and pulled out the pages I'd faxed home, starting with what was on top, the ones from Vinnie Esposito's file. He lived in the Bronx, he was married, and he had one child. He'd worked for Keller's for four and a half years, and according to notes in the file, there had been three discussions about his desire to manage either this or the plant at Hunts Point. I couldn't be sure, because the notes were semi-cryptic, but it seemed that Vinnie had every reason to expect that when the previous manager, Charles Willensky, retired, he would be the new manager. Instead, Kevin Mulrooney was brought in from Hunts Point, but not from their own plant.

So now I had someone who resented Kevin Mulrooney, who knew Mulrooney was doing something that could get him killed, and who, from watching television, knew exactly how to do the crime. In fact, I was sure that if someone would have had a problem getting the deadweight of Kevin Mulrooney up onto one of the hooks the carcasses hung from, that person wasn't Vincent Esposito.

On top of everything else, he had lied to his hooker. Gee, on that alone he could get convicted.

Still, the cops hadn't arrested him. For all intents and purposes, he'd never been a suspect.

I'd faxed home the old manager's file, too, which I'd found in another drawer, not taking the time to read anything there but figuring it was better to have too much than too little. I wouldn't have minded poking around in Keller's in the middle of the night again. I found that sort of thing strangely exhilarating. And I got a real kick out of Clint and surely wouldn't have minded teaching him new chores, or doing a second run on the back-chaining I'd already taught him. But letting go of the roof and swinging into that small bathroom window, that I didn't want to do again, not in a million years.

I began to read Willensky's file, thinking it would be long and ordinary—address, phone number, number of dependents, when hired. But one of the first things I spotted changed my mind. Charles Willensky was forty-one years old. I'd heard of cops having their twenty years in by age forty-one, then getting another city job and double-dipping. But butchers? I didn't think so.

The file indicated that there was a Mrs. Willensky, too, a Myrna G. Willensky. And then I found something even more surprising. Just a week before retiring, Charles and his bride had moved from Queens to Greenwich Village. What was *that* all about?

So now I had four weird things to deal with. That Mulrooney came in from the outside wasn't unheard of, but it was a bit odd, considering that Vinnie had been all but promised the job. I had Willensky's sudden, early retirement and his move to a more expensive neighborhood. I had Vinnie's getting passed over for the job he was expecting.

More than ever now, I wanted to talk to Frances Mulrooney and see what she knew about her husband's career move. They must have talked about it. The only question was, would she talk to me about it?

And I thought it might also be a good idea to arrange to accidentally run into Mrs. Willensky, perhaps shopping for a standing rib roast at Ottomanelli's or buying a box of butter cookies at Balducci's.

Dashiell was on the daybed, snoring. That seemed like a good idea. But instead I wrote down names and motives, reminding myself that I was nowhere. There was surely something as smelly as a decaying rodent going on at Keller's. And knowing that, I might have been inching closer to who killed Kevin Mulrooney, and why. But I'd been hired to find out who had killed Angel Rodriguez. As far as that went, I still knew nothing at all. Except that the tranny hookers were not the only players here who weren't what they seemed to be.

I turned on the computer and went on-line, searching for information about the meat market, finding much more about Hunts Point than the Gansevoort market. Then I did another search, this time on the carting industry, getting the story behind Giuliani's self-serving statement that he'd put a stop to the mob's monopoly, finding out exactly what the law was, what it was the old-timers like CityWide were now up against, at least on paper.

When I finished reading, I picked up the faxed pages, tapped them together, and slid them back into the drawer. You never know who's going to drop by, and for now, I wanted this to be my business. But when I got up, I saw I had missed one. This one had gotten kicked under the desk. I bent and picked it up, straightening it out. Dashiell had stepped on it on his way to the bed. There were holes where his nails had punctured it, but it was only the activity report from my own fax machine, nothing important. I balled it up and lifted my arm, ready to pitch it into the wastebasket, when something occurred to me, stopping me in mid-toss.

Keller's fax machine did the same thing.

I opened the page and smoothed it flat on top of the desk.

On top, there was the date it had been received, the time it had come in, and my phone number—the phone number, that is, that connected the rest of the world to my fax machine. Below, it said, Activity Report. Then, Transmission OK. And under that, there was a list of facts and figures, the second one being the number of the connecting telephone, Keller's fax number. If anyone checked these reports at Keller's, they'd have my home phone number. From there, finding my name and address was a piece of cake.

But why would they look at it? I hardly ever checked mine. Except that I just had. For a moment I stayed there, frozen, my hand on the piece of paper, my forehead as wrinkled as Dashiell's when he knows there's something he needs to do but isn't sure quite what it is.

22

She Call Herself Peaches

G RACE was standing on the corner where I was supposed to meet my clients, smoking a cigarette. Ebony
was there, too, calmer than I'd ever seen her.

"Hey."

Grace looked me up and down, a sly grin spreading her
lips wide. "I see you gave up dog grooming. Or you moon-
lighting?"

"Got bitten once too many times. Man, *you* try taking
knots out of a nasty Old English sheepdog, doing the nails of
a Rottweiler who never had them cut at home, blow-drying a
komondor, see how you feel about being a dog groomer.
'Sides, all that hot water was making my hands look like shit."

"You think you been in hot water, sweetheart? You ain't
seen nothing."

She was tall and dark, her skin the color of bittersweet
chocolate with a slightly blue-gray cast to it, her outfit more
like something you'd wear to a rock concert than something
you'd wear on the stroll, a long silky skirt, flowers on it, shiny
black work boots with thick lug soles, a short leather jacket

on top. Her hair was wild and loose, jet black curls going every which way. Her lipstick was nearly black, to match her nails.

"So what you goin' do," she said, one long finger aiming at Dashiell, "two-fers?" She laughed so hard, she began to choke. Meanwhile Ebony was about as lively as the Lincoln Memorial, only by some miracle she was standing.

"Whatever," I told her.

"Whatever is right," Grace said.

"What's the big deal? I shake my tail, make a fortune, all cash."

"Who tol' you that?" Despite her catatonic stupor, Ebony had been listening. When she smiled at me, I saw she had no teeth. Her dyed hair had broken off in places. Her skin was blotchy, dark in some places, nearly white in others.

"You should be on Lexington Avenue, at Hunts Point up in the Bronx, maybe waiting by the phone somewhere, you know, one of them high-class pieces of ass, does blow jobs in hotels 'stead of out here in the cold, a business girl, not a common ho." Grace looked me up and down a second time. "Any fool can see you don't belong here. You the wrong hue, for one thing. The wrong gender, for another. You the wrong everything, wo-man." She sent air audibly through her nose to let me know that, words aside, in her opinion I was beneath contempt.

"It's temporary. I just need enough cash to get me down to Florida."

"You hard of hearing? She telling you—" Ebony, back from the dead again.

"What you telling her?" LaDonna, pushing me out of harm's way, my guardian angel in white leather. Some of the hookers looked really bad, especially the ones that worked on Sunday, in daylight. Dogs, every last one of them, out there for the desperate, out there as the last-chance saloon, no more gas for the next fifty miles, bridge out. They wore sneakers, for God's sake, and crappy clothes. They had bad hair, a five o'clock shadow on their sweaty upper lips, and maybe it was just the daylight, but you could see the fear shining in their eyes from two blocks away. Not LaDonna, come to save me from Grace and skinny little Ebony, neither of whom wanted more competition than they were used to, LaDonna looming over Ebony now, an Airedale menacing a Chihuahua.

"What's the problem?" I asked them both. "We're down one since Halloween. It won't kill you if there's one more *business girl* on—"

Grace pitched her cigarette into the street and glared. "What are you talking about?"

"Rosalinda is what."

I felt barbed wire tighten on my arm, like some of the tattoos I'd seen on some of the dames along Washington Street.

"She only here for a week, two at mos'. Keep your gaffs on," then louder, "all of you." Then to me: "You know how it is. Someone disappear, that's okay. Someone arrive, it gets the girls in a snit, they's not going to get enough business no more, they's not going to be able to turn the men on, they's too damn ugly."

LaDonna, nearly a foot taller than the rest of us, tossed her head, jiggled a shoulder, touched her hair. She wasn't worried. She was a beauty, and she knew it. Case closed.

"Oh, *I* get enough business no matter how many of you are around." Grace pulled out another cigarette, but just held it. "What you know about her," she asked, "about Rosalinda?"

"Rosalinda?"

"Yeah. Her."

"Not much," I said. "Don't know anything about the john got himself killed right before I left San Francisco either."

"A john?"

"Must have been rude to one of the working girls, right?" Ebony asked. "Maybe her pimp—"

I shook my head.

"There was no pimp. Devon, he'll be the first pimp I ever give a dime to. I don't like to share, but LaDonna tells me, it's just for a week, you know, and since I'm new here, I could use the protection."

"Yeah," Ebony said. "Mouth like yours, you sure could."

"What I wonder is, what's he going to protect me from, making a living?"

"He watch out for your health, girl."

"My health? Like he did for Rosalinda?"

"You knew her?" Ebony asked.

I didn't say.

"That hers?" Grace said, pointing to my skirt. A skirt like that, you didn't see it every day of the week. It didn't surprise me that she recognized it. Again, I didn't say. I just tossed the boa across my neck so that both ends hung down in the back. It was chilly being out wearing so little. But if I thought a bunch of tired feathers would keep me warm, I could think again. How did they do this in January and February?

"'Stead of cross-examining her, you ought to be giving advice. She a sister."

Grace laughed. "She's no sister of mine. But I do have some advice for her." With that, she turned to face me. "Stay the hell off my corner."

"Or what?" LaDonna asked, and I watched the two of them staring at each other, wondering which one would break eye contact first, like watching a pair of adolescent dogs, each of whom would rather be doing something else but neither one wanting to lose face.

"I know the rules," I said. "We had rules there, too." Giving them an out. "Don't give your real name. Don't carry ID. Don't make a statement. Don't agree to take a polygraph. Don't cooperate with the authorities under any circumstances. And don't take shit from any johns."

"You mean they slap you or something, they dis you?" Ebony asked.

"I mean I don't plan to end up like Rosalinda."

"Who said that was a john?" she said. "You know something?"

"Who do you think it was?" I asked her. "Her pimp? How's she going to make money for him now?"

No one had an answer. Not even LaDonna.

"John's what makes sense," Grace said.

"You think?" Ebony said. "Then we all in grave danger."

"Who do you think did her?"

"I'm no cop. I don't know. I mean, some of them get mean after, they won't pay you, they call you names, throw you out of the car, or they try to hurt you before they go back to their regular lives, be upstanding citizens, model husbands, take they's kids to Disneyland. But I never knew anyone who got killed before." Ebony was shaking. "And worse thing is, I ain't got no other way to pay my rent, get what I need, you know what I mean?"

I nodded. I did know what she meant. Even cleaned up, with her strange appearance, finding employment would take a miracle. "You didn't hear anything, any rumors, anyone talk about a john who was *really* mean, someone who liked to do more than smack or punch?"

Ebony shook her head. LaDonna gripped me again. Instead of a tattoo circling my upper arm, there was going to be one mean bruise.

"It's time to go to work," she said. She turned to go, taking me with her, Dash coming, too, all of us connected. But Ebony wasn't finished. She came trotting along behind us as we headed west.

"I did one time hear about this ho got killed, but I never met her."

I wanted to stop, but LaDonna kept moving. "Don't listen to her. She crazy," she told me, loud enough for Ebony to hear it, too.

"After she died," Ebony said, rushing to keep up, "her family laid her out like a man, dressed in a suit, tie, the works, even where it wouldn't show, for God's sake, black socks, lace-up shoes. She would of died all over again in embarrassment, she knew. So when the viewing was over, three of her friends, they tell the grieving family, You go, we'll stay to make sure no one steals his silk tie, his cuff links, his ring before the coffin is closed. It's traditional, they tell the mother, for some loved ones to stay for this purpose. 'Oh,' she says, the mother. 'Then I'll stay. After all, he's my son.' But they tell her, 'No, no, it always the friends what do this job. It's way too stressful for a mother to do it.' And when the family finally agrees, and they all gone, the friends do her the way she'd want to go—Dolly Parton wig, makeup, rhinestone earrings, a little halter top, paste-on titties, short skirt, fishnet panty hose, wedgies. No matter to them no one's going to see those shoes. She had this thing for wedgies, they said. She never wore no other kind of shoe. They sent her off right. That's what friends are for."

I hadn't seen Grace since we headed west. I thought she might be waiting for Devon, having a last smoke before she went to work. But now there she was, right in my face.

"How they going to bury *you*?" she asked.

This time I pulled my arm free. "They're not," I told her. "I don't plan to end up dead. I plan to end up in Palm Beach, where if you leave your butt hanging out in the weather, you don't get frostbite, you get a tan."

"Palm Beach—la-di-dah. Keep dreaming, girl," she said.

"How'd she die?" I asked Ebony. "Was it a work-related accident?"

LaDonna mouthed, You aksing too many questions.

Ebony shook her head. "They didn't say. They only said how they fix her up, make her look good one last time."

"What did I tell you?" LaDonna asked. "Come on now."

We weren't on Washington Street for two minutes when the car pulled up, a pillow man driving, big soft chunks of flesh going every which way, sticking out of his short-sleeved shirt, pushing out over his belt, made you feel like taking a nap, if not for the odor that hit us the moment he rolled down the window, as if he kept dead cats in his car.

"How much?" he asked. You had to give it to him, he wasn't a looker, but he sure had the gift of gab.

"We worth twice what everyone else aksing," LaDonna said, backing up so that he could see more of her, dancing around a little, shaking whatever would move.

"You mean I get both of you?"

"You got it, sweet lips. Ain't no other way. We Siamese twins. So it's two for the price of one." Then she looked thoughtful and went right up to the car window, leaning her arms right into the stink. "Well, it's not exactly two for the price of one. It's two for the price of one and a half, still the best deal you gonna get, isn't it?"

"But what about him?" Pointing at Dashiell, who was as far away as the leash allowed, facing the other way. He didn't like the smell either.

"We take care of her. You don't gots to pay one dime extra for her."

"Her? With those testicles?"

"She saving up for her change. Matter of fact, you want to pay a little something toward that, she wouldn't turn it down."

"What's her name?" Stalling. Thinking about whether or not he wanted a pit bull in his car. The pit bull may have had similar thoughts. I know the pit bull's owner did.

"She call herself Peaches," LaDonna said. "Now, don't you say nothing, you hear? She sensitive. You'll hurt her feelings, you make fun of her."

"Okay, okay, but sixty's as high as I can go."

LaDonna opened the car door, bent as if to get in, but turned to me instead. "Don't let him touch you. He'll beat the shit out of you if he find the wrong kind of genitalia between your—" She stopped, touched her hair, inhaled through her nose. "Never mind." She slid into the front seat and reached behind her to unlock the back door for me and Dashiell, but before she got the chance to do it, the car made a loud noise and sped away, leaving me standing there alone with my dog, the mural of leering pigs behind us. Truth is, I hadn't planned on getting into that car anyway. But instead of feeling only relief as I watched it turn left on Horatio Street and disappear,

I was scared, scared for LaDonna and for the rest of the girls, taking the kind of chances they did ten, twelve times a night.

Could the pillow man be the killer? Sure, he might have accidentally gotten an appendage of the wrong gender in his big, fat hand, but how did that explain Mulrooney's death? And that's what I was thinking when the next car pulled up and stopped, that somehow these deaths had to be connected, wishing like hell I could see how.

"How much?" he said. Another sweet talker.

"Two hundred," I told him. "White meat costs more."

"Two hundred? Are you nuts?"

I noticed he'd stopped to talk to Grace first, that she'd leaned into the car, the way LaDonna always did, her derriere sticking out behind, waving around in the wind. Guess he didn't like her price either.

But he was still here. He hadn't driven away. And he didn't smell bad, at least not so bad it hit me where I was standing, outside the car. I couldn't keep sending johns away all night, not if I wanted credibility with the competition, not if I wanted to live until the end of the week.

"Oh, what the hell," I said, all smiles now. "I was thinking tonight would be perfect for a fire sale. How's fifty bucks, sweet lips, just for you?"

He leaned across the passenger seat and opened the door for me. Dashiell hopped in first and went straight to the back.

"He okay?"

"He's perfect," I said, sliding into the front seat and pulling the door closed behind me.

"He don't bite?"

I ignored his question. There, shivering on the corner outside the closed dry cleaner on Gansevoort Street, was Ebony, watching the car go by. The timing couldn't have been better. I leaned my head against the cold glass of the window and sighed.

"Do with me what you will," I told him. The car lurched forward as he pressed down hard on the gas.

23

He Was Nearly Bald

TOLD my john to turn right on Bethune Street. I'd seen a lot of condoms there, in the tree pits and dotting the sidewalk, especially after the weekends, people practicing safe sex alfresco. I figured this would be as good a place as any. He pulled over to the curb and reached for his zipper.

"Uh-uh. Cash in advance," I told him, and when he grunted and reached for his wallet, I opened the door and stepped out, Dashiell right behind me. If I hurried, I could get a decent night's sleep before I was due at Saks.

Dressed in a way that my own mother might not have recognized me—hell, she never would have expected me of all people to be looking like a lady—I sat on the steps of St. Patrick's Cathedral waiting for Frances Mulrooney to meet me for lunch. I saw her coming out of the side door and heading for the corner. No jaywalking for this lady. She seemed to do everything by the book, and I would need to use that to get her to open up about her husband and what he may have done that hastened his trip along the River Styx.

I stood, happy to remove my butt from the cold stone and

from everyone else sitting there, all tourists with cameras, resting up after taking shots of each other in front of the cathedral. Frances and I headed over to Madison Avenue, to a little coffee shop called Nick's.

"It's terrible," she said. "But the portions are huge." She laughed, a nice laugh. I didn't think I'd seen her do that before. "And most important for you, it's dirt cheap."

"Anything safe?"

"The water. At least it's predictable. It comes from a reservoir upstate, and there's bound to be a little fleck or two of something or other floating in the glass, but nothing that'll kill you. You've only got a part-time job, and temporary at that. We don't want to spend your entire paycheck on lunch, just to get some clean water and a bit of tasty food, do we?"

I shook my head, though I was sure it was a rhetorical question.

"You still need an outfit for that date, don't you?"

"I backed out." I had, in a way, dumping that john across the street from Westbeth last night, the money already in his hand when I'd slammed the car door. Hey, who could blame me, the rude fuck talking about money right from the get-go, not even giving me the chance to ask if he wanted a date, after all my practice with LaDonna.

"You don't feel ready yet, do you?"

I shook my head, glancing at the menu, trying to figure out what would do the least harm.

"I understand. Sometimes I think I'd just like to have someone to go out to dinner with, not that I did that a lot when Patrick was alive. He worked such terrible long hours. Sometimes he didn't come home from one day to the next. Double shifts," she whispered, leaning across the table. "And then when he did get home, it was a quick meal and off to bed."

Double shifts? In the meat market?

A waitress came with a pot of coffee. Frances said yes. I said no. She ordered a salad with fruit and cottage cheese. I ordered bacon and eggs. In a joint like this, they were sure to come with orange-hued home fries. What with the potatoes, the onions, and the grease, I'd have all the major food groups of the day.

"It's so cheerful, getting out in the evening once in a while. The nights are so long now. Sometimes I go to an early movie with a neighbor friend. She's also alone. Two years now. Heart attack. He was only forty-four." She shook her head. "There's a Chinese place we go to. They give you so much, you have enough left over for dinner the next night. Usually, I eat sitting in front of the TV set so I can hear another human voice."

"Me, too." Actually, that sounded pretty good compared to the way I usually ate, grabbing something on the fly or eating at my desk.

She picked up her cup and sipped some coffee, making a face. "Places like this, at least the coffee's usually good. But here, they don't have the knack for that either. It tastes as if they never clean the pot. Sometimes I eat in the employee's cafeteria. The food's not bad, and it's very inexpensive, but there are no windows and it makes me blue not to get out and see the sky a little. The atmosphere in the store is very confined, but they have a very good benefits package. Of course, I don't really need it. I'm still covered, because of Patrick's job." She shrugged. Yet another person not living out her dream.

"Were you married long?" I asked.

"Twenty-three years," she said.

"Then you married very young?"

"Right off the boat."

"Really?"

"Met him at a party the first week I was here. And that was that. Oh, what a handsome man he was, so elegant." She went off into her memories for a moment, but then the food arrived. Frances looked at the cottage cheese and sighed, then pulled a tiny paper napkin from the dispenser on the table, smoothed it open, and laid it across her lap. I wondered what she thought it would protect her from.

"And you? Where did you meet . . . ?"

"Ted," I said. I reached for my wallet and pulled out his picture, the only one I had of him without my sister hanging on his arm, gazing lovingly at his face, without their surly kids looking annoyed at whoever held the camera. I handed it across the table. Why had I chosen Ted to be my dead spouse? Wasn't there a chance of sending him bad karma, doing that? Was I really as hard-hearted as Lili claimed?

"Oh. He looks much older than you." Handing it back. "Patrick and I were the same age. Both of us kids when we fell in love."

"How did you manage?" I asked, figuring it might lead to what he did for a living, the place I needed desperately to go.

She was fishing for her wallet as she spoke. "He drove a truck for the first two years, but then when the baby came, we needed more security, so that's when he applied for the academy. I was against it myself. If you think about security, well, it's one of the last things you'd want your husband—"

I'd already stopped eating. If Dashiell were here, he'd be up on his feet. "The academy?"

"The police academy." She pulled the picture out of her wallet and extended it across the table, careful to keep her sleeve out of the cottage cheese. "He said it was steady work, good benefits, and"—she dabbed at the corners of her mouth, then smiled—"appropriate work for an Irishman. He had a wonderful way about him, a wonderful, self-deprecating sense of humor."

"And so that's what he did, he was a cop?" Holding the picture. Not looking at it.

Now she put her fork down. "Yes." Indignant. "A fine one, too. He had his gold shield in only five years."

"Oh, I didn't mean any disrespect. It's a noble calling." Almost a lilt in my voice, I was sounding that Irish.

"'Tis." She speared a piece of canned peach, holding it aloft.

"Was he killed on the job, Frances?" Trying like hell to soften my attitude, to hide what I was feeling, everything spinning so fast I couldn't grab hold of any one fact. Mulrooney was a cop? Then he must have been working undercover at Keller's. That changed everything. But how? And how did it connect to Rosalinda's murder?

She ate the peach before responding, putting the fork down, picking it up again. "He was," she said. Then she did a funny thing. She began to poke at her salad, talking at the same time but no longer looking at me. I knew a story would be coming my way before she even began. "It was a drug bust," she said, "in the Bronx. A big shoot-out. Patrick was first in, and"—she shook her head—"he caught the first shots before the backup could . . ."

"How tragic," I said, thinking this lady needed to polish up her weaving if she was going to lie to someone as experienced in the art as myself. But why? Sure, she couldn't talk about his work while he was alive, but what difference could it make now?

I looked at the picture in my hand, expecting to see a full-faced Irishman, red hair cut short like the dos the other butchers wore, a dour face. Cops—they see it all, everything the rest of us want to pretend doesn't exist, and what they see, it's written all over them. But his face was lean, almost gaunt, not round at all. He had a clownish nose, round and red, and a broom of a mustache. He was nearly bald. And he was smiling. But if his mouth was carefree, his eyes weren't. They were the eyes of a heartbroken man. I looked back at Frances, wondering if it was business or personal, whatever it was that had put that look in Mulrooney's eyes.

"He took out two of them, the two with the guns, protecting the rest of his men. He was quite the hero." Frances sat straighter now. "So young, too. Only forty-one."

I thought the *Times* had said thirty-something. Thirty-eight is what I remembered. I'd have to go back and look at the articles again.

On the other hand, they often made mistakes like that, making people older or younger, spelling names wrong, or simply reporting the wrong name. You could read the corrections every day in the paper, if you really cared, too little and too late. Whatever the impact of the original article, that's what was remembered, not the Oops, we're sorry, we goofed again.

Forty-one. A cop. Was he there because of the carting industry? I wondered if the old manager would have anything to tell me. Or if the new one, McCoy, was also a cop, continuing whatever it was Patrick had been working on. Was that why they'd passed over Vinnie?

"We're running out of time," she said, looking at the tiny watch on her wrist, a gift from Patrick perhaps, years ago when they were young. "Do they want you back this afternoon as well?"

"Yes. I have to learn how to use the cash register, and there are two lectures about how we're supposed to behave toward customers."

"Ah, yes, I remember those. And when do you start on the floor?"

"Tuesday. Two to six. And Thursday, but not this one, because of Thanksgiving."

Frances looked sad.

"Holidays alone," I said. "That's one of the worst parts. I'm dreading . . ."

Manipulative, my sister had also said, the last time we spoke. Then she'd added, At least you have an appropriate outlet for it now, referring to my work, work she deemed highly inappropriate for a member of her family.

"Perhaps you could come? It'll only be me and Sarah, the neighbor I mentioned. I'm making a turkey anyway. There'll be plenty to eat. If you're concerned about traveling, don't be. Sarah and I decided to do it like Sunday dinner, so you'll be able to get home before dark. It's only Rego Park. It's not far at all. Where do you live, Rachel?"

"The Village," I told her. I watched her eyes flicker as she took that in, that I lived in the neighborhood where her husband had been killed.

"Well, then," she said, pulling out a clean handkerchief and blowing her nose.

I thought of the pillow man again and what I'd be doing after dark until I found out what happened to Rosalinda, and probably, even if it had no bearing on my own case, what had happened to Frances's husband as well, wondering now if the two deaths were connected after all. If Mulrooney was a cop, working undercover, maybe his death was exactly what it appeared to be, phony alibis aside. And maybe, in the frenzy of the Halloween parade, Rosalinda had flirted with the wrong man, nothing more.

"Sure. I'd love that," I told her. And on the way back to Saks, I even asked her what I could bring. My mother would have been proud. But only for a moment. Because as soon as we'd decided that I would bring a nice bottle of wine, I began to wonder what I'd wear a few hours later when I joined my clients for the stroll. I didn't think I could wear that same green skirt, the same boa, the same platform shoes every night until the case was over. I wondered if there was anything I could pick up at Saks, now that I had an employee discount, to freshen up my outfit, and while I was still thinking about that, we were back at the side door. Frances Ann leaned toward me and gave me a kiss on my cheek before opening the door and becoming all business.

24

Hop In, He Told Me

WEARING a black miniskirt with the waist rolled up so that it was obscenely short, a black workout bra, my signature red platform high heels, a little purse—the outfit I had on, there was no place to carry a tissue—and Rosalinda's lucky boa, I showed up only an hour later than the night before, a sure sign I was not anxious to get to the stroll. I found LaDonna where I'd last seen her the night before and told her I'd made a decision.

"Wha's that?"

"I'm working alone tonight," I told her.

"You doing *what?*" A hand on a hip, a cold stare.

"You heard me."

"You lost your mind, woman? First, you go, No, no, no, not me, I'm not going out with you bitches sucking on no guy's cock to solve this case for you, even though you laid a huge bunch of money on me, even though it's my job to get the answer you need no matter what I have to do to get it." All done falsetto, of course. "And now you don't want my protection? You want to do the johns yourself? What you on, girlfriend?"

"That's not it. I tried it last night, and—"

"So I heard. And speaking of which, you with me, I pays Devon. You on your own, you on your own." She held out her hand. I dropped a twenty into it. She glanced down and snorted. "You want me to give *this* to Devon, tell him it's your night's earnings?"

"That's his percent."

"His what?"

"His percent, you know, ten percent, like any other kind of agent."

"He ain't your agent, honey. He your lifeline. He don't like your line, you don't have a life. Simple as that. What was your take last night, Miss Thing?"

"That."

"This?" She held it up by one corner, the way I'd hold it if the pillow man had touched it.

"I'm new at this. What'd you expect?"

"You don't want me telling him *that* either, not after the story we laid out for him. How old are you, anyway?" Sticking her face in mine, so close I could feel her breath on my skin.

"Thirty-eight. Almost thirty-nine."

"A late bloomer?"

"I beg your pardon?"

"That's what I should tell Devon, that you're a late bloomer? You almost thirty-nine, one foot in the fucking grave, and you still a beginner?"

I shrugged.

LaDonna sighed. "I been out here since I'm sixteen."

"Sixteen?"

"You got hearing problems, you so old? Sixteen. Full-time. Had to, after I left home."

I nodded, as if I understood. But of course, I didn't.

"Why I use a pimp," she said. "You don't want to be on your own at sixteen, God knows what's going to happen to you without no one to watch your back."

"You've been with Devon since you were—"

"Hell, no. My first pimp, he got hisself killed. Big mouth," she said, as if that explained everything. "The second one, he disappear. One night he here, the next night, he gone. Permanent. Never heard another word about him."

"He never showed up again?"

"That was my meaning. Devon, he the third. Been with him two years."

"You give him everything? Every dime?"

"If I wants to live, I do."

She still had the money in her hand. "Well, that's it. That's everything. He was real lonely, the guy who picked me up, and we started to talk."

"You did *what?*" Her face screwed up, about the same way mine must have looked when I learned how the girls tuck and tape their equipment, then hide the works under a satin gaff.

"He started to talk. Well, he didn't just start. Truth is, I started first. And before you know it, two hours had gone by, we're parked on Bethune Street, gabbing away. So then I said, Look, I gotta go, I'm going to be in real trouble spending so much time with you. And that's when he handed me the twenty. I said, Time is time. Don't matter what we did or didn't do, you owe me fifty."

"And what'd he say?"

"He said, 'Fifty? For just talking? Fuck that noise.' So that's all I got. He'd been so nice up until then, so candid and forthcoming. He's got two kids in college. A boy and a girl. He plays the violin, his son. And the daughter—"

LaDonna put a finger to her lips, then shoved the twenty into her bra. "Some nights are like that. You can't make money nohow. Devon understand, long as you don't make a habit out of it. So, you wants to go alone again?"

"I do," I told her, "because last night, with this lonely guy, I thought maybe if I get these johns talking, I can learn something. No one's going to talk with you doing them, that's for sure." And that's when a car pulled up, a tan SUV, a really tall guy behind the wheel, white, uptight, wearing a tie, for good-ness' sake. What was *he* doing here?

I leaned my elbows on the frame of the open window, my butt sticking out behind me, my flesh covered in goose pimples, even those few places where it was covered by skimpy clothes, my raisin-colored lips trembling. (Revlon, six-forty-two after my discount.) I didn't know how much was from the cold and how much was from naked fear. What was *I* doing here?

"How about a real treat?" I asked him. "Like nothing you ever experienced."

"How much?" he asked, his voice breaking.

"Not nearly as much as you'd think," I said. Then Dashiell put his paws up next to mine, his butt sticking out behind him, his tail wagging.

"Whoa. What the hell is that? He with you?"

"He just sits in the back. He's a pussycat."

"Oh, I don't know about that. I never heard about anything like this." He reached toward the button that would close the window.

"You owe it to yourself," I told him. "Tell you what, you don't like the way I treat you, you don't have to pay me a dime."

"You're kidding. Nothing?"

"Uh-uh."

"Hop in," he told me.

I let Dashiell in first. My john blinked, but before he could react further, Dashiell had hopped into the backseat, and I was sliding onto the front one. "Home, James," I told him.

He sputtered.

"Just a little joke," I said. "How about swinging around onto Horatio Street, parking under a tree?"

He pulled away. I wiggled my fingers at LaDonna. I waited until the car was parked on Horatio Street, the engine off, before commencing with my plan. In fact, I gave him enough time to pull his zipper halfway down.

"Undercover cop," I said.

His hand stopped moving. "Jesus."

"Either you leave the area the minute I get out of this vehicle and never show your skinny white ass in this neighborhood again—not even to get a beer at the White Horse Tavern or check out the beautiful new park along the river, got that?—or else your name and your likeness go up on the Internet. Have you seen the Arrested Johns site yet?"

He shook his head. "What do you mean, my likeness?"

"Now's as good a time as any, in case you're in a big rush next time I see you here." I opened the little purse and took out my Minox, preserving the startled look on his pale face once, then once again, trying for a mug shot duo but getting two identical pictures because he seemed frozen, his mouth hanging open, his breathing raspy and loud, as if he were about to have a heart attack. "Second one's for good luck," I told him, "mine, not yours."

"Hey," he said. "This isn't fair. You said—"

I shrugged. "Better safe than sorry. And I'd be one sorry-assed cop if next time I see you, you see me and drive away before I can capture your likeness. Am I correct?"

"I've never . . . this is the first time, and nothing . . ."

"Save it for the judge, buddy. We're offering a week of grace. But the bad news is, the clock's been ticking, and it's half over. I find you here again after Tuesday, your name goes up. This goes up." I lifted the camera. "The mayor's thinking of releasing the list to the *Times*, too. Me, I think it's excessive. Hey, guys will be guys, you know? But I'm not the mayor, and he likes to see evidence of how he's making the city safer in the *Times*."

Which is where I got this idea. I'd picked up a copy someone left in the coffee room when I was on my afternoon break at Saks and read an article that said that women responded to stress by social contact rather than by fight or flight.

"You read the *Times*?" I asked my john. "Anyone you know read it, your boss perhaps? The wife?"

I didn't get an answer. No surprise. "Before I go, I was

wondering if you'd like to contribute to the Policeman's Benevolent Fund, me being a policeman, in a manner of speaking, and being benevolent enough to let you off with just a warning."

"How much?"

"Oh, sir, that's entirely up to you. Shall we say fifty?"

He began to lean across me, to open my door, but I pushed his arm away. Hell, I was a cop, I could open my own damn door. It was stuck, I could shoot it open.

I stared at him for a moment, then opened the door, whistled for Dashiell, and watched my very first trick drive away, figuring yesterday didn't really count because no money had changed hands. Now all I had to do was walk slowly back to the stroll and do it again. It wasn't that I thought I could clean up the meat district single-handed. It was that I needed the other hookers to think I was legit. I needed to seem to be working, and this was the least painful way to accomplish that. And this time I wouldn't have to pay Devon out of my own pocket.

It had to do with a hormonal difference between the sexes, the article had said. It said that women often attempted to "tend and befriend." Well, hadn't I just done that? I thought, heading back to work.

But what would that mean for my clients and their colleagues? They dressed like women. They referred to themselves as women. And some of them were saving up for the surgery that would make them appear more like women. But were they women? When push came to shove, would they fight like hell or try to charm their way out of trouble? That is, I thought, picturing what Rosalinda might have looked like in her bloodstained gown, the wand still in her hand, if they saw the trouble coming in the first place.

25

What About the Money? She Asked

ERHAPS the success of my own war on prostitution the night before had gone to my head. Or maybe it was the research I'd done on-line that left some nagging questions needing answers. It could even have been the second-hand smoke from Chi Chi's joint. Who knows? Nevertheless, there I was with her, presenting my startling request.

"Jus' a little something to tide me over," she said. She held it out to me. I shook my head.

A minute later, forgetting she'd already told me why she had ducked around the corner, under the sidewalk bridge, to grab a smoke, she said, "I got the fiercest headache. This make it go away." She peered toward the corner. "Devon see me, I'm as dead as the rest of the meat around here."

Clint finished sniffing and put his front paws up on my fishnet stockings. I scratched behind his ears, folded over like the flaps of envelopes.

"I came looking for you for a reason," I said, Chi Chi doing her best to look alert. "I've changed my mind."

"'Bout what? You not going to solve this case for us?"

Chi Chi stumbled. I grabbed for her arm, but she pulled it away.

"Doing Vinnie."

"Say what?"

"Are you supposed to see him this morning?"

She nodded.

"Well, I'd like to go instead. The door'll be open, right?"

Chi Chi nodded again.

"Chi Chi, I've got all these pieces of information, but I can't put them together in a way that makes sense. I'm trying." I shook my head. "I don't want anyone else to get hurt. I don't want you to get hurt. That's why I need to—"

"I din't say no, did I?"

"Thanks. Really."

"And like I said, you could keep half the money." She sniffed. "Right?"

"I don't want the money. You paid me enough."

"Okay. Whatever you say, Rachel. You want I should wait here?"

"Is it time?" I looked at my watch. Then up at the sky, which had just started to lighten.

"More than time. It late. See, I got delayed with a trick. He let me off," she waved her hand in the direction of downtown, "an' I had to walk back. Then I stopped to have me a little smoke, ease my pain. Jus' try the door. I'll wait here for you. You need Clint?"

Chi Chi had obviously had a bit more to shore her up than the one joint. I told her I didn't need Clint, I would go in the way she did, through the front door. She thought about that, then nodded and said she'd wait.

"You don't have to," I told her. "I doubt I'll have anything to tell you when I come out, but I have to try everything. You never know where the information that gives you the answer will come from, what'll set your mind straight."

"What about the money?" she asked.

"How much do you get?"

"Sixty," she said.

Yeah, yeah.

I pulled some cash out of my purse, a bigger one this time, more to carry, and gave her three twenties, easiest money she ever earned. She held it in her hand, saying nothing. Then she handed me a twenty back.

"Sometimes he only pays forty," she said, "and you a beginner."

I could see from the sidewalk that the padlock was off the door. I made my way across the cobblestones, careful not to get my heels caught in the spaces between the stones, looking the way Chi Chi had the night I spied on her from up on the bridge, that same funny walk. Dashiell was heeling. At the door, I bent and took off his leash, hanging it around my neck. Then I pulled open the door, let him in ahead of me, and signaled him to heel again. We picked our way through the hanging carcasses, not much here at this hour, before the morning deliveries. Coming to the end of a row of hooks, sides of pork hanging on the last three and blocking my vision, I found myself nose to nose with the head of a pig, his eyes staring dead ahead, as if he were looking right at me, his mouth open. There were six of them. Now, what was that all about? Halloween was long past. I hurried on, the sound of the compressor covering any sound I might make, pushing through the plastic strips, heavier than they looked, reminding Dashiell to stay at my side. Once we'd gotten to the top of the stairs, I pointed to the floor, then held my palm in front of his face to let him know he should stay put.

The light was on in the office. So was the heater. I could hear the fan, feel the heat coming out into the cold hallway, see the orange glow from where I stood.

"Where's Chi Chi?" he asked. He'd gotten up from where he'd been sitting, coming halfway around the desk, stopping, one hand on his hip, the other pointing at me.

"Busy," I told him. "Anyway, she thought you might like a change of pace."

He shook his head. "I didn't tell her that. I didn't tell her to send someone else."

"No. You didn't." I walked closer, sliding one cheek and thigh onto the edge of his desk. We were close enough to touch. "Something wrong?" I asked him. "Not enough money in petty cash to pay me?"

"What are you—"

"I have some questions, Vinnie. You answer them, I leave, no problem. It won't cost you a dime. In fact, if you cooperate, this little meeting never happened."

"Why should I talk to you? Who the fuck are you?"

I slipped my hand into my purse. Vinnie backed up so fast, he nearly fell into the chair he'd recently vacated. As I pulled my hand back out, Vinnie raised his in a defensive gesture, as if he could stop a bullet with it, as if that ever worked.

I held up my cell phone.

"What the—"

"I have your wife on speed dial," I said.

Vinnie froze, one hand still up in the air, the way the Supremes used to do it when they sang, "Stop in the Name of Love."

I was waiting to see if I needed to call in the big guns, but Vinnie's hands never moved.

"Why don't you roll your chair back a little," I suggested.

That seemed to wake him up, and he reached for the drawer on the top left side. I swung my leg around the front of the desk and kicked the door shut, catching two of his fingers when it closed. Then I whistled, and there was Dashiell in the doorway before Vinnie had the chance to pull his damaged hand out of harm's way.

"Watch him." I slapped the desk, and then Dashiell was on it, his back paws on the old blotter, his front ones at the edge, as if he were ready to spring again, his compressor going full blast.

I leaned forward and opened the drawer, flipping my hand at Vinnie, telling him he could have his wounded paw back, then pulling out the gun and, without looking at it, pointing it at him.

"Charlton Heston would be so proud of you," I told him. "On the other hand, didn't you ever read that when you keep a gun, there's a *huge* chance whoever breaks in will end up using it on you?"

He didn't answer me. He was cradling his hand and staring at Dashiell.

"Did you hear me?" I asked.

"It's since Mulrooney," he said. "I'm here alone, and I don't know who the hell—"

"You could always lock the front door," I said.

"But—"

"I know. You've got needs. And Rosalinda had to earn a living. And anway, don't they call it a victimless crime?" Nothing, not even a polite little nod. "Until, of course, Rosalinda became a victim. I'm wondering what might have caused that. I'm wondering how you could help me, Vinnie, given the fact that both she and Mulrooney died at virtually the same time and that it stretches credibility to think that since Mulrooney worked here, and Rosalinda worked here, we might say, and they both died on the night of Halloween, that those deaths were unrelated."

"I didn't . . . ," he said. Then he stopped. He closed his mouth so tight, his lips all but disappeared.

"You didn't?"

He shook his head.

"I never thought you did," I said, slipping my other leg up onto the desk, putting an arm over Dashiell's back. I heard the cup Vinnie kept his pens in hit the floor and break, the pens and pencils skittering across the dirty floor, but I didn't turn around to look. "Hey, the cops released those two guys from CityWide Carting. Paper said they were someplace else that night. Lucky guys, don't you think? Most times, cops want to know where you were and there's no one around to corroborate your story, you're home alone watching TV, boo-hoo, no alibi. Am I right?"

Vinnie took a breath, his first, as far as I could tell, since the Eisenhower years.

"Especially when you're talking four, five in the morning."

"Six."

"Six?"

"That's what we were told."

"Broken watch pinpoint the time?"

Vinnie shrugged. He wasn't the ME. How the fuck did he know the answer to a question like that?

"Of course, saying it was them, saying those alibis were bought and paid for, why would they have killed Rosalinda, too?"

This time Vinnie's mouth opened, then closed again.

"Any theories?"

"Maybe she saw something?"

I stared.

"Maybe she witnessed a crime while commiting a crime."

"Excellent point. But I figure it this way, Vinnie. If Capelli and Maraccio had done Rosalinda, wouldn't they simply have left her here? Why take the enormous chance of carting—get the little occupation-appropriate humor?" I waited. Vinnie nodded, taking a not-so-subtle peek at his watch. "Why take the chance of carrying a corpse all the way to the Gansevoort Pier? Or perhaps they walked her there, then did her? What's your opinion on it, huh?"

"Look, it's getting late for you to be here." He was sweating, the way the girls do, but as far as I could tell, he wasn't on anything, a decision he might have been ruing at the moment.

"Not to worry. I have plenty of time."

"No, you don't understand. Dressed like that"—he gestured from where he sat, looking small, almost as if he were a ten-year-old sitting in his dad's chair—"the men will be here in less than an hour. Some of them, they get in a little early, you know. I need you to leave. Now. Understand?" Loud. He got up. Dashiell revved up the sound effects. Vinnie sat again.

"I appreciate your concerns," I told him. "I really do. So,

tell me what your take is on this, and I'll be out of here. Not only that, you being such a good boy, I won't call the little woman, either."

"It was them," he said. "Capelli and Maraccio."

"This is your theory? This is your brilliant conclusion, that even though Keller's has used two other carting companies since the Trade Waste Commission was established, these two hoods killed Mulrooney over a few months of your puny business? All of a sudden, you think you're Lamb Unlimited, Western Beef, your business is worth killing for?"

"The what commission?"

"Don't take me for a fool, Mr. Esposito. I'm not a fool. And since you were aiming to manage this place, you couldn't be ignorant of the laws about the carting industry. You couldn't be that stupid."

He sat there, trying his best to make me a liar.

"Used to be, the carting industry was all the mob, am I right? Feel free to nod, just so I know you're awake." He did. "Nothing anyone could do. You put out for bids, you only get one bid. You want to stay in business, you pay them whatever they say it costs. But then Giuliani gets a bug up his ass. He wants to clean it all up. Make the carting industry honest. So now the commission gets to check all the licenses of the carters, and they set maximum rates. Since they started, the rates have gone down by twenty to as much as fifty percent. Can't blame Mulrooney for trying to save a little money for the Keller family, for doing his job, can you?"

"But the paper said—"

"Hey, grow up. The cops must have been after those two anyway. And they can tell the papers whatever the hell they please. What's the *Times* going to do now that they released a second cock-and-bull story, arrest the police?"

"Maybe it had to do with a different change."

"And that would be?"

He checked his watch again. "Maybe someone knew about the meat."

I leaned forward. "I'm listening."

Vinnie put his hands up to his head, as if it had suddenly started to ache, or perhaps was about to explode. "It's genetically altered. But we sell it without saying so."

"And you think someone killed the manager because of that?"

He nodded.

"And your hooker? Was she here that night, in her white gown? Was that a night she helped you wait for the wedding, Vinnie, so that you wouldn't be tempted to dis your virgin bride?"

"Oh, shit."

"Tainted meat without a label?"

"Not tainted, genetically altered. The law says, you know, you got to say, but the hotels and restaurants, they don't want it. They want milk-fed, corn-fed, not dicked-around-with provisions."

"Then why were you selling it?"

He rubbed the thumb of his right hand against the forefinger. "It's cheaper. The profit is higher. They tol' me I was passed over because the profit margin was too low, I wasted money, I had too many men on the floor, I never came up with any good ideas, that Mulrooney could do better. He had a history of making more money for management. But that's not what they told me earlier, when they said I had a good shot at promotion, I should be patient."

"So this was his decision, to buy the altered meat?"

"No, mine. I thought if I could show them I could put more money in their pockets, they'd change their minds. I'd get the job they promised me after all. That's all they care about, the almighty buck."

"You mean, you did it on your own? You wanted to prove to them that you would make a better manager?"

He smiled, the little snake, proud of himself.

"Then why did Mulrooney get it and not you? And why didn't whoever was so upset, upset enough to kill, just move their business elsewhere? Why execute the manager?"

"Maybe as a lesson to the other markets."

There was a noise downstairs.

"Shit," Vinnie said. "Shit, shit, shit."

"Your men?"

He nodded.

"And your boss?"

He nodded again.

"You've been very helpful," I said. "I wouldn't want to see you get into trouble."

"I can't explain this." He pointed at me, the boor.

"Pay me, and I'm out of here."

"Pay you for *what*?"

"I told Chi Chi she could have the money tonight. I was here longer than she usually is, so that'll be a hundred. Actually, make it one-fifty. I'll tell her you were feeling generous, what with me being new and all."

We could hear the men at the open door, waiting for whoever was parking his car, shouting across the courtyard. Vinnie reached for the middle desk drawer.

I shook my head. "Key to the cash box? I don't think so. It's on you this time, Vinnie. And by the way, if you try to take this out on Chi Chi in any way, I'll be back. And he'll be back," nodding in Dashiell's direction.

"What are you talking about?"

"Never mind that bullshit."

I stuck the gun in the waist of my skirt, took the money he was holding out to me, carefully counted it.

"You know what to do," I told him. "You've been through this before." I headed for the bathroom, hoping that none of the early arrivals had been drinking coffee while driving in. A moment later, I heard them, three men. They were at the closet, pulling out their white coats and rubber boots, and then I heard Vinnie call them into the office. Then their voices became muffled, and Dash and I made a quick exit, down the worn steps, through the refrigerator, then out into the courtyard, where I was just about to let my breath out, free at last, free at last, except that Timothy McCoy was there, stepping out of his car.

"Hey, you," he shouted, "get away from here." Looking first at Dashiell and then at me, he scowled, taking a step toward us, then stopping. "Weren't you told that fifty times already? Go on, go home. We're running a decent business here." He stood there waiting until I'd left the courtyard and headed back toward Washington Street, the sun up now, the hookers and johns nowhere in sight.

I turned west again, the cold wind blowing over the river, cutting right to the bone. We didn't have to wait for the light to turn green. There was no traffic. Once I was on the other side, I stood near the fence, took the gun from my waistband, and tossed it as far as I could into the dark water, hearing the plop as it hit, seeing the small splash as it was swallowed up.

Vinnie was a liar, true, but I was sure he'd told the truth about one thing. The gun I'd just pitched into the river was acquired after Mulrooney had been killed. No way whoever did the murder left the gun right there in the desk drawer. And if he had, no way would the Crime Scene Unit have missed it.

Had Chi Chi lied about getting paid from petty cash? Vinnie had really looked confused about that one. Chi Chi said he left the office to get her money but that she didn't know where he had gone. But he reached for the drawer when I asked to be paid. Of course. I'd seen a key there, not the small kind that would open a padlock on a cash box, a big one, the kind you used to lock an old door, the door to that locked back room perhaps. But if all that had nothing to do with the money, what did it have to do with?

On the way home, I decided to pick up a muffin and tea. I took out the twenty Chi Chi had given me back and found a shopping list on it: tape, six rolls; box cutters, three; black markers, two. Someone was moving. In this city, no one stayed put for very long. Nothing stayed the way it was. And nothing was what it appeared to be.

26

You Never Know Who Might Be Listening

I SLEPT most of the day, waking up twice to feed Dashiell and take him out, looking at a world I felt I no longer belonged to. When it got dark, the long shadows no longer in the garden, everything gray and cold, I took a bath and, in my terry robe, sat at the table with a bowl of cereal, trying again to figure out what had happened a few weeks earlier.

I couldn't be sure, but I didn't think the murders had to do with the carting industry. And it surely wasn't about the meat. That wouldn't be the cops. It would be the FDA. If anyone gave a shit what the American public ate in the first place.

And Vinnie. He was definitely a little worm, a petty thief, a liar, an unscrupulous businessman, but was he the killer? Had Mulrooney found out about the deal Vinnie had made to get the cheaper genetically altered meat? Was he about to spoil all Vinnie's plans? And was Rosalinda there, touching up her makeup in that filthy little bathroom?

A petty thief. A liar. What if Vinnie was pocketing the difference between the natural pork and the altered pork? What if Mulrooney found out?

But would he? Why was Mulrooney there in the first place? And why was all my thinking leading me in circles?

Later in the evening, back on the stroll, I found Chi Chi on the corner of Thirteenth and Washington and told her everything went well. I thought she ought to give it a break for a few days before going to see Vinnie, then it would be okay. "Well," I told her, "maybe give it a rest for a week. And if there's any trouble, any at all, here's what I want you to do. I want you to say, 'Vinnie, lay a hand on me, and I'll get my friend and her dog back here.' Okay?"

"Why? What happened?"

"I was late leaving."

"Shit."

"That's what *he* said."

"What happened?"

"The manager, McCoy, he saw me in the courtyard and told me to get the hell out of there. That's all."

Chi Chi looked away.

"He's seen you, too, huh?"

"Once or twice. He probably thought it was me again."

"Maybe he did. But we're not exactly twins."

"He don't really look. He just sees a ho. We all look alike to him."

"So he knows you were inside?"

She shook her head. "Some of the girls, they look for a courtyard, you know, to relieve themselves."

I nodded, reaching into my purse. "Here. This is just to tide you over until Vinnie calms down."

"Oh, shit. The men came in while you was there?"

"Yeah. But that's not it. I got out without them seeing me. He didn't like what I did with him."

"I could teach you. You could learn, Rachel. You got brains."

"Yeah, well, maybe some other time. This time, we just talked. I had some questions to put to him, about the murders."

Chi Chi's eyes got wide. "An' he tol' you stuff? He knows who did her?"

I shook my head. "I don't know. I'm not sure of anything yet, except that Vinnie's a liar."

"What? He's married?"

"Yeah," I told her. "That, too."

A car stopped at the corner, and Jasmine staggered out. Or was shoved out.

"What are you doing on this corner?" I asked Chi Chi, watching Jasmine mincing her way toward us. "I thought you're always on Little West Twelfth Street. I thought you guys were territorial."

"Who you calling a guy?" she said, pulling Clint out of her jacket, putting him down next to Dashiell.

"It's just an expression. Nothing personal."

"I could sure use something." Jasmine wiped her nose with the back of her hand in a gesture my mother would have found unladylike. Actually, she probably would have found the whole scene unladylike.

"Ain't nothin' to be had, girl. You look bad."

Jasmine sniffed again. "Yeah, well, there's nights and there's nights."

"Rachel here got to talk to Vinnie, over by Keller's, about the murders."

I lifted a finger to my lips, but neither of them was watching. "Look," I said, reaching out and touching Chi Chi's arm, "it's not a good idea to talk about what I'm doing. You never know who might be listening."

"But this here's Jasmine," she said. "She hire you, for God's sake. Why wouldn't I tell her the news?"

"It's not like there is any yet." I turned to Jasmine, noticing the bruise on one cheek, and that one of her small eyes was now smaller than the other. "I don't believe he was telling the truth."

"He lie to a hooker? Imagine that."

"What happened to you?" I asked her, pointing to her face.

"Someone patted me on the cheek, but he didn't know his own strength. The johns, they always do that when they're finished with you, pat you on the cheek, say thank you, sister, for a job well done." Hands on her hips. Then she changed her mind, took a strand of that blue-black hair, and pulled it forward over the bruise. "Stick around, Rachel, you'll get patted on the cheek, too. So, we safe yet? Lord, I'd like to be safe."

"Rachel's been going out on her own," Chi Chi told her. "She having ten, twelve dates a night. LaDonna told me."

"And no one hit you?" Jasmine said. "Man, you got the luck."

"Well, I—"

"You got the lucky boa. Maybe that's why." She reached out and pushed her fingers into those sad feathers. The way things were then, the middle of the night, standing on the greasy sidewalk waiting for strangers to buy a little of our time, a little piece of our lives, we'd all seen better days. I hadn't looked in a mirror lately, but I was pretty sure there were dark circles under my eyes and a sallow look to my skin. But, no, no one had punched me in the eye, smacked my face so that it turned colors. Not yet, anyway.

Jasmine's hand was still stroking the boa. "You got some secret you want to share with Jasmine?" A coy question, but she had a hard eye on me.

I shook my head.

"You're just one lucky broad, is that it?"

"Look, I—"

"How about if I wear the boa for a couple of nights? Rosalinda would have lent it to me, I asked her pretty please."

I slipped the boa off, and Jasmine slipped off her fluffy short sweater, draping it around my shoulders and buttoning the top button. "Wouldn't want you catching your death," she said, and then to Chi Chi, "Where is that bitch Grace?"

Is that why they were here instead of their usual place, because Grace wasn't? All this time, I'd never seen anyone swapping stations.

"Better class of customer here," Chi Chi told me.

"Yeah? How so?"

She sighed, amazed I could ask such a dumb question. "Because they come from there." She pointed toward West Fourteenth Street. "And they turns onto Washington, and the good ones get taken up right away, before they gets there," she said, pointing to where she usually stood. "Get it? We gets the dregs."

From what I had seen, they were all the dregs, but I didn't say so.

"Alice, she posts herself on that corner, dances around. She practically naked, no matter how cold it is. And she got cleavage now." Chi Chi nodded, agreeing with herself. "Grace usually here. Usually by herself. You can't work this corner when Grace is here. Sometimes she with Devon, he around. Maybe she with Devon now."

"How come? She the favorite?"

But I didn't get an answer, because Dashiell started to bark and Clint began to whine. LaDonna was headed toward us, coming from the other way, pretty in pink. She had a twenty in her hand, rolled up like a cigarette.

"Hey, LaDonna," I said.

LaDonna ignored me. She took out a pack of cigarettes, shoved the twenty in the pack, took out a smoke. Chi Chi's hand went out, and then the pack was offered to Jasmine and to me. We stood there watching for traffic, LaDonna and Chi Chi smoking, the dogs taking turns sniffing each other's butt, the wind blowing down the canyon of dark streets with a hollow sound, but you couldn't hear it when the door to Hogs and Heifers opened, the rockabilly pouring out at us in a shaft of yellow light, a bozo in a leather jacket glancing back at his Harley before going inside to the smoke and boozy smell, the wall of noise, a place to pass some time out of the cold and loneliness of the streets. Feeling cold and lonely myself, I slipped my arms into the sleeves of Jasmine's sweater and wiggled my fingers at the girls. Then Dashiell and I picked our way home, leaving the others hoping for one more trick before calling it a day.

27

They Make Mistakes, She Said

My first day on the selling floor of Saks, I sold eight pairs of socks in only four hours and got a note from Frances with her address and a little map showing where her house was in relation to the subway stop.

Much as I missed Dashiell, after an afternoon of discussing the virtues of cotton blends versus rayon, of triple-cuff versus the standard fold-over, I decided to walk home. Four hours of recycled air had been too much for me. I needed some of the free-floating kind, some of New York's finest, complete with gasoline fumes, but minus the blood-and-guts smells of the meat market, where I'd be spending the latter part of my workday.

Not being one to fritter away time, I decided to make it a working walk. I pulled out the little notebook where I had the information I'd gathered about my case. Well, information and questions. I'd worked on my case at Saks, too, twice going to the ladies' room to add notes and questions; then, hoping to answer one or two of my questions on the way home, I pulled out my cell phone and dialed the first number.

"Hullo?"

"Mrs. Willensky?"

"Yes?"

"Hi. I'm a journalist," I said. I was in a churning sea of people, the woman passing closest to me, walking uptown, talking on her cell phone, too.

"Harry, stop it. Harry, you're killing me," she said as she walked by me, her small Gucci bag tucked under her arm.

"I'm doing a piece on the meat district," I said into my phone, "the Gansevoort Meat Market, its history and the latest developments, how they affect the wholesale meat market, et cetera, et cetera, and I was wondering if I could talk to Mr. Willensky for just a few minutes, ask him some questions."

"He's not home from work yet," she said.

For a moment, I couldn't think of anything to say. I looked at the faces coming my way, the backs of people passing me, everyone walking as fast as they could. Where were they all going so fast?

"Oh," I said. Fucking eloquent. If I ever gave up PI work, I could become a speechwriter or do stand-up. "When I was researching the area"—lame, lame, I thought—"I read that he'd retired. So I thought he might have the time to talk to me. The other managers I spoke to were too busy to answer my questions." Brilliant, I thought. I just gave Willensky the perfect out.

I took a breath, redolent of hot roasted sugarcoated peanuts and regular unleaded. "It's an extensive piece," I told her, grimacing. If I wasn't convincing myself, how could I be convincing Myrna Willensky?

"Retired?" News to her. Maybe she never read the paper. Maybe Mr. W. never talked to her. Maybe he did read the paper, over breakfast and again after work. "No, no," she told me, "he's managing a plant at Hunts Point now. He doesn't get home until seven."

"But the paper said—"

"Oh." Pause. "They make mistakes," she said. Then neither

of us said anything for long enough for me to cross the street in the tight, moving crowd going uptown and downtown, everyone anxious to get out of Midtown as fast as they could. "If you leave me your number, I can have him call you."

"I don't understand," I repeated, hoping for more.

"There are problems in the Hunts Point plant. They brought him in to straighten things out. Once he does, he'll be back at the Greenwich Village plant. That'll be nice, too, because then he can walk to work. Now he's got a long subway ride both ways, unless one of the men who drives in from Brooklyn gives him a ride. So, do you want him to call you, or do you want to try him later?"

I picked a number off a passing taxi, replacing the final zero with a seven so that it would sound more like a home number. "He can call anytime," I said. "Day or night."

Why was I surprised? Since Mulrooney was there undercover, of course the story was released as if the old manager had retired and he'd replaced him. Had Mulrooney not gotten murdered, there would have been no story at all. In fact, Willensky had probably gone right to Hunts Point without missing a day's work. And would be back as soon as the undercover gig was over. Which meant that Timothy McCoy, despite the long résumé in his file saying otherwise, was also an undercover cop. And Vinnie had a long wait if he wanted to become manager.

I was passing a little boutique in the high twenties, a junktique actually, and they had an amazing outfit in the window, sort of a skintight strapless coverall, in a bright fuchsia spandex. If I wore it with Jasmine's sweater, I might actually be able to go outside without having my teeth rattle. I went inside, tried it on, and bought it. At the rate I was going solving this case, I'd get plenty of wear out of it.

Back on Fifth Avenue, passing the dog run at Madison Square Park, I stopped for a moment to watch a dalmatian bitch showing her teeth to an amorous cairn terrier, then continued on downtown. If it wasn't about the corruption in the carting industry, and it wasn't about the genetically altered meat, what was it about?

I thought that Mulrooney was offed because he switched carters, and that most likely, Rosalinda saw the crime. But that didn't work. Because if Rosalinda had been there, then the pig man had been there, and he, Vinnie, was still very much alive.

What if it was the other way around? What if it was Mulrooney who was the witness to a crime, not Rosalinda? Or what if they both were, which would make Vinnie the doer?

And suddenly I knew what made the cops so interested in Keller's market. It had been around me all along, because it was always part of the commercial sex scene, and because long before Jeffrey arrived with six-hundred-and-fifty-dollar shoes, long before Lotus was getting hundreds of calls a day for reservations, long before the art galleries, bakeries, and furniture shops moved in, the West Village belonged to sex clubs and hookers—and where there are sex clubs and hookers, you can take it to the bank, there are drugs. But to find out for sure that I was right, I'd have to get back into Keller's when it was closed.

I thought about sending Clint on his run again, about waiting for the almost imperceptible click that would let me know the latch was open, the woof that followed it, his announcement he'd done the job. Then I thought about swinging off the roof and dropping, hoping the hinges would stay in the old wood. I thought about the window creaking under my weight. I thought, No way, not this girl. Once was enough for that sort of thing. There had to be an easier way.

Dying for Dashiell's company, I stuck out my arm for a cab, remembered it was rush hour, and head down, lost in thought, I continued walking until I was all the way home.

28

Better Safe Than Sorry, I Told Her

A T nine that night, wearing my new fuchsia cat suit and Jasmine's sweater, Dashiell in tow, I headed for the stroll. Always priding myself on my ability to be an innovator, I wore ballet shoes instead of the pair the girls got for me. For one thing, the red clashed badly with the fuchsia. Even more important, they made noise. Lots of it. And they were as difficult to walk in as they looked. I wasn't planning on swinging off Keller's roof. But I was planning on spending some time there, and on not clattering around and getting caught. For one thing, I was sure the gun I had taken had already been replaced, and that no way would it be in the drawer when I showed up again.

Two of the girls were in the usual spot on Hudson Street, waiting for something. They always seemed to behave that way, living in the later instead of the now. Considering their now, I couldn't say I blamed them either. Especially that night, because as I approached, I saw that Devon was there, too.

LaDonna was talking too loud, gesturing with a cigarette

in her hand. As I crossed the street, I saw him slap her with the back of his hand, his ring leaving a bloody gash on her face.

"Any other complaints?" he said, looking at her, turning toward Chi Chi, and then staring at me as I stepped up onto the curb. "And what the hell is that all about?" He was pointing to Dashiell.

LaDonna, with blood trickling down her cheek, stepped between Devon and me.

"It's her signature," she said. "You remember you tol' us what a good thing that was, that the johns look for something that makes us stand out, how you always want the family to be special 'cause it pays off?" She slapped one big palm with her other, perhaps Devon's way of telling the girls to stop with the excuses and fork over the cash. He was a man of few words, that Devon, a man of action.

"Well, so far I haven't *seen* anything special coming from this particular lady and this particular sig-na-ture." He drew out the word, enunciating one syllable at a time.

I kept my eyes down, as I'd been instructed to do, but Dashiell didn't. I could feel the tension in the leash.

"I gave you everything, from her and me, last night and the night before. It's been slow."

"Don't you lie to me, bitch." He lifted his hand but didn't strike. He was too busy looking at Dashiell. "The johns let him in the car?" he asked me.

I nodded without looking up.

"I aksed you a question."

"So far, they do."

"Yeah? This I gotta see." With that, he turned to leave. "*Two* fucking dogs I got to deal with now. I'm a regular Saint Francis of whatchmacallit."

"He be watching you tonight," Chi Chi said. She'd been standing back, not saying a word, trying to keep herself and her dog out of harm's way.

"Fine," I told her, glancing at LaDonna's cheek, the sweat

mixing in with the blood. I reached into my bag and pulled out a tissue, handing it to her.

"What you carry in there, a whole pharmacy?"

I shrugged. "Condoms."

"Condoms? What you need condoms, you just sit and talk to them?"

"Better safe than sorry," I told her. "Hadn't we better get to work, if Devon's going to be watching?"

"He always watching," Chi Chi said. "He watching and he counting. He don't miss a trick."

Walking over to Washington, I heard the click of high heels behind me and turned to see Jasmine, ebullient in the lucky boa, her hair in ringlets. "Couldn't get a train," she said, and for the first time I thought of something I'd never contemplated, how the girls got here from home. But just as suddenly, it became something I didn't want to dwell on. Didn't I walk out of my house all tarted up, mincing my way through the neighborhood hoping like hell no one I knew would see me, or that no one who saw me was on the prowl, looking for a tranny to beat up, preferably one my size and not LaDonna's? Of course, I didn't think I looked male, any more than Dashiell looked female. But this outfit in this neighborhood could mean only one thing, and most people didn't look that closely, especially when they were looking at what they presumed to be a hooker.

I walked closer to Chi Chi. "I need you to see Vinnie tonight."

"You jus' tol' me *not* to see Vinnie. You tol' me you made him real mad at you, now you want me to go in there and take the heat."

"I need to get in there again. If we both go in, I can check things out while you distract Vinnie, calm him down, you know? I'll be right there, just in case you get into trouble, okay?"

When I looked up, Jasmine was practically on top of me. "I see you like the sweater as much as I like this," she said, twirling the ends of the boa. "Want to make it a permanent trade?"

"Sure," I told her. "Whatever makes you happy." The sweater was a lot warmer, and besides, the boa made me sneeze.

"You look great tonight. Where'd you get that?" She was touching my hip, admiring the cat suit. I told her where it came from and how much it cost.

"I might get me one of those, too," she said. She checked out my earrings, sparkly rhinestone fans I used to let my niece play dress-up with when she was little. Then she ran her fingers over the matching rhinestone bracelets, two, the whole set under twenty dollars at a street fair years ago, bargains everywhere. I took off one of the bracelets and gave it to her. She snapped it onto her wrist, as happy as a kid at Christmas. Last, she looked at my shoes. "Are those real?" she asked.

I stuck one leg forward and twirled my ankle around. "Yeah."

"You a ballerina now, too, in addition to being a dog groomer, a detective, and a ho?"

"Yeah. I'm a person of many talents. There's no end to my abilities." I smiled. She didn't. Jasmine, the joker, was dead serious.

"As soon as the case is over, you can have everything, your sweater, the boa, the green skirt, the cat suit, the ballet shoes—"

"Keep the shoes, honey. They wouldn't cover my big toe. But I'll take the rest. Unless you want to save any of it, for when your boyfriend comes over."

"Oh, he prefers a white blouse with a Peter Pan collar and a plaid skirt, knee socks, oxfords, that look."

Jasmine shrugged. "Doesn't surprise me. Takes all kinds."

And then we were there, at work, and LaDonna was smearing a tube of makeup over the cut. She asked if I was still going it alone, and I told her I was. We spread out in front of the pig mural, and LaDonna began to dance around. I looked down the block and saw a car coming, its windows tinted dark. LaDonna danced up to the curb. She had to make some real money tonight, give it all to Devon, or she'd have much worse than a cut on her face. She knew it, and so did the rest of us, hanging back and letting her take the first trick.

The window on our side rolled slowly down. "How much for two of you to do the two of us?" the passenger said, the driver leaning forward to have a look-see.

"No problem. I do you both," LaDonna said, opening the passenger door, motioning with her thumb for the man who spoke to get out, get into the backseat so that she could slide into the front one. "My legs way too long for me to sit in the back," she said. "And not to worry, gentlemen, I'm enough woman for the both of youse. I do you both at the same time," she told them. I could still hear her laughing as the car pulled away, LaDonna doing verbal foreplay, a full-service hooker if ever there was one.

I got into the next car. I don't know if the shlump behind the wheel didn't notice Dashiell or if he thought it was a kinky idea, that Dashiell would do something, too, that he'd get double his money's worth. In this world, anything was possible.

He was short and small, with weird little hands that clutched the wheel and made me think of a hamster on a treadmill. He took furtive peeks at me while he drove south on Washington, turning left on Horatio when I told him to. When I gave him my spiel, a whistling noise came out of his mouth, but no words, no excuses. He didn't promise anything. He didn't tell me it was his first time. And when I asked for my fee, because I wanted to have something to give LaDonna, to cover my share, he didn't argue at all. In fact, I'd asked for forty and he gave me fifty. I took his picture before getting out. That's when he came to life, reaching for the camera, letting go when Dashiell reached for his arm. One down, I thought, checking my new Timex, nine to go.

I gave all the money I'd earned on Horatio Street to LaDonna before heading around the corner to meet Chi Chi in the courtyard of Keller's as planned. She was already there, shifting from foot to foot, chewing on her cuticles.

"You sure this is a good idea?"

"Chi Chi, I can't figure this out for you without taking some risks."

"But you risking *me* this time."

"I know. But you're at risk anyway, until we find out who killed Rosalinda."

"You right about that. You always right. Leastways, I hope you're always right, because I got a bad feeling about doing this tonight." Chi Chi was shaking. Maybe she was right. Maybe I shouldn't have been asking her to do this. I looked up at the roof, thinking of the other way I'd gotten in there. I'd have more time that way, if the window held a second time.

"I'll be downstairs. Just holler if you need me and Dashiell."

Chi Chi nodded, and together we approached the door, the padlock locked to one handle now, letting us know that Vinnie was there.

But he hadn't asked Chi Chi to come. Was there some other reason Vincent Esposito, the model employee, had arrived an hour and a half before he was due at work?

We went inside, the air so cold it seemed white. Chi Chi wiggled her fingers, such a girlish gesture, as if we were saying good-bye after a movie or a trip to the malt shoppe. I nodded and watched her head down the row of carcasses and disappear.

About a third of the freezer hooks were in use. I'd seen a box of heavy rubber gloves last time I'd been through, and I headed there first, taking a pair and slipping them on. I could feel a thick layer of steel mesh between the layers of rubber, something to prevent the loss of a finger when cutting the meat. They were ridiculously too big, but I pulled them as tight as I could and started at one end of the first row, reaching inside, feeling around for anything that I could remove, going from carcass to carcass until I'd given each and every pig an internal exam. Nothing.

I checked out everything else I could see, a pair of boots left against the wall, the gizmo that you wrapped the high-pressure hose around. I reached behind the grinding machine, into the backs of the drawers on the huge cutting tables, everywhere. Nothing.

If the cops were here undercover because of drugs, the third big business of the area, where the hell were they? Was I merely too early?

If Vinnie was using the carcasses of the pigs to transport drugs, might not the drugs come with the morning deliveries? But from where? Were they being shipped to New York to be sold on the street from Iowa? Because, for God's sake, that was where these pigs had lived and died. And where were they headed? And when? If they came in in the morning, when did they go out again? And where did Vinnie stash them in between? That's when I remembered that key again, the one I'd seen in the middle desk drawer. But if the key opened to the door to the drug stash, why would it be kept where anyone could find and use it?

Fine, I could risk Chi Chi and frisk the pigs now. But if the stuff hadn't come in yet, there was no way I could get in here and do what I'd just done when everyone was working. Could Vinnie? If the meat was coming in and most of it getting processed, ground and sliced and chopped, the same day, then going out again, how could Vinnie know which carcasses to check before the butchers began to cut them up?

But drugs made sense when nothing else did. Drugs would bring the cops in, undercover. Drugs were rife in the neighborhood, and transporting them this way might just work. If they'd been so easy to find, wouldn't Mulrooney have cracked the case in a day or two? He'd been here for two months.

Of course. He knew about the drugs. He probably knew how they got here. What took time was plotting out the whole route, where they started out, when they got hidden in the meat, who removed them from the meat, and where they went when they left here. And why did it have to be Vinnie? It could have been any one of the other butchers, looking for a stamp, a mark on the pork, taking those to process first.

Could be, could be. Standing in the refrigerator, the compressor as loud as a subway pulling into the station, I realized I'd have to get into the files again. Somehow I'd see a pattern, figure out where the drugs were headed. And then the more difficult part—who was rerouting them once they arrived? I took another pass around the refrigerated room. Nothing.

The compressor shut off, and I heard Chi Chi.

"No, honey, I can find my own way out."

And there she was, mad as a cat in the bathtub.

"Move it," she said, pointing toward the door.

"What?"

She pushed the front door open, pulled Clint out of her jacket and set him down, pulled the door closed behind us. But she didn't explain. Because that's when we saw her lying in the courtyard, facedown, her legs splayed at an odd angle, blood seeping out near her face, the lucky boa splattered red, lying next to her now, her skin bleached pale by a sliver of a moon.

29

What Are You Talking About? I Asked Him

W E'VE got to get out of here." I grabbed Chi Chi's arm and tried to pull her toward the street, but she might have been cemented in place. She never budged. My hand still partway around her biceps, I was reminded of what it was sometimes easy to forget. Chi Chi was a man.

"We can't just leave her here." One hand covered her mouth, the other held the leash. Both dogs stayed put, heads up, tasting the air. Then Clint began to wail.

"That could be you lying there. Don't you get it?"

Chi Chi turned slowly away from Jasmine and toward me. I knew what was coming before she said it. But she never did. She just shook her head, slowly took the hand that had covered her raspberry-colored lips, and pointed at me.

With Jasmine in a cat suit very much like mine and the boa I'd been wearing all week, her hair in ringlets, in this location, dark as a pimp's asshole and twice as foul, someone could have thought they were killing me, the interloper, the snoop, not realizing until after the fact, one quick slash to the neck, expertly delivered from behind, that the dead woman had rough, dark skin, that she was in fact not a woman at all.

I looked around, as if at any moment someone might pop out from behind Vinnie's car and rectify their mistake. But there was no one there. I don't know why I did it when I should have gotten out of there as fast as possible, but I bent down and picked up the boa. Then, yanking on Chi Chi's arm, I made for the street.

"I want you to go home," I told her. "Now. Do you have a cell phone today?"

She nodded, turning back to look at the courtyard as I pulled her toward Washington Street, hoping the meat market would be coming to life soon, that there'd be trucks moving, deliveries arriving, butchers in their white coats and hard hats standing on the sidewalk, watching as sides of beef, hooks with thirty chickens hanging from them, trembling as if they were still alive, moved into the processing plants.

"Good. Then call LaDonna. She have her phone, too?"

"Yeah."

"Good. Call her. Meet her over on Hudson Street, and both of you go home. And I don't want either of you back here tomorrow night, okay? Take the night off." I reached into my pocket for the money I'd collected earlier in the night, remembering I'd already given it all to LaDonna. "Don't come back here without calling me first," I told her. "I must be getting close if someone's coming after me."

"But Jasmine—"

"Nothing we can do for her now."

"You're sure?"

"I'm sure." I put my arms around her and hugged her against me. She bent and picked up Clint. That's when I saw that she was crying. "Go home. Get LaDonna and just go home."

I watched as she tip-tapped across the street, rushing toward the curb when a huge truck came barreling down the street. It stopped without pulling over, blocking my view of

Chi Chi. The driver honked. I could see the back of his head as he called out to Chi Chi, but she apparently never answered him, never stopped running.

That's when he turned to me.

"How much?" he asked. No beating around the bush in this neck of the woods.

"Fifty," I told him, way too high for this time in the morning. I was hoping he'd go away and leave me alone.

That's when I realized what I'd done. I'd sent Chi Chi home. I looked left, down the canyon of the dark streets where the hookers worked. There was no one in sight. But Jasmine had just been killed. We'd been inside Keller's for only twenty minutes, maybe less. So whoever had done that, whoever had tried to kill me, could still be around.

I walked closer to the truck. "Good-looking guy like you," I said, offering him the Kaminsky family grin, all teeth and charm, "how would twenty be?"

He frowned.

"Ten? Ten okay?"

This time he grinned and nodded, but when he leaned over to open the door—a real gentleman, just when you think there's not one left anywhere—he seemed to notice Dashiell for the first time.

"He curls up on the floor. Unless he snores, you'll never know he's there."

He thought about it, then pushed the door open.

I tied the boa around my waist, sent Dashiell ahead of me, and climbed in after him. He put the truck into gear, but instead of driving over to Horatio Street, he pulled over to the curb on the next block and, leaving the engine on, parked, his hands coming off the wheel and going right to his lap.

"Whoa," I said. "No small talk?"

"You gotta be kidding. I been on the road eighteen hours. This delivery is due in ten, fifteen minutes. You want I should spend that time talking?"

"Actually, I do," I told him. I pulled out the camera.

"What the hell?"

"Sorry, fellow, you're busted."

"What are you—"

"Police. Giuliani is cracking down on prostitution, haven't you heard? Since you're obviously such a decent person," I said as his hands slipped back onto the wheel, "I'm going to do you a big favor. I'm going to make this a warning." I snapped a picture. "Turn forward," I told him. But he didn't. He glared at me, but I saw him take in Dashiell, too. Whatever he might have been thinking, Dashiell inspired him to think again.

"This is for the Busted Johns website," I told him. "Have you seen it?"

"This is entrapment. For ten bucks, hey, no guy's going to say no."

I shrugged. "Way it goes."

"No way, sister. This'll never hold up in court. Besides, you said this would be a warning."

"Right. I'll just hang on to this, in case I see you here again."

"Of course you'll see me here again. It's my job to be here. And you got a lot of guts, little lady, I'll tell you that, working these streets at this hour of the night after one of your own just got it." He tilted his head in the direction I'd recently come from, toward the spot where Jasmine lay dead in the courtyard, waiting for the first of the butchers to show up and find her there.

My heart was suddenly racing. Dashiell leaned tighter against my legs, keeping his eyes on the trucker. How would he know Mulrooney was a cop? "What are you talking about?" I asked him, hoping I hadn't totally lost my cool, thinking I must have.

"Don't play dumb with me, little girl. I wasn't born yesterday." Then he began to laugh. "You don't know, do you? Too bad the department didn't fill you in. Maybe you ought to read the papers more carefully." And then he laughed again.

"What's this, your first day on the job, sister? Is that how you got this plum assignment?"

I opened the camera and pulled out the roll of film, pulling it open, then dropping it on the floor.

"Speak," I told him.

"What do you think, I'm your dog? Gotta make my delivery. You're the cop. Surely you can find out for yourself. Just check the computers or whatever it is you people do." He sighed and leaned his head back, tired from his long drive. I opened the door and got out first, calling Dashiell to jump down after me, the empty camera still in my hand. Then I stood there watching as the truck backed up, the warning sound almost deafening at this close range. As he backed around the corner, toward Keller's, I headed home, picturing him still laughing about what had happened, until he stepped out of the cab and saw Jasmine lying dead at his feet and the whole world pitched sideways, suddenly and without warning, the way it did when you weren't paying attention, and sometimes, even when you were.

30

I Felt Small and Cold and Stupid

I NEEDED activity to help me deal with what had happened less than an hour earlier, the murder of someone dressed like me and heading for where I had gone snooping. I put up the kettle and began to chop raw food for Dashiell. How did anyone know I'd be going to Keller's tonight? Who was running off at the mouth this time? And Jasmine, had she been coming to warn me? Is that why she'd been there?

I stopped chopping, turned off the stove, and sat down hard on the couch, the door open, Dashiell outside. Alone in the living room, only the kitchen light on, I felt small and cold and stupid. How could I have let this happen?

The change of carting company followed by the death of the undercover cop on the job could have been a coincidence. Replacing the usual provisions with genetically altered meat, something some people thought meant the end of the world as we knew it, that could have been a coincidence, too. But Jasmine's death? No way was that unconnected to what I was doing. Why hadn't I seen it coming?

I walked back to the kitchen, pushed aside the stack of

unopened mail I'd been dropping on the counter for days, and finished making Dash's dinner. Or given the time of day, was it breakfast? His world was upside down, too.

I went upstairs, checked my messages, and lay down on my bed. But all I could think of was Jasmine in the lucky boa, Jasmine with her long hair curled, like mine, apparently thinking I knew something she didn't. And the trucker, knowing Mulrooney was a cop. My mind jumped from one thing to another.

I had to get to the library and check old newspapers for an article on a drug bust in the Bronx, something Mulrooney was involved in before he came to the Gansevoort Market. There had to be something there, something the trucker saw and I missed. I closed my eyes again, thinking I'd sleep a little first. The library wouldn't be open for hours. Instead I began to think about Rosalinda, that if she was killed because she was there when Mulrooney bought it, that means that Vinnie was there, too. And the only way Vinnie could still be alive is if he had something to do with the shooter. If drugs were moving in and out of Keller's and Vinnie was in on that, had Mulrooney confronted him? Was Vinnie onto Mulrooney in some other way? And did he set Mulrooney up?

I still had the boa tied around my waist, Rosalinda's lucky boa. Some joke. Now all I could think of was saving it, getting the blood out, making it look like new. I got up and took it into the bathroom, filling the sink with cold water, adding Woolite and stirring the water with one hand. Then I dropped in the boa, watched a part of it sink, pushing the rest of it under the water to soak. I dropped the rest of what I was wearing onto the floor, got into the shower, and stood under the water as hot as I could stand it for what seemed like a very long time.

I rinsed the boa and set it carefully on a towel to dry. Then I got dressed, left Dashiell at home, and took a cab up to the main branch of the library, the one at Forty-second Street with the lions out front. If what I was looking for existed, it would be there. Two hours later I had found the two articles that let me understand what the trucker was talking about. The first one I found was actually the second article to appear in the paper. It was a short piece about the burial of a cop killed in a drug raid, the drug raid Frances told me about, rewriting history so that it became her husband who'd died in the initial shoot-out when in fact it was his partner. There was a picture, the widow weeping, being held up by a young man—a son, a cousin, it didn't say. And there were eight cops carrying the coffin. I'd seen one of the pallbearers before, his gaunt face, the clownish nose, that great broom of a mustache nearly covering his grim mouth, the coffin bearing his partner weighing heavily on his shoulder. It was a lot to carry in every way. Especially since, I could now see, he was rather slight, maybe five-five or five-six and slim, the smallest of the seven colleagues. The trucker had seen this picture, too, and then, to his great surprise, he'd seen Detective Kevin Patrick Mulrooney at Keller's, only there it was Manager Mulrooney. My, my. He didn't need anything more to put two and two together. But I did, just to be sure of the facts. I needed the article that had appeared a week earlier that said that Mulrooney's partner, Dave O'Neill, forty-four, had gone in first, not Mulrooney. And that it was Dave who caught the fatal bullets, three of them. It was Mulrooney who had gotten two of the drug dealers, brothers Julius and Lamarr Wright. The article went on to say that a third dealer had escaped through the window; he'd probably gone up the fire escape instead of down, then across the roofs to safety. The stash would have brought three-point-two million on the street, it said, and the police were looking for the party that got away. And good luck on that one, I thought, wondering what Mulrooney had told his wife about the bust and what I might be able to get her to tell me over turkey and yams the next day, not letting on that I knew it was O'Neill who died in the shoot-out and not her Patrick.

I took a cab home, watching Fifth Avenue out the window, thinking if I got lucky tomorrow, if I could get Frances to talk, I might not have to go back to the market ever again. I was sick to death of the whole thing—the drugged-out hookers, the sleazy johns, the smell of death in the streets.

When I got home, I wanted to call Chi Chi, make sure she was okay, but the way she was moving when I last saw her, I was sure she was home, under the covers, too scared to come out even to answer the phone.

I went to bed as soon as Dash came in from the garden, but I still couldn't sleep. Mulrooney was small, I was thinking. I'd worried about who could have picked him up after they shot him, put him on that damn meat hook, made it look like a mob execution, duct tape and all. Hell, I could have done that in the heat of the moment. Frances could have done it, if she had a reason, put her arms around his slight body, bent back, and lifted him onto that cold, mean hook. Lifting him, that wasn't the issue anymore. Why? That was still the question.

And then it was Jasmine I was seeing, Jasmine looking much like me from behind, the boa hanging down, obscuring the narrow line of her hips. She'd been the brightest of the three, the most articulate, the one, I'd found myself thinking once or twice, who might have a chance in hell to get out of the life. Well, she was out of it now, all her chances at anything taken away, someone trying to stop some annoying little snoop from sticking her nose in their business, an annoying little snoop who'd been seen around Keller's in the dead whore Rosalinda's lucky boa.

I walked downstairs and opened the cabinet where I kept wine, taking three bottles out to take to dinner instead of two, hoping Frances would be feeling relaxed and festive having two friends with her for Thanksgiving, that with a bit of encouragement she'd drink too much, and that after that she'd talk too much. I was desperate now, thinking of the old Hollywood line, Who do I have to fuck to get off this film? Because one way or another, this case was coming to an end. Only this wasn't Hollywood, and it wasn't a movie, and though it might have looked like a movie set, those huge eerie pigs dominating the street, the meat market wasn't. It was as real as death, ten times over.

31

She Took a Gulp of Wine This Time

By the time Frances brought out the pies, cold pumpkin and deep-dish apple, hot from the oven, her face was flushed, her stories were flowing like the wine, and her neighbor Sarah had fallen asleep right there at the table, her chin nearly touching her large bosom, her mouth open, a string of saliva dangling from one corner.

"Don't wake her," I whispered as Frances set out three dessert plates. "She looks exhausted."

"Exhausted? I don't think so. It's the wine. She drank it like it was water," Frances said. She ought to know. She'd done something similar herself, but perhaps she had more practice; happily, she was still very much awake.

We carried our dessert plates to the living room, and when Frances asked if I wanted coffee, I asked if there was any of that nice wine left instead. I said I thought it would go well with the hot apple pie. She said yes, as a matter of fact there was some wine left, that she'd make the coffee anyway, it would only take a minute, and bring both.

What exactly did they say the road to hell was paved with?

At the rate I was going, no doubt I'd find out one day. I was shameless. I was dishonest. I didn't care. I just wanted to be done with all this without losing another client.

I walked around the small, cluttered living room looking at framed photographs—a wedding picture, Kevin and Frances when they were young, Frances half a head taller than her husband. And one I guessed was Frances with her mother and father, the father wearing a suit and a hat, the mother, too. Everyone used to dress that way when they went out, when they took pictures. Looking down at my jeans, I thought about my own parents. Had they been invited to a friend's house for Thanksgiving dinner, my mother would have worn a suit with a silk blouse and a pin on her lapel. She would have worn a hat. And gloves. My father would have looked as if he was going to work, in a suit and tie, his shoes polished, his hair slicked down.

I picked up a photo of Kevin Mulrooney in his blue uniform, very young, very serious. And that was it. No pictures of their kid, nothing more recent than twenty years ago, it seemed. Unless the others were in the bedroom. Some people did that, kept most of the private stuff to themselves.

Waiting, I thought about the trucker, what he'd seen and what he said. A murder years before on Gansevoort Street had been solved because of an observant trucker who had pulled over for a much-needed nap only to be awakened by a shot, someone getting executed, the doer not knowing there was anyone in the truck parked at the curb, not knowing there'd be a witness who would ID him later that same day at the Sixth Precinct. It had been a fluke that he was there, too tired to drive; that he'd seen the crime take place; that there'd been a full moon—all the elements working in favor of the law.

I never thought about truckers being good witnesses. All that sitting, watching the road pull under the truck for sixteen, eighteen hours a day, they had to do something to keep awake. Maybe they looked for details, looked to see what had changed in the environment since the last time they went by, looked at the faces of the drivers they passed, the drivers who passed them. Maybe they tried to read the faces, tell themselves a story, pass the time that way. This trucker, the one on Gansevoort Street, he'd had the face down cold, the parroty nose, the eyebrows that nearly met in the middle, lips that looked wet, the pencil mustache, sideburns, the scar at the hairline over his left temple. He saw it all. He remembered.

Frances made three trips, ferrying everything in from the kitchen, bringing the wine bottle from the table. Finally she came in with a cup of coffee for herself, set it down on the coffee table, and picked up the plate with pie. Apple. But when I lifted my wineglass, she put down the pie and lifted hers. We touched them together. "To friendship," I said. She smiled and drank. I didn't.

If I solved the case, the person who'd killed her husband would be caught and punished. Did that make my toast any more genuine?

"Your child is grown now?" I asked, wanting to open the conversation again, to get it going, to make it personal.

"Oh, yes." She seemed to forget about the pie, holding the wineglass and sipping. I picked up the bottle and topped off both our glasses.

"Living here?" I asked, wondering why there were no pictures, Mom and Dad and baby. Or baby grown up.

"Oh, no." Had she had too much wine? Was she about to nod off?

"What does he—"

"Denise. She's at the store. Didn't I tell you?"

"Saks?"

"Yes. That's how I got the job. She's a buyer. Cosmetics. Oh, she does very well for herself. She has an apartment in Manhattan. In the Chelsea section, on Nineteenth Street. Four rooms and a little garden."

"How wonderful." But something began nagging at me even as I spoke. "So you see her often?"

"Well, not as often as I'd like. But what parent does?" She took a gulp of wine this time.

Like a terrier after a rat, I pursued.

"She's busy?"

"Busy? Yes. Very. She travels for them. To Paris mostly, on buying trips. I asked her once to bring me some Chanel, and she scolded me. She said it's cheaper at the store, with my employee's discount, than she could get it in Paris. Mom, she said, you just want some attention. Mom, I give you more attention than most girls give their mothers."

Frances laughed and drank, and I refilled her glass and took a little sip of my own wine.

"She's right. We're close. I can't complain."

"But today . . . ?"

Frances looked stumped, as if I'd asked her for the formula for Chanel instead of why her daughter, to whom she was so close, hadn't come home for Thanksgiving dinner, especially this one, the first since her father had died, since her mother had been widowed.

"Paris," she said. "She didn't get back in time to come. Couldn't get back in time, I meant."

And then I knew I wasn't the only liar in Frances Mulrooney's living room. She hadn't only lied to me to protect an ongoing police investigation. She was lying now, too. What was she protecting this time? Or whom?

"Are your friends after you again about that blind date, Rachel? You should go. Do you a world of good to get out. Didn't it cheer you up to come here this afternoon, 'stead of sitting home in front of the TV?"

I waved a hand, brushing away the question. "I can't even think about that, about dating. Can you? Have you?"

Again, Frances looked as if I'd asked her something too difficult to answer. But she was game. She was going to try. I could see the struggle in her eyes.

"It's much too soon for me to . . ."

I took a sip of wine, as a sign of good faith, and waited.

"I suppose it would be nice someday to have dinner with a gentleman, to get dressed up and all that."

She looked dreamy for a moment.

"But?"

"Where would I find a gentleman?"

"I guess that's the question." Something niggling away at the back of my mind. Something was off. Way off. But what?

"Sarah," she whispered, "surfs the Net." Frances nodded, sipped, sat back against the couch pillows in a *There, I've said it* pose.

What was I supposed to say?

"You mean chat rooms?"

She nodded.

"My sister's done that," I lied.

"But how would you know who you were going to meet?"

"She's only actually met anyone twice. Both times in public places, just for a drink."

"And?" Leaning closer. I topped off her glass again, adding three drops to mine. But Frances didn't seem to notice that she was drinking by herself.

"The first guy was short-waisted, overweight, and really ugly. Didn't seem to matter to him that he was homely as a toad, she said. He was so full of himself, he never stopped bragging. She left after two drinks. And that was it."

"But she tried again?"

"Yes. The second man was very good-looking."

"But?"

"Married. He told her he loved his wife and kids. He said he thought, working as hard as he did, keeping his family in Scarsdale, for God's sake, his kids in private school, well, didn't he deserve a little recreation, a little something for himself?"

"On the side, you mean?"

I nodded. "How'd you know there'd be a but?"

"Patrick, you know, the police, they always look for the underbelly, the negative in life. I guess I got the habit from him. And I know anyway that men can be like that," she said. "Even in the department, men sworn to uphold the law, there was a lot of cheating and a lot of divorce."

"But not Patrick?"

"Patrick? Oh, no. That wasn't the problem with Patrick."

"What was?"

Frances looked puzzled for a moment. Then she nodded. "Well, the work, of course. You worry all the time. And then it happened."

"At least they got them," I said, "the dealers who—"

"Oh, no. They didn't."

For a moment, I didn't know if we were talking about the same case.

"Two were killed. He shot two when he went in. But there was a third who got away. Patrick's partner stayed with him. He was bleeding so heavily."

"There were no other officers on the scene?"

"There were. But the third drug dealer found a way out, first through the window and then up to the roof, they think. Two officers did go that way. But no one was there."

"And the other two, the ones Patrick killed?"

"Brothers," she said. "They thought the third one might be a brother, too, Rendell they said his name was, that it was a family business."

"But they didn't know for sure?"

"No, not at the time."

"And now?"

"Oh, I wouldn't know that. I suppose if they ever catch him, one of Patrick's old friends would tell me, to give me closure. But I'm not privy to their ongoing investigations."

I nodded, not knowing what else to say at the moment. It was getting late, and I thought I should go, try to get in touch with Chi Chi and LaDonna and make sure they were safe. But there was still one more thing to do.

"And where would the powder room be?" I asked. "All this wine . . ."

"Through the bedroom, Rachel. I'll just clear while you do that."

I got up, and so did Frances. I watched her walk over to the dining room table, Sarah snoring lightly, and begin to stack the dishes. Then I headed for the door to her bedroom, making sure it closed partway behind me. She had a long low bureau and a tall one, probably Kevin's. The tops of both bureaus were covered with photos, all of their daughter, pictures of her as a tiny baby, Frances beaming at her, then Kevin. There were no pictures as she was growing up, with her parents and by herself, smiling, a happy child, a lucky child to have such doting parents. But there she was as an adult, tall, like her mother, not slight, like her father. But other than that, not resembling either parent, not in the least.

For a moment, it was difficult to catch my breath. But I tried, slowing everything down, trying to ignore what was in my hand and concentrating on getting air in and out of my lungs, on that and nothing but that. Still holding the picture, I went into the bathroom, laying it down on the sink, splashing cold water on my face. I studied the photo again, absorbing the stunning news it revealed, the last thing in the world I would have expected, the absolute last.

Frances was in the kitchen, soaking the dishes so that the dishwasher could get them clean. She wiped her hands, picked up her wineglass, and we walked back to the couch.

"You didn't mention that your daughter was adopted," I said, still holding the framed photo.

"Oh, didn't I?" Dreamy again. "I couldn't have a child of my own. It was what I wanted, more than anything in the world, to have my own baby. But there was something wrong with my tubes, the doctor said. They tried to open them." She winced at the memory. "But we weren't to be blessed in that way. And then Patrick was coming home from the job one night, on his way to the subway, and he heard her. She was in a Dumpster, wrapped in newspaper. She was just a wee thing, a newborn. He was alone, Patrick. He climbed in and lifted her out, and he held her against his chest. He knew what he should do, that he should take her to the station and turn her in. He stood there for a while, just holding her and watching her, and then he walked to the corner and put out his arm, and when a taxi stopped, he gave the driver our address."

"And you just kept her?"

"At first. We knew it was wrong. But Patrick said that most of the children that were abandoned, the mother's never found. Or she's fourteen. And a crack addict. What kind of a life could someone like that give a child? What kind of person puts a baby in a Dumpster? Giving her up, giving her to the precinct, she could have gone back to a person like that, a dope addict, someone who'd abandon her again. We couldn't. Then, after a month, Patrick arranged for us to adopt her legally." She looked into her lap for a moment, as if the rest of the story were there. "We thought there'd be trouble, but he worked it out. She was able to stay here with us. That's all I cared about. If he used some influence," Frances shrugged, "if he bent the law, I don't know and I don't care. We knew we could give that baby what she needed. And we did."

"And were they close, father and daughter?"

Frances's eyes flickered for just a second. "Oh, very," she said. "They loved each other to pieces."

Sarah woke up, and we all had coffee. Though I was anxious to get home, I stayed a while longer. Then, when I felt I could, I thanked Frances and said I had to go. She walked me to the door and hugged me hard.

"I'm glad you came," she said.

"Me, too." This time, I wasn't lying.

When I got outside, I didn't head for the subway. On Queens Boulevard I found a cab, and despite the cold, I rolled down the window halfway and sat right next to it, letting the cold air hit my face. And then I was home, in my office, Dashiell circling me and sniffing as if he hadn't seen me in years, the *Times* obit in my hand, the information I'd recalled right there in black and white. Mulrooney, it said, had been survived by a wife, Frances, and a son, Dennis, who was in public relations.

And although I'd never seen her dressed the way she had for her mother's camera, I'd know her anywhere. I was sure I'd be seeing her in my sleep for years to come. We had, after all, become quite attached in the short time since she'd hired me, using yet another name, her street name—not Denise, LaDonna.

32

She's a Lousy Cook, She Said

THE answering machine was blinking. I hit the play
button.

"Rachel, it's us. We don't want you mad or nothin', but it
being a holiday, business always be brisk, menfolks feeling
lonely or sick of they's family, so me and LaDonna's going on
the stroll, but she says to tell you we promise to look over
both shoulders at all times."

Up there floating. Then LaDonna's voice.

"We be in the usual spot, you want us. Dress up, you coming. It's Thanksgiving."

My mother, as a transvestite hooker.

No. Mulrooney's daughter as one.

I checked my watch. It was only seven-thirty. I had time
to feed Dashiell, change, and get to Little West Twelfth Street
in time to meet them. Was it the drugs that masked how
much danger they were in? Whatever it was, this would not
be the night off I'd planned.

I opened the foil package Frances had given me at the
door and set it down for Dashiell—turkey, yams, green beans,

a slice of apple pie. I never gave him sweets, but what the hell, it was Thanksgiving. I watched him nose each thing, eating the turkey first, then the yams. I could see from the expression on his face how their sweetness had surprised him, spreading sideways, filling his mouth and his senses. He took the beans one at a time, then touched the pie with his nose again. He stopped, looked up at me, then back at the pie, as thoughtful as a preacher, finally leaving it there untasted, walking into the living room and sighing as he lay down, someone's uncle, having eaten too much, about to loosen his belt and take a nap.

I showered and put together my holiday hooker outfit, topping it off in the traditional way with a feather boa, now dry, the bloodstains all but invisible. It was white again, the way it used to be years ago. Looking at it, draped over my shoulders, I knew it should be in a plastic evidence bag someplace at the precinct instead. I took one end, tossed it around my neck and over the opposite shoulder, and poked at my hair one last time. Like LaDonna said, it was Thanksgiving.

Dashiell was snoring when I came downstairs, but when I picked up his leash, he was on the job. We walked over to Washington Street, which was deserted, everyone having gone through the Holland Tunnel to have dinner with their parents by now, no one waiting on that long line to get back home yet. I had to find Chi Chi and LaDonna, and I had to find them right away. Once they started working, it would be much more difficult to locate them, and even if I did, much more difficult to get them away from the smell of holiday money.

I saw Chi Chi first, talking to a hooker I hadn't seen before, a short, fat girl with a red wig and way too much mascara.

"Excuse us," I told her, pulling Chi Chi toward the corner, then around it, until we were under the sidewalk bridge.

"You don't want to go there," she said, her eyes cutting toward Keller's.

"No, I don't. And neither do you."

"I didn't say I was." Shoulder hiked, jiggling Clint. "They'd be closed anyway. Vinnie wouldn't be working on Thanksgiving."

"Everyone should have Thanksgiving off," I told her, a little too loud.

"Yeah, right. Like it's a paid holiday for everyone," she said. "I gots to pee."

She crossed the street, walking toward the far corner. Had she suddenly gotten modest, or did she want another look at Keller's, see if the light was on after all? I was curious, too, because I'd lied to Chi Chi. I did want to get into Keller's. I wanted it badly.

I began to walk west, too, stopping when I got to the courtyard. Vinnie's car wasn't there in its usual spot. The lights weren't on either. I glanced down the block, but Chi Chi had disappeared. So I headed for the old chicken market next door, finding a stick at the side of their parking area and digging up one of the loose cobblestones, then leaving Dashiell at the base of the tree and taking the route I'd taken twice before, up to the roof. I duckwalked across the roof and climbed over the parapet onto Keller's roof. When I got to where their skylight was, I lifted the cobblestone and brought it down on the glass as hard as I could. The third strike did it, the glass shattering, a piece hanging down into the back room, held together by the wire but leaving space for me to see. I had a penlight with me, and lying on my stomach, leaning over the hole I'd made, I shone the light below.

I heard the chatter before I saw anything, then the light hit one of them, his onyx eyes looking up at me. I could see three of them, big city rats, and lots of droppings on the floor. I dropped the cobblestone through the hole and watched them scatter. The small room was filled with boxes. They were stacked everywhere, boxes the processed pork would fill on its way to restaurants and hotels, the thought of what I was seeing more than enough to make me want to spend the rest of my life eating nothing but carrots and broccoli. I stayed another minute or two, shining the small light on every corner of the storage room. I suppose the drugs could have been there, but I doubted it. Too many people would have entry to this space; the door probably opened at the start of business each day and locked again each night, not because what was stored there was so precious but to keep the rats at bay, to make sure no one left the door ajar by accident. Why not just let the cat in there? But then I took one more look and I thought I knew why. One of the rats was inspecting the cobblestone now, nearly as big as the cat and more than likely twice as tough. Perhaps the smell of the cat kept the rats out of the office, out of the refrigerator. But clearing the rats out of the meat market was not even a possibility, not unless the method you used resulted in a hole bigger than the Grand Canyon and a mushroom cloud that could be seen for miles.

Crouching low, I skittered across the roof, back to the roof of the old chicken market, and down the tree into the dark courtyard. With Dashiell close to my side, I headed next door just in time to see Vinnie's car pull in, to watch him make it do that little dance, pulling in and out of the spot until he had it perfect. I stayed back, behind one of the bushes, crouching low and waiting. Then I heard her. She was crossing the street, one hand in her hair, her legs stiff and moving fast. I expected a yoo-hoo, but Vinnie heard her, too, and no one needed to say a word. He waited, the padlock in one hand. As she got there, he snapped it shut on one handle, pushed the door open, and walked in first. It was Chi Chi's hand coming back out that pulled it closed.

I stayed where I was, Dashiell on a down right next to me, waiting for the light to go on upstairs. Then we ran through the courtyard, opened the door, and were in the refrigerator. I'd seen the toolbox the first time I'd searched with Chi Chi upstairs covering for me. She was doing it again, only this time she didn't know it.

I opened the cabinet under one of the cutting blocks and took out the tools, finding a hammer and a crowbar. Then I grabbed one of the towels the butchers used to wipe their knives on. There was no longer time for anything but quick, no matter how crude. I slipped the end of the crowbar between the floor and the trapdoor, right where the lock was, wrapped the towel around the end of the hammer to deaden the sound, and smashed down on the top of the crowbar as hard as I could. The lock gave, and knowing one of the things I'd find for sure, I opened the trapdoor anyway, peering down into the blackness of the subcellar, where the pipes of the hundred-year-old refrigerator system that cooled most of the meat market were located. The smell hit me first. Like the smell of a dead animal, musky, moldy, vile enough to make it difficult to inhale. I wrapped the boa around my mouth and nose because it was all I had. The only thing that would get anyone to go down there was a sound all the butchers dreaded, the dripping of melting ice. But Vinnie may have had another reason to do it. And therefore so did I.

There was a metal ladder going straight down. I left Dashiell above but took the crowbar with me, hearing the population below stirring. Then, halfway down the ladder, I took yet another chance. I banged the crowbar against one of the metal rungs of the ladder, hoping the rats would disperse at the strange noise. I didn't plan to stay long, but crouching in the area beneath Keller's, I could see no place where Vinnie could have secreted the drugs. I didn't find them, in fact, until I had used the crowbar to open the old wooden door that led to the area under Jeffrey's, and there they were, kept off the damp ground with boards resting on cinder blocks. They were in a pair of two-drawer file cabinets, neither one locked. Why bother, with rats to keep anyone sane away? Hearing scratching noises too close for comfort, I banged on one of the cabinets, then opened one of the drawers. It hadn't been a cash box Vinnie had gone to find. He was paying Chi Chi in merchandise.

I kept the light high, shining it ahead of me, hoping not to see the denizens whose space I was temporarily sharing, and made my way back under Keller's and up the ladder in record time, closing the trapdoor, leaving the toolbox where it was, and running out the door after Dashiell, the crowbar still in my hand. I must have dropped it in the courtyard or on the sidewalk, because later, when Chi Chi emerged, I no longer had it, nor did I know where it had gone.

"I went inside to see if you was there," Chi Chi said, blowing smoke at me as usual. "I mean, when I got back from my pee, I saw the car. So I thought you might need me to keep Vinnie busy."

"Very thoughtful of you," I told her. "So what's the deal, he just stop by to pick up a side of pork for the holiday, a little change of pace from eating fowl?"

Had Mulrooney found the stash? Of course he had, proving once again that a little knowledge is a dangerous thing.

I wondered if he'd found it that day, the day he'd died, if he'd been down with the underground refrigeration, down with the rats, when another rat caught him, a bigger rat, coming down the ladder before he had the chance to get back upstairs.

I'd thought Vinnie had something to do with the shooter. Was I wrong? Had it been Vinnie after all? But if it had, why was he still there? Why wasn't he in jail?

There could be only one reason. I thought about all those notes I'd read in Keller's files. The hookers were not the only ones adept at rewriting history, making up whatever bullshit seemed to serve their needs at the moment.

Suddenly the cold I'd felt crawling around the old refrigerator system, picking my way through a nest of rats, was gone. I felt myself heat up. I began to sweat.

"Guess we don't need you on the job anymore," Chi Chi said, both of us being sarcastic now, both of us scared out of our minds, me more than ever now that I knew what I was into. "I guess the po-lice will be putting their best men on this any minute now, solving the crime in no time flat." She leaned toward me, her breath a medley of alcohol, tobacco, and something with an almost feral odor. She took a step back and nearly fell off her shoes, tapping at her near-white hair when she'd steadied herself.

"Yeah. Fine. Let's get out of here now, okay?"

"Sure. Whatever."

We walked back to the corner, moving around to keep warm.

"What are you doing here tonight, Chi Chi? It's so dangerous. I thought I told you—"

She hiked that broad shoulder again. "You don't tell me what to do. Devon, he tell me what to do. 'Sides, it's always dangerous."

"No. Well, yes. But not like now."

She lifted the end of the boa, as if she'd just noticed it.

"This Rosalinda's?"

"Yeah."

"How'd you get the blood off of it?"

"I washed it."

"No shit." News to her, you could wash something dirty and get it clean.

"No shit."

"What you wearing it for?"

"Luck," I told her.

"The kind of luck that thing's been bringing, you don't want even a little piece of that."

"That aside, Chi Chi, you have to go home. It's no good being out here now. It's too hot."

"I gots to—"

"No. You don't. You can't. It's—"

And there was LaDonna, crossing the street, tall and slender and ever so ladylike in pink. Should be Prima Donna.

Had Frances been lying to me? Or herself?

"Okay," I said, "I have to talk to LaDonna. How about you go to Florent, wait for us there. Get yourself a steak or something." I pulled a twenty out of my pocket and held it out to her.

"Steak's not what I need," she said. "What I need, they don't have none of at Florent."

Had he given her cash this time? Or had he stiffed her altogether?

A car pulled up, stopping first in the middle of the street to check out LaDonna, have some polite conversation with her about fees, then when that didn't work out for one reason or another, pulling over to the curb right in front of us. Without so much as a wave good-bye, Chi Chi opened the door and jumped in. She and the john seemed to be arguing for a minute. He pointed at me. Chi Chi shook her head. Then she leaned toward him, whispering in his ear, and the car took off, revealing LaDonna. She stepped carefully up onto the curb, not wanting to slip on a hunk of fat or a greasy bone and take a fall.

"Time to have a little talk," I said, stuffing the twenty back into my pocket.

She pulled a pack of Camels, offered me one, and when I declined, tapped hers and placed it between her lips, dead center, pouting around it. I watched her pull out one of those colorful, disposable lighters, fire up her smoke, inhale, blow two rings off to my right, a lady with nothing but time.

"Sure, hon. What kind of talk you got in mind?" she asked, not looking at me, gazing toward Fourteenth Street, hoping for traffic.

The wind blew by us, making a funny sound, whistling in the dark. Something rustled in one of the cans of bones left out the morning before and not yet picked up. I wrapped the boa once more around my neck, which turned out to be as effective as trying to keep warm by wearing an extra Band-Aid or nail polish.

"I was at your mom's house today," I said.

"Aren't we the little detective."

"We are."

"And with no foreplay, Rachel? You're acting like them now?" She hooked a thumb toward Fourteenth Street. "You just go right for the crotch, don't leave a girl no pride at all."

"I'm tired of the games. Your games almost got me killed."

"Well, almost don't count. Ask Jasmine."

"I can't. I can't ask her anything at all. Besides, I'm not sure she could have told me anything. I think you're the one I should have been speaking to."

"Shoot." Turning over one large hand, the palm pale except for the dark lines that crisscrossed it, that curved around her big thumb, almost touching her wrist. She wore a bracelet of beads in various shades of pink, one as dark as her nail lacquer, the others in lighter shades, one clear, one white, for contrast.

"Frances says you work at Saks. She says you're a buyer. Cosmetics. She says you couldn't make Thanksgiving dinner because you're in Paris, on a buying trip."

"She's a lousy cook," she said. "The turkey's always dry. The yams are too sweet. And she drinks too goddamn much."

"Like your dad?"

"Where'd you get that?"

"I'm the little detective, aren't I?"

"The mistaken little detective. It wasn't like that at all."

"Okay. He was sober as a—"

"My mom's okay. Just weak."

"She couldn't stand up to your dad?"

LaDonna inhaled, blew smoke out of her nose, looked down at me and my theories.

"When he threw you out?"

LaDonna laughed. "What do you think you know, little detective?" She put a big hand on each pink cheek and talked in a falsetto voice. "The beatings started when he caught me in her bra once. They continued, getting worse, after he found me walking around in her shoes or playing with the Barbie doll I kept hidden under my mattress. The slimmest excuse to smack it out of me was enough for him. He was eclectic about his instruments of torture, too. A broom. The truck he gave me that I decorated with nail-polish flowers. Pink ones. A frying pan. Still hot. Frances cleaned up the grease without saying a word. I understood what 'enabling' was long before I ever heard the word. Is that it? Is that what you think happened, that it was a classic case of rejection and abuse? Well, think again, little one. It wasn't like that at all."

"What was it like?"

"Where's your head, asking me that? Don't you know what goes on in the world, you live in a cocoon or something?"

"I was hoping—"

"Yeah. We're all hoping. Look around you, woman. Every single person out here is hoping."

"What?"

"That our parents would accept us as we are. Did yours?"

I opened my mouth and closed it again when I realized it was a rhetorical question, my sister's favorite kind because it allowed her monologue to continue uninterrupted.

"He was a law-abiding man, a good man, except he couldn't find it in his heart to . . ." LaDonna looked away and sighed. "Most of the time," whispering now, "he made believe I wasn't there. I would rather he had hit me. Maybe I even took Barbie into the living room just so I could get something from my old man. Something's always better than nothing."

She inhaled on the cigarette and blew the smoke off to the side again.

"And this job, LaDonna—why was I hired?"

LaDonna looked up at the nearly black sky. A car came around the corner from a few blocks away but stopped at Thirteenth Street. I heard the door open and close, the car coming closer, passing where we stood. I saw a tear streaking its way through the pancake makeup on LaDonna's left cheek, making a small black trail of mascara as it moved slowly toward her chin.

"Look. He was still my dad. Even that last day."

"What happened then?"

"He held his gun to my head. He said if he ever saw me in a dress again, his face would be the last thing I'd ever see. No—that's not what he said. We're talking now, right?"

I nodded.

"There was no gun. He was holding my hand and crying. He said I could change if I wanted to." She wiped under one eye with her pointer. "Well, honey, don't you know. I'm saving up for just that very thing." Loud.

She pitched her cigarette into the street and lit another.

"He said if I wouldn't, not couldn't, wouldn't be a man, I should get the hell out and never come back because if I did, he'd shoot me dead. He meant it, too. When my dad wrapped his mind around something, he was like a pit bull." She turned to Dash. "No offense."

"But you still wanted to know who did him?"

She nodded. "Maybe he didn't do any of those things, Rachel. Maybe I'm just another lying junkie. Maybe I just left, that's all."

"And now you need to know who took away your chance that someday—"

"Wouldn't have happened. Not him."

"One can hope."

"I'm beyond all that."

"No. You're not. You wouldn't have put up big bucks to hire me if you'd been reconciled to the fact that—"

"I wanted to know who did Rosalinda. Can't you understand that?"

"Hookers die. It's dangerous work. One got killed just last week, outside Grand Central Station. It happens."

"Doesn't mean you don't want justice."

I waited.

LaDonna stared.

"Whatever happened between us, that doesn't mean I forgot what he did for me, how he saved my life, took me in, fought to keep me. Lots of parents, lots of men, they can't adjust." Eyes squeezed closed. "It makes them fucking insane."

"Your mom?"

"She tells stories. It makes her feel better. About him, too, and what a big hero he was."

I nodded.

"So you wanted to find out who killed Rosalinda?"

She nodded.

"And in the process, you hoped I'd find out who killed your father. In the process, there'd be justice for the man who saved your life."

"Could be that was in the back of my mind."

"Does Chi Chi know about him?"

She shook her head.

"And Jasmine? Did she?"

She shook her head again, a length of bronze hair coming loose, arcing down one side.

"But you knew then, before sending me in there, that this was police business, that it had to do with a murdered cop, and you didn't think to take me aside and—"

"I knew you'd find out. I heard you were good at what you do. I had faith in you."

"Gee, thanks."

"Look, Rachel, I was in no position to tell you. And if I had, then what? Would you still have taken the case, sent yourself poking into police business?" But then she wasn't looking at me anymore. She was looking behind me, her mouth open.

"Shit," she said. "Shit." A look of panic in her eyes.

I turned, but whatever we might have done, it was much too late. The car she hadn't noticed sooner had already stopped, the front doors sticking out sideways like elephant ears, the driver and the passenger already heading our way, fast, too fast, I thought, the bigger one heading for LaDonna. The short, mean-looking one, eyes as dark and dead as the creature who was now standing up on his haunches on top of the can of bones, came straight for me.

"What?" I asked. "Gay bashers?" Hoping they'd think twice with Dashiell here.

"Worse," she said through her teeth. "Look at their fucking shoes, Rachel. Didn't you learn anything here?"

33

His Big Nose Was Right in My Face

"Y ou have the right to remain silent and refuse to answer any questions. Do you understand?"

"Cut that out. You're hurting my arm."

"I'll take that as a yes. Anything you do say may be used against you in a court of law. Do you understand?"

"Sure, sure. Just take it easy, okay?"

For a moment, nothing happened. He was my height, but wide as a door, his hair shaved to within a quarter of an inch, his skin dark and oily, as if he were made of the grease beneath our feet. Eye to eye, neither of us saying a word, he looked me up and down slowly and carefully, reaching toward me, the look on his face making me try to pull back but his other hand, his thick fingers tight around my upper arm, preventing me from doing anything but stumbling on my red platform stilettos, my ankle turning over. He pulled the boa loose and ran his fingertips over my neck.

"Had it shaved?"

"What are you talking about?"

"Your Adam's apple."

"Look, Officer, I'm not really—"

"That's detective, sister." The esses whistled through the space between his upper teeth, teeth as big and white as Chiclets. "I see you've started the treatment. Or are these as fake as the rest of you?" He slid his hand inside my skimpy leopard halter top and pinched one of my nipples, hard.

"Ooow. Are you out of your—"

This time I never saw his hand move. I only felt the shock as he hit me across the cheek, tasted the blood from biting my tongue, felt the incredible heat on one side of my face, as if he'd held a torch to it and set it on fire. For a moment, I saw two of him, the mouths moving, no sound coming out. Then I heard wild barking and the sound of the chain he'd attached to the signpost nearest his unmarked car with a set of handcuffs, then made me hook to Dashiell's collar. His eyes hard as granite, his gun drawn, telling me to chain him up or he'd take care of him, my choice. I'd opened Dashiell's collar, slipped it through one of the huge links, and buckled it back on. The detective had pulled me away after I'd done it, yanking me backward, Dashiell's eyes following me, full of confusion at first, then betrayal, not understanding how I could be the one who'd stopped him from doing his job, who'd made it so he couldn't hang on to his self-respect.

". . . to consult an attorney," he was saying, "before speaking to the police and to have an attorney present during any questioning now or in the future. Do you understand?"

I nodded. I could taste the overcooked turkey and the too-sweet yams I'd eaten hours earlier in my throat, sour now, and all the while, Dashiell kept barking, saliva flying from his mouth, this detective ignoring him, acting as if he wasn't even there.

"If you cannot afford an attorney, one will be provided for you at no cost. Do you understand?"

When I didn't answer right away, he grabbed the boa from both sides and pulled me into his face.

"Speak up, Ms. Alexander, I can't hear you. Or is that just plain Alexander?"

I'd thought this was just business as usual, crack down on the transvestite hookers, chase them to the next precinct, make them someone else's headache. Then how did he know my name?

I could see the other detective talking to LaDonna, who loomed over him, her arms akimbo, giving him some lip, in LaDonna's case, bright pink lip, to match her leather miniskirt, the one she'd shoplifted at Jeffrey two weeks earlier.

Suddenly I was off the ground, the detective sneering. "I knew there was something hinky about you the first time I saw you." He dropped me, just let go, grinning when I lost my footing for the second time. "If you do not have an attorney available to you," he said, "you have the right to remain silent until you have had an opportunity to consult with one. Do you understand?" His voice had gotten considerably louder. His big nose was right in my face.

What first time? We met before? I wanted to ask, but didn't. I said, "I do." Respectful. Trying to diffuse his rage, knowing at the same time that what I wanted was impossible.

"Now that I have advised you of your rights, are you willing to answer my questions?"

"I want to speak to a lawyer," I said.

When his hand moved, I flinched. But this time he didn't go for my face. This time he grabbed my crotch.

"Where do you hide it?" he asked, squeezing so hard tears came to my eyes. He turned to his partner. "Hey, Ryan, this one here's post-op. Unless he shoved it up his own ass, for a change."

I bit the inside of my lip but said nothing. Whatever was going on, this cop was acting crazy, and the last thing I wanted to do was to provoke him further. He spun me around and cuffed me, using white plastic cuffs that cut into my wrists, the metal ones that held Dashiell back clanking as he tried to break the chain that held him to the pole. Then everything began to move so fast, it was like watching a slide show, silent images popping up and disappearing before I got the chance to digest them. A nun in a long black habit appeared from nowhere, standing across the street and watching, her palms pressed together as if in prayer. Another hooker came around the corner, and Ryan, waving his gun, called her over. Something dark and quick shot out of a trash can full of bones. When I turned to see where it went, I saw the beam of Ryan's flashlight panning over the pig mural, a bizarre tableau of larger-than-life porkers that morphed into roasts and chops as the light moved from left to right. Behind the sliding wall were parking spaces for the trucks, and behind that, the refrigerated plants where the carcasses of the slaughtered animals were taken to be prepared for sale to hotels and restaurants. I wondered if I'd end up any better off than them, here at the end of the world in the middle of the night with no way of protecting myself.

Then I was moving, but not under my own power. I was being dragged past where LaDonna was cuffed to a street sign, over to where Ryan was, the hooker he'd summoned just standing there, pathetic looking, couldn't have been out of her teens.

The two detectives stepped away from us and turned their backs. The short one was saying something I couldn't hear; his partner, Ryan, was nodding, not a good sign considering the circumstances.

The other hooker took a step closer. She was small and slight, her skin the color of mocha latte, her hair dyed a honey blond, wearing fishnet stockings, a short red skirt and halter top, her cleavage telling me she was taking hormone treatments. "Is it a he or a she?" she asked, nodding her head toward Dashiell.

"A boy," I told her, looking at Dash, who was barking nonstop now, his forehead crushed with concern.

"I have two cats," she whispered. "I used to have a dog, but he ate something in the bathroom and my boyfriend took him to the vet and had him put to sleep. I think he did it to get even with me."

She scuffed a foot and pouted. I thought she was shaking with the cold, her lips trembling, her hands dug deep into her skirt pockets, but there was a trickle of sweat coming down along the left side of her face. The detectives were heading back our way. She pulled one hand out now, keeping it curled around a wad of bills.

"I think you dropped this, Detective."

Ryan, his hand covered with a latex glove, took the roll and slipped it into his pocket. Then he gestured with a tilt of his head, and she took off toward Fourteenth Street, turning left and disappearing around the next corner.

Ryan went over to the car, pulled the door open, stuck his head in.

"You can go."

Nothing happened.

"Go," he shouted. "Crawl back into whatever hole you came out of." He reached in and pulled her out by her arm. "Don't let me find you here again."

"It's on the seat." She turned away and took off into the night.

Chiclets cut the cuffs off LaDonna and said something I couldn't hear. The nun was crossing the street now, moving quickly, not wanting to miss the chance to rehabilitate the last remaining sinner, deliver a lamb to God.

Chiclets was facing me again. He kicked at one of the bones that had spilled out of an overflowing garbage can and watched it skitter down the greasy sidewalk. I held my breath, waiting for him to give me a stern warning and remove the handcuffs.

But that's not what happened.

"If not for you," he said, his lip curled in disgust, "I could be home eating turkey and cranberry sauce like the rest of the civilized world instead of having to spend my time hanging out with you animals in this jungle. But you need to be controlled, no matter what it takes."

He grabbed my hair and pulled me toward the open door of the car, pushing my head down when we got there and throwing me in so that I sprawled across the backseat on my side, the crumpled tens and twenties sliding off the seat and landing on the floor of the car.

"Wait a minute," Ryan said. "What about the dog?"

"Unhook it and throw it in the back, with her. We'll take them down to the station."

What wouldn't have been good news for any of the rest of them made me so grateful I wanted to slide out backward, fall to my knees, bow, and kiss Chiclets's feet.

"A fucking *pit bull*? Are you nuts? I'm not going near that thing. Look at him."

"I'll get him," I shouted, choking, the words like shards of glass in my throat.

But Chiclets slammed the back door, opening the driver's door before turning back to answer his partner.

"Fuck it. Leave him where he is."

"We can't do that. You can't just leave a pit bull chained to a pole in the middle of the meat district. What happens when the market opens?"

"You got a point there." He glared at me, his eyes all hate, then back at Ryan. "What in hell's name you waiting for, he should die of old age? Shoot him."

34

We Were Face-to-Face Again

I REMEMBER opening my mouth, but the sound I heard was not my own scream, it was a gun firing, right behind the car, right where Ryan was standing when he was told to shoot my dog.

And then I heard Chiclets. "Terry. Terry. What the fuck." I saw his arm move, reaching for his gun. And then there was a second shot, and just like that I could no longer see him. Like a magician's coin, he had disappeared.

I tore at my panty hose with my fingernails, reached under my pants to where the razor blade Chi Chi had given me was taped to my hip, because she'd said, Do it, Rachel, in this life, you never know. Pulling it free, I sliced at the plastic cuffs, cutting them in the center so that my hands were free. I turned to open the door, get out of the car, and see what had happened, and found I couldn't. The handle wouldn't budge, nor would the button that locked the door come up. I tried the window, too, but it wouldn't roll down, and there was a barrier between the front and back of the car. I was in a cage.

I got up to my knees so that I could look out the back, terrified of what I might see, but having to know, my chest so tight I couldn't inhale. But before I had the chance to look, the door was pulled open, and there was the nun, her arms all but hidden beneath the wide sleeves of her habit, a metal pipe in one hand, the crowbar I'd used at Keller's, left God knows where. But it was what was in her other hand that got my attention. I could only see the tip of it, but that was more than enough to scare me witless, because she was holding it in my direction, at about the same spot her crucifix lay against the heavy black cloth that covered her own chest.

The wimple was hiding her face. "Sister," I managed to say, barely above a whisper, "what's going on here?"

"Suck my dick, bitch," she said, spitting the words into the car. "Good one, having your cop friends coming to the rescue. Unfortunately, they're not able to do anything for you at the moment. They're too busy being dead."

Now I didn't need to see her to know who it was, all in black, including her heart.

"Hello, Grace," I said. "Good to see you again."

I waited for her gracious reply, but none came.

"Nice outfit," I said. "Black is definitely your color."

"I'm grieving," she said.

And then, too late, I understood.

"Those were your brothers who got killed at Hunts Point?" I waited, but not for long. "Grace?"

"But for the Grace of God, would've been me, too." She looked right into my eyes. "He busy tonight, asked me to take over for the evening, be the one who decides who lives, who dies. I'm well suited for the job, don't you think?"

When her hand moved, I tensed, but it was the hand with the crowbar. She smacked it hard against the side of the car, then let it go. I heard the sound of metal against pavement as it scraped along the ground. Slow motion, Grace reached into one of the pockets hidden in the folds of her skirt and pulled out a syringe.

"You so upset after killing two cops, you needed a little

something to shore you up. You girls, you like that. It's what keeps folks like Devon and me in the chips. You need him to earn the money, then I be kind enough to give you something to spend it on."

I inched back on the seat, knowing there was no way out, knowing that door handle didn't work either, that I was trapped and there was someone holding a lethal shot blocking the only escape.

"How'd you find him? Mulrooney? How'd you know he'd be here?"

But Grace didn't answer me. I tried not to look at the gun, its mouth as big as the opening of the Holland Tunnel, but I couldn't help it, couldn't help seeing the letters tattooed on her fingers, HATE, dark against her dark skin.

"What about Rosalinda? She see you off Mulrooney? Was that why you—" I stopped when she started to laugh, a guttural sound, deep and throaty, ending in a cough. At last I'd tickled her fancy.

"Bitch fucking confessed to me. Saw me having a smoke on the corner, took my hands, begged me to listen to her life of sin. Kept talking and talking all the way to the waterfront, saying she wanted to start a new life, asking if I'd absolve her of her sins, the fucking moron. You start out dumb, drugs don't make you any smarter." She laughed again at the stupidity of it.

"You mean she didn't see you off Mulrooney?"

She shrugged. "Didn't think to ask. She said she been to see the pig man, was all I needed to hear. Did she, didn't she, wasn't a risk I was about to take."

Adrenaline pumping, my mind searched for a way out. And then I had it, maybe. There'd been two shots. And two detectives down. Dashiell was still alive, but he hadn't figured out what I'd done yet, all that barking, all that pulling, he'd been going the wrong way. I still had that. I had Dashiell. And a razor in my hand, albeit a small one, just a single-edged blade. But it was better than nothing. Of course, Grace not only had a hypodermic needle that she was very experienced using, she also had a gun.

"So you're not one of them," I said, trying to stall for time again. "You're their dealer."

It was all coming together, every last bit of it, but what good would it do me now? Grace was leaning forward, coming toward me, the gun pointed at my heart, but it was the needle I had to worry about. If it appeared that I'd killed the cops who were harassing me, then tried to send myself to heaven and accidentally went straight to hell instead, if it seemed I'd OD'd, no one would look any further. Wasn't that Grace's plan, that she'd be able to conduct business as usual on West Thirteenth Street, case closed? The way I saw it, I had one chance, and I took it.

I held up the hand with the puny razor in it. "Back up," I yelled at the top of my lungs. And again, even louder: "Back up."

"Who you giving orders to, bitch? I'm the one with the—"

And now Grace disappeared, and I heard the gun scraping against the street, heard her scream this time, and I was out of the car so fast I have no memory of how. Dashiell, who'd listened to me, twice, had backed out of his collar. He was on top of her, and I was kicking her arm, then standing on her wrist until her fingers opened and I had the syringe she'd been trying to get into Dashiell's shoulder.

I stared down at her, but if I was waiting to see fear in her dark eyes, I would have had a long wait. There was none. And there wasn't going to be any. Nor was there anything to celebrate. Behind me, lying in the gutter, were the two detectives. At my feet was the drug dealer Rendell Wright, aka Grace, dressed as a nun, my pit bull standing over her, the look in his eyes and the vibration from his belly keeping her completely still.

Or was Dashiell keeping *him* completely still? On this street, at this time of night, you never knew for sure.

I reached for my cell phone when I saw him coming

around from the other side of the car. He pulled a pen out of his pocket, stooped, and picked up the gun with it, holding it out in front of him. He looked at the car, then at the dead cop behind me, then at Grace.

"What the fuck is going on here?"

"The night Detective Mulrooney was killed, was there a nun anywhere in the vicinity?" My voice raw, my words swallowing each other, figuring I had a minute, or less, before he got me off his back once and for all.

Vinnie turned to look at me. For a moment, I thought he didn't quite know who I was. "*Detective* Mulrooney?"

I watched his face, watched him get it, watched the color leave his skin, as if he'd been shot with bullets instead of words.

"Did you see a nun anywhere near Keller's that night, asking for money, or just passing by?"

Of course not. He was down in the subcellar, getting drugs for his hooker. Or he was back in his office, the compressor covering any sound coming from below. He never saw a thing, never heard a thing, not until it was over, way over for Mulrooney, Rosalinda gone, getting some heavy shit off her chest.

He looked at Grace, at where her hand was, close to where the gun had been, then he slid the gun off the pen and into his hand, letting the pen drop, moving that gun back and forth between his hands, as if he needed to get the feel of it, then he held the grip, his finger on the trigger, but he never said a word. He stepped past Grace. We were face-to-face again. Only this time, he was the one who was armed.

35

LaDonna's Eyes Were Shining

VINNIE turned. The hand holding the gun moved. This time that black hole wasn't pointed at me; Vinnie's hand stopped almost as soon as it had started.

"No," I shouted. "Vinnie, don't."

He looked up at me, a shopworn man, used up, his face sagging, his eyes dark and dead.

"Detective Esposito," I said. Then I did the only thing I could. I dropped the hypodermic and reached for Dashiell, pulling him back by one flank. The sound of the gun was deafening. Grace's body jumped once, then lay completely still.

Vinnie stood there, the gun hanging down at his side. "Call it in, Rachel." He laid the gun carefully on the roof of the unmarked car, then changed his mind and took it back, turning away, going back the way he'd come. "They'll know where to find me," he said, his back to me, the wind taking his words and blowing them by me so fast I didn't get their meaning until a minute later, until he was already out of sight.

My hand shaking, I dialed nine-one-one. "Officers down," I said, giving the location, hanging up without answering any questions. Then I turned to look at the dead detectives, see-ing LaDonna coming down Little West Twelfth Street, Ebony and Chi Chi behind her, Devon, too, the troops coming to save me. Unless it was Rendell they'd come to save, in which case they were years and years too late.

Devon shook his head from side to side. "You do that?"

"You better not hang around. Grace did them. Vinnie did her. It's over. The cops are on the way."

I looked around on the ground for the syringe, stamping on it with my red shoes like a deranged flamenco dancer.

"I hear you won't be working for me no more," Devon said.

"That's right," I told him. "No need. Your girls are safe now, in a manner of speaking."

He nodded, pointing a long finger to where he'd come from, Ebony heading back that way, Devon right behind her, LaDonna and Chi Chi staying.

"Don't do this. You're okay now. Don't stay here and wait for the cops. Go on. Go on." I slipped off the boa and draped it around Chi Chi's neck. "It turned out to be lucky after all," I told her. For a moment, she stood there. Then she ran after Devon and Ebony.

I turned around to tell LaDonna to go, too, but she was behind the car, bending over Ryan.

"The white one's alive," she said. "The other one, he's gone." She thumped her fist on Ryan's chest. "This one had a vest on. He's still breathing." She stood and came over to me. "You got guts, girl."

"You better get out of here, you don't want to answer to the police."

"Remember what I told you, Rachel, how I was going to protect you?"

"LaDonna, you can't—"

"She killed my dad?"

I nodded.

"How come? Just pure hate?"

"The night your father's partner was killed in a drug raid near Hunts Point, two brothers were killed. A third dealer, the third brother, got away because your father stayed with his dying partner instead of going out the window after him. Her."

"Whatever. And that was Grace here?"

I nodded again. "I thought she was one of the girls."

"No. She didn't do no tricks. Didn't have to, all that money she made selling shit to us and the johns."

"She was your dealer?"

She nodded. "Sometimes Devon, he wouldn't give us the stuff, to show his power, you know? Then we'd go to Grace, buy what we needed with our pocket money, not eat that day, maybe not be able to pay the rent." She shrugged. "Way it is, no sense whining about it. So what'd she do, Grace, follow my dad here from Hunts Point?"

"I don't think so. I think she just changed neighborhoods. The heat was on after that drug bust, it was too dangerous for her to stay there. So she gave herself a new look and set up business here. What could be safer? Then shortly after she got here, an amazing thing happens. She sees Mulrooney, someone she'd know anywhere, even in a white coat pretending to manage a meat plant."

"And then what?"

"I imagine she stalked him, waited for a chance to find him alone, made it look like a mob hit."

"Why was my dad here?"

"Drugs. I found them tonight. I'm sure your dad had the location, but he was probably trying to get the whole route, where the drugs started, where they ended up, get some of the major players, not just the bit parts."

"And Vinnie, he was in it with Grace?"

I shook my head.

"Why'd he kill her?"

"He's a cop, LaDonna. That's what tonight was all about, trying to scare me off, get me to keep my nose out of their business."

"Vinnie's a cop?"

I nodded. "He went in undercover and turned. Your dad was sent in . . ."

"What are you saying?"

"The only way Vinnie could still be a free man is if he was on the job, too, if he was there undercover and so deep in, he'd gone over. That's a lot of temptation, the endless amount of money you see dealing drugs. It was more than Vinnie could resist. So your dad was brought in because Vinnie got corrupted, the good cop sent to set a trap for the bad cop. Only that's not how it turned out."

"The good cop."

"Not entirely good."

She nodded.

"And the bad cop, he never would have stood for the murder of a fellow police officer. He proved that tonight, didn't he?"

"Not entirely bad," she said.

"Not entirely."

"That means there's others in there, in on the dope? Civilians?"

"At least one. Not my concern."

"And Rosalinda? She is your concern."

"I thought she'd seen the murder, got seen seeing it. But that's not what happened." I shook my head. "She was there and left. I doubt she saw anything. She was in her white gown, walking to the corner, and she sees Grace, decked out the way she was tonight, like a nun."

"It was Halloween."

"True. But beside the point. Wearing that outfit was the perfect way to get close to your father without arousing suspicion."

LaDonna winced, lit another cigarette. I could see her hand tremble as she took it out of her mouth, blew the smoke off to the side.

"Vinnie had given Rosalinda something, in lieu of a payment or as part of her payment. She's feeling no pain, until she sees the nun, feels an overwhelming need to unburden herself of her life of sin. And all Grace needed was a blabby hooker who'd been in the vicinity of the crime she'd just commited."

LaDonna's eyes were shining. "So after doing my dad, she did Rosalinda."

I nodded.

"Go now," I told her. "Quickly."

I heard the sirens before I saw the cars, two of them, coming the wrong way on Washington Street, the headlights hitting me, standing over Grace. Chiclets was lying near the rear bumper, Ryan, moaning now, behind the car. Just before the cars reached me, I heard a single gunshot, a muffled sound, but no mistaking it, the report echoing against the old buildings on Little West Twelfth Street between where I was on the stroll and the river. The cars stopped, the doors on both sides opening immediately. I raised my hands above my head and waited.